Herbvana

A NOVEL

Brian B. DeFoe

ISBN: 979-8-9887431-1-8

Cover art and HERBVANA logo by Daniel Eyenegho.

Published by Boondoggle Industries, Inc.
Bainbridge Island, Washington
inquiries@boondoggleindustries.com

B O O N D O G G L E

To Reuben

who asked "when are you going to start writing?"

Author's Note

    This work is intended as an entertainment. Nothing in these pages should be interpreted to be sound thinking, competent legal analysis, ethical behavior, or a good idea. Various legal doctrines which would be quite relevant if this tale were to play out in real life have been purposefully ignored or simplified – often aggressively – for the purposes of expediency and storytelling.

HERBVANA

Chapter 1

"Barry! Oh, Jesus, you're stoned again, aren't you."

"Huh?"

"I knew it. We talked about this. You can't be stoned in the shop. What if the LCB were to walk in right now."

"They're not here, dude. At least, I don't see them."

"No, they're not here. But that's not the point. They can inspect any time they want – no appointment required – get it? And if they show up and you're wasted then we're out of business. Understand?"

"Yeah. I get it. Sorry."

"Sorry isn't enough, Barry. Sorry doesn't keep them from shutting us down and pulling our license. You've got to start taking things seriously. Grow up a bit, even."

"Come on, Marshall, don't get all parental."

"I'm serious. This is my shot at the gravy train, and I'll be damned if I miss it because I picked a stoner partner."

"You need me, man. You don't know the first thing about weed and you know it."

"And I don't want to. I just want to keep selling it. Losers come in here and want to give me cash for the stuff. That's all I really need to know. And yeah, I needed you. But that's past tense, Barry. Past tense. Don't need a weed guy anymore now that the stuff is legal. Hell, I could put an ad in the paper for someone to fill your shoes. I'd get a thousand applicants in an afternoon. So seriously, get your act together or you're out."

"You can't kick me out man, I own half of this joint. You wrote it up yourself."

Marshall winced. He had indeed written things up. Made things all legal between Barry and himself. But there was a problem. In his haste to form their company – this venture between obvious stoner and supposed businessman, he'd made a mistake. A rookie mistake, really – but one that had haunted him ever since.

Law school takes three years, usually. Fail a handful of classes along the way and you can stretch it out to five. By all accounts, Marshall was the first full-time student at his school to stretch it out that long without just giving up. But he was determined to finish, and his future alma mater was even more determined to keep taking his tuition. So, finish he did – last in his class at a second-tier school, a quarter-million dollars in student debt and desperate for an opportunity. Unfortunately, opportunity can be elusive.

Eventually, he found a strip-mall law office in Bremerton with a lazy-eyed ambulance chaser who was willing to let him hang his shingle in exchange for cheap rent and a share of his fees, and he started hustling for clients. And that's how Marshall Owens met Bartholomew "Barry" Jones.

Barry had walked into the office on a sleepy Tuesday afternoon when Marshall uncharacteristically found himself in the office during business hours. In his cargo shorts and tie-dyed t-shirt, with his blond dreadlocks covered in a filthy bandana, Marshall guessed Barry to be a potential criminal defendant. The fact that he smelled like weed only solidified that impression.

But he hadn't been a defendant. In fact, he'd managed to stay out of trouble his entire adolescence and early adulthood – a remarkable accomplishment considering that his sole reason for his first-ever visit to a lawyer was because he was exceptionally skilled at committing a very particular crime.

Barry was a pot farmer. And he was a good one. He'd started growing the stuff while he was a teen – planting seeds he'd scrounged from a neighborhood dealer in pots at the back of his mother's greenhouse. Behind her tomato starts he'd managed to grow quite a lot over the years. Being something of a connoisseur, he'd even started to develop his own different strains. Now, some twenty years later, he had his own greenhouse and was making a handsome living for himself quietly growing and selling weed to a handful of illicit dealers in western Washington.

But the business was changing, and Barry knew it. Washington had just legalized recreational weed. The state was in the process of awarding licenses to grow, process and sell the stuff. It was even changing the name of its booze cops – the Liquor Control Board – to the Liquor and Cannabis Board. To get a license, you had to show the State that the money you would use to build the business hadn't come from an illegal activity. And that was a problem for people like Barry. The very thing that made him qualified for a license – his ability to grow weed – was the same thing that might prevent him from being able to go legitimate.

Barry explained all this to Marshall that fateful day back in 2012, and that's when Marshall hatched a plan. The two of them would apply together for licenses, identifying Marshall as the source of funds. After all, what could be a more legal source of funds than the practice of law? Marshall sold Barry on the approach and after a few hours of work – for which Marshall dutifully billed Barry three times his normal hourly rate – Marshall plagiarized some poorly written documents he found on the Internet and used them to form a series of corporations owned by the two of them. Using those corporations, he then submitted applications to grow, process and sell at retail as much of the Devil's lettuce as the state might allow.

But of course when greed takes over – as it can easily do in times of plenty let alone times of desperation – mistakes will be made. Marshall's big mistake, the one he cursed on a regular basis, was getting into business with a client. He knew from reading the disciplinary notices in the state Bar Journal that there were only a few ways to more quickly lose your license to practice. And even if the Bar didn't pull his card, Barry could basically pull the rug out from under him at any time. All he had to do was to explain to a judge that his lawyer had taken half of his business venture without telling him to seek the advice of independent counsel, and his deal with Barry would go up in smoke faster than the weed they sold in their shop.

Marshall knew all this and was desperate to keep Barry from understanding it. Unfortunately, that meant he was in business with a frustratingly good-natured stoner with essentially no business acumen or obvious ambition. He couldn't even be trusted not to light up a joint in the middle of their showroom floor and, consequently Marshall found that every interaction with Barry left him seething and resentful, and at the same time fearful that his entire enterprise might disappear.

"You're right, Marshall. I did write it up. And I know how to end it. So don't push me. Now get off the sales floor – go back into the storeroom at least – until you're clear."

Barry eyed Marshall with bleary but quizzical eyes. He could never understand why someone who wasn't interested in marijuana would want to be in the business. But that was Marshall. As far as Barry knew, Marshall had never even touched the stuff. Which he thought was weird. But then again that just meant that there were more samples for Barry to try, so he didn't want to complain too much. Barry slowly got to his feet, crossed the showroom floor and walked through the door at the back of the shop into the storeroom, closing the door behind him.

"I don't know what you see in that idiot."

"He's fun," replied the only other person in the room, a tall blonde with a slightly beak-like nose and an assortment of visible piercings. "I'm not saying he's a good long-term plan. But he's fun for the moment."

"Yeah. Fun. Lilith, that fun guy of yours is going to get us shut down. He's a liability. We're just lucky we've got a good relationship with the LCB. Otherwise, we'd probably already be out of business. Maybe worse."

"What are you talking about? Good relationship? Earl's in here nearly every week busting our ass about something or other. Comes in, makes a big scene, scares off customers and then goes away. Doesn't sound like a good relationship to me."

"Have we ever been cited?"

"Cited?"

"For a violation. Screwing something up – you know."

"I don't think so."

"And have we ever screwed anything up?"

"Well, yeah, I guess so. I mean having a stoned owner on the premises. I'm guessing that's a pretty serious violation."

"You bet your tits it is. LCB boys find that even once and our license is gone. But they don't find it, do they? No. They don't find it because I'm on the case – taking care of things."

Lilith pondered this for a moment. It did seem odd that every time their assigned LCB agent came into the shop for an inspection, even a surprise inspection, everything seemed to work out. And it was true that they'd never received a citation even though their compliance hadn't always been great. In fact, it had at times been downright lousy. She could recall one time that the agent walked into the shop while Marshall was chatting up a couple of obviously underage girls on the showroom floor. They shouldn't have been allowed in the shop – should have been carded at the door and then denied entry. But there was Marshall, showing the two pretty young things an assortment of bongs when Earl had walked in. He exploded – scaring the shit out of the girls. But he didn't write anything up. And the next time he visited it was like nothing had ever happened.

"I'm telling you, Lilith, without me around this place is dead. And your boyfriend is dead along with it."

"Barry's not my boyfriend. We just hang."

"Well, you've got him fooled. Anyway, I'm going to need you to straighten things up here on the floor and then see if you can't keep him occupied for a bit. I've got some stuff to do, and I don't want him screwing things up. Can you do that for me?"

"What's going on?"

"Legal stuff. Don't worry about it." Marshall glanced at his watch. "Actually, let me finish straightening up. Just, please, keep Barry out of my hair for the rest of the afternoon. Ok?"

"Whatever you say."

As she exited the sales floor and went into the storeroom, Lilith caught a reflection of Marshall in one of the shop's mirrored displays. Standing at the counter in slacks, a collared shirt and a blazer, he looked entirely out of place surrounded by the shop's décor of psychedelia and reggae posters. He was staring at her as she walked toward the storeroom. Or at least watching her lower half – his eyes glued to her lower back peeking from below her cropped shirt and the roundness of her hips moving beneath her skirt. Watching Marshall watch her, she let her hips travel in a slightly wider arc for his viewing. She wasn't the least bit interested in him – although she did think that perhaps the two of them had similar taste in women. And if Marshall thought she was attractive? Well, that could be useful at some point.

Marshall finished tidying the shop and tended to the few last bedraggled customers, before switching off the flashing neon green "HERBVANA" sign in the window promptly at 7:00 p.m. Some of their competitors stayed open later, but Marshall was determined to stay in the good graces of the local community. Even if he didn't use weed, and completely understood why several towns had passed ordinances to prevent shops like his from opening; he wanted to keep this good thing going as long as he could. Owning half of *Herbvana* was the best thing that had happened to him, apart perhaps from that one night in high school when the Bridewell twins – Ashley and Melinda – had gotten slightly tipsy and seriously naked in the back of his car.

Having finished the work of shutting down the store, Marshall double-checked to see that the door to the storeroom was locked – Lilith and Barry had left some time ago – armed the alarm system, killed the lights, locked the front door, and exited out into the night. In the twilight of the late spring evening, the sun was trying but failing to cut through thick clouds. Rain drizzled down.

As he walked to his car, an aging but nevertheless libido-enhancing German sports sedan, he caught sight of a decrepit pickup truck parked at the Poulsbo Creamery, an ice cream parlor across the street. It was slowly flashing its lights.

"Right on time," Marshall said quietly to himself. He turned away from his car and walked instead across the street toward the signaling vehicle. Earl McAllister, a corpulent man in his mid-fifties, sat slouched behind the wheel eating what appeared to be a double scoop of rocky road.

"Earl, how nice to see you."

"Cut the bullshit, Marshall. We need to talk."

"Of course." Marshall walked to the passenger side and got into the truck, his feet disturbing layers of trash piled up like geologic strata in the floorboard. "What's up?"

"Here's the deal. The morons in Olympia have assigned me a new partner. Say I need to train the guy. And so, I'm going to train him. But there are some things I don't really want to train him on, if you know what I mean – things that he doesn't need to know about."

Marshall sat in the filth. He didn't respond.

"So, here's how this is going to go down. You're going to keep up your end of our bargain. No change to our arrangement. But I'm moving the drop. We're switching from ice cream to espresso. From now on, the envelope goes to Cindy out in Gorst. Got it? You know Cindy, right? The one with the wings on her ass? She takes the drop and gives it to me. And if she doesn't get it, or she doesn't give it to me, then you've got a problem. Understand?"

Marshall nodded.

"So, the second thing is this – the new guy's going to be with me. Maybe not every time – but regular. If he gets wind of any part of our arrangement, *Herbvana* gets shut down. I've found a lot of problems in your little slice of heaven over the last three years. And I've written every one of them down. Got a good long record of them. Decent chance if those come to light that you and that stoner buddy of yours will get prosecuted. You know Jorgenson, right? The county attorney? Yeah, I hear he's got some pretty high aspirations. Wants to be governor one day. I'm guessing he'd love to be able to make a name for himself and that would probably happen pretty quick if he managed to put a pot-peddling lawyer behind bars. Boy, that would make all

9

the papers, wouldn't it? Hell, it might even make national news. He'd be set and you'd be screwed. Maybe even literally. Pretty boy lawyer like you in the joint? You'd be everybody's dance partner. The new guy learns nothing. Got it?"

"I got it, Earl."

"Good boy. Now, how were sales this week? Good, I hope."

Marshall pulled a large envelope from the inside pocket of his jacket and handed it to Earl. "Good enough."

Earl peered into the envelope and thumbed through a stack of bills. "All here?"

"It's all there – twenty thousand."

"Excellent. You know, I do love a cash-based business. If you guys ever find a way to take credit cards or keep a legit bank account that will make things damned inconvenient." Earl smiled – his mouth turning to a sickly sneer. "Now, I'm afraid I must be going – got some more appointments to keep. You have yourself a nice evening."

Marshall opened the door of the truck and stepped out into the parking lot, accidentally knocking an empty paper cup out of the floorboard and onto the pavement. As he walked back across the street to his car, Earl drove away into fading light of the evening.

Chapter 2

Marshall stood on the top deck. He preferred piloting *The MaryJane* from this position – up on the flybridge. It afforded him three hundred and sixty degrees of visibility around the boat, the wind in his prematurely thinning but longish brown hair, and the feeling of freedom.

The air was unseasonably warm and there was no rain in the forecast, an unusual state of affairs for the end of May in the Pacific Northwest. He passed the buoy that marked the end of the no-wake zone and gently prodded the throttle forward, causing a surge of engine noise if not an actual obvious increase in speed or wake.

He turned the ship's wheel, steering the boat out of Eagle Harbor and along the narrow channel of deep water between the sand bar to port and the shores of Rockaway Beach to starboard, hugging the side of the passage in an effort to stay out of the way of an incoming ferry. Before him lay the still waters of the Puget Sound which, should he so choose, could lead him all the way out into the Pacific and, from there, almost anywhere in the world. Beside him, on a chaise on the flybridge but below the level of the railing and obscured from view by passing boats or the houses on the shore, lay a blonde who assured him that she was twenty-one (though she could have passed for seventeen) and who had removed her bikini top so as to soak up the sun. All was good in his world. "Well done, Counselor," he muttered to himself.

Having passed the length of the sandbar, Marshall turned the wheel sharply to port and *The MaryJane* swung around in a leisurely manner. A miniature trawler, twenty-six feet in length, she was neither the fastest nor the most responsive vessel. But she was sturdy, well-equipped for fishing, crabbing and shrimping, and offered ample space for entertaining the occasional female passengers either up top or down below in the enclosed cabin and berth. He loved this boat.

Today, notwithstanding the presence of his passenger, was intended to be a shake-out cruise. A few hours on the water to make sure that the boat was performing correctly before the serious business of the upcoming crab and salmon seasons. The girl was just a bonus. Just one of the perks of being a successful lawyer turned entrepreneur.

Leaving the helm for a moment, Marshall scampered down the ladder into the cabin below and came back with two champagne flutes. Setting one down on the helm station, he took a leisurely sip from the other.

"That's not fair!" complained the blonde.

"You know the rules, Lucy. I'm a stickler for rules."

Rolling her eyes and offering a well-practiced pout, Lucy dutifully removed her the remainder of her swimsuit and reclined, fully naked for his gaze.

"Good girl," Marshall said, handing her the champagne.

He savored the moment – sipping champagne while watching the wind tickle the well-manicured tuft of curly blonde hair between Lucy's slender thighs. "This is a great boat," he thought to himself.

Unexpectedly, his reverie was interrupted by the ringing of his cell phone. Looking at the screen, he saw that it was *Herbvana* calling. He reduced the throttle to idle and shut off the engine, allowing the boat to drift with the currents and the winds of the afternoon, and put the call on the phone's speaker.

"This is Marshall."

"Marshall, its Lilith."

"What's up?"

"We've got a problem. The bank just called. They're going to pull the account."

"Shit. Not again. That's the third bank."

"I know. Anyway, they said they're going to freeze the account at the end of the month."

"But it's already the 25th! That doesn't give us enough time to find a new bank."

"I know. I told them that. They don't care. Said they're getting a ton of pressure from their examiners and they're not interested in being the test case for the feds."

In his heart, Marshall didn't blame the bank for their discomfort. Nothing in law school had prepared him for the surreal environment of a business that is permitted and regulated under state law but illegal under federal law. Banks wanted to take their deposits; the sheer amount of cash that was flowing through the state's cannabis industry was enough to make bank executives salivate. But with the need to comply with federal "Know Your Customer" requirements and to file suspicious activity reports with the regulators every time the business made a cash deposit above $10,000, banking a cannabis business was probably even riskier than operating one yourself. The banks were scared.

"Ok," sighed Marshall. "Sounds like we've got to move quickly. We've got to get all the money out of the account before they freeze it. What's the current balance?"

"Four and a half million and change."

"Geez. Ok. I'm out on the boat. I'll be back at the shop as soon as I can. In the meantime, pull our accounts payable – let's pay everything we owe. Even if it isn't due yet, prepay it. We'll pay everything we can and have to move what's left. I'll try to call in a few favors from some friends and see if we can't park the money while we look for a new bank."

"Ok. Sorry to spoil your cruise."

Marshall looked back at his passenger. Lucy was liberally applying suntan oil to her now glistening breasts. "Yeah. Well, the timing isn't great. But that's business."

He hung up the call and swore. "Lucy – I'm sorry babe. I'm going to have to cut our little cruise short today. Business before pleasure and all that. You understand, don't you?"

Lucy doubled down on the pout. "But I just got all oiled up, Marshall. I'm really slippery. Are you sure we can't stay out just a bit longer?"

Marshall studied Lucy. Her empty champagne glass was in her hand as she lay on the chaise with one leg outstretched and one knee up, rocking her hips slightly from side to side as she eyed him, giving him a brief glimpse of heaven with every movement. Having essentially bathed in the tanning oil, she was now visibly slick from the tips of her painted toenails to the bridge of her nose and absolutely everywhere in between. He wanted nothing so badly as to spend the afternoon exploring that slipperiness. She looked like a great fuck. But she didn't look like a four-million-dollar fuck.

"I'm sorry, babe. Another time?"

"Probably not."

Ignoring her, he scrolled through the contacts on his phone and dialed his former law partner – who did not pick up the call and let it go to voicemail.

"Cal – hey its Marshall. I need a favor. I need to park some cash in your trust account. It shouldn't be for too long, but we've got a bank situation at the business and I'm in a bind. Please give me a call as soon as you get this message. Thanks, buddy. I owe you one." He hung up the phone.

"He's probably off partying," Marshall said to himself.

"Sounds like he's got his priorities straight."

He glanced down at Lucy. She'd flipped over onto her stomach on the chaise. As she turned her head to look back over her shoulder and aim that now perfected pout in his direction, his eyes lingered briefly on her naked ass. An exquisite testimony to the female form, Lucy's bottom deserved to be carved in stone so that it might exist in perpetuity in its current splendor. Tiny pools of tanning oil had formed in the dimples at the small of her back, only to spill over their borders and allow droplets to run toward her spine, merging there into a mini torrent that slowly made its way through the canyon between her buttocks downward toward the wonders that lay beneath.

"Focus, Counselor," he muttered to himself as he restarted *The MaryJane's* engine and began to steer the boat back toward Eagle Harbor and its slip at the marina.

His attempts at self-control flagging, he was relieved to feel the phone come to life in his hand. It was Cal. He put it on speaker.

"Cal! Hey man, thanks for getting back to me so fast."

"No problem, Marshall. What's going on?"

From the speaker, even above the hum of the boat's engine, Marshall could hear the sounds of beeping equipment and the occasional intercom announcement in the background. Cal was at the emergency room at one of the local hospitals; it was his favorite place to hunt for new clients.

"Here's the deal. The bank called today and said they're going to freeze *Herbvana's* account – say they've decided to stop banking weed. This has happened before. It's actually the third time. But the first two times the banks gave us a lot of warning and we were able to get a new account set up in time to make the switch. These pricks are only giving us five days. And if we don't get the money out of the account before they freeze it then we're screwed."

"I see. So how can I help?"

"I want to hire you."

"Marshall, I don't know anything about the weed business and I don't know anything about banking. This is your area, man. Not sure I can be of much use."

"Hear me out. I don't want you to actually do anything for us. I just want to have you be our lawyer."

"I don't follow."

"If you're *Herbvana's* lawyer then you can represent us, right?"

"Yeah."

"And what do you normally ask for from a client before you represent them?"

"A retainer."

"Exactly. So, if we retain you for legal services, you're probably going to want a retainer to make sure you get paid."

"But you just said you didn't want me to actually do anything."

"I don't. At least not at the moment. But I might. Right? We might need legal services in the future. And in the meantime, we'd have a retainer on account with you that could be used to satisfy your bills or – if we decide that we're not going to use you in the future – that could be refunded to us."

"Yeah. Got it. You want to hide money in my trust account while you look for a new ban. Sounds like a sham, Marshall."

"Ok, first of all I don't know that we're not going to need you. Who knows, there might be some kind of accident at the store and we need you to defend us, right? Bunch of stoners going in and out every day – it's amazing that hasn't happened already. But second, since when are you somebody to shy away from something just because you think it sounds sketchy? I've known you a long time, Cal. Don't act like you don't do shady shit all day, 'cause I know you do. Where are you right now?"

"St. John's emergency room – down in Tacoma."

"Right – and you're there because of a sick relative I bet."

Cal didn't respond.

"No, you're there because you know you can slink around in the emergency room and find yourself a few new clients. 'Easy pickings in the ER' – I remember you told me. You've made your whole career doing that. You got form engagement letters in your briefcase? I bet you do."

Cal started to chuckle. He did, in fact, have form engagement letters in his case. Worse than that, he'd recently downloaded an application on his phone that let him take credit card payments or – more importantly for today's business development effort – credit card deposits from potential new clients. "Ok, Marshall. I get it. You know me well. So, what's the deal. How much are you looking to hide?"

"We've got some bills we're going to take care of first, but my guess is it will be about four million."

Cal coughed. "Four million? As in dollars? That's a lot of money – and all that from weed. I picked the wrong line of work."

"Business has been brisk."

"Marshall that kind of money is going to raise some eyebrows. My bank won't ever have seen that kind of cash come into my account – not with the clients I work with. You know that."

"So your client base is getting more sophisticated. Congratulations."

"I'm serious, Marshall. They'll shut down my account or report it to the bar or worse. You're asking me to take a big risk here. Why would I do that?"

"I'm sure that *Herbvana* will make it worth your while. You'll probably get some good work out of this."

"You're not hearing me, Marshall. I'm not fucking doing this unless I get fucking paid for it. And real money."

"Such language!" teased Lucy – who had set about putting her bikini bottom back on, a process that apparently required her to bend fully at the waist in front of Marshall displaying once again that most potent signal among primates. She clearly knew her best asset.

"Who's with you?" Cal demanded.

"A girl. Don't worry about it."

"Girl got a name?"

"Lucy."

"She sounds young."

"She's a grown woman."

"Oh, I'm sure she is, Marshall. I'm sure she is. Look, it sounds to me like you've got yourself in quite a predicament. And to solve your predicament you're asking me to take on risk. And you know I don't like risk, Marshall. You know that. So, if I'm going to take on…"

"How much, Cal?"

"A million."

"You're out of your mind."

"I'm serious, buddy. You want me to do this thing it's going to cost you. Of course, maybe you don't need me. Maybe you can get Lucy there to help you. I bet she's got some great places to hide stuff."

"Get serious."

"I am serious. Find somebody else."

"Two hundred fifty grand"

"Nope."

"Cal, that's more money than you make in a year."

"Maybe. But I've got dreams, buddy. Big dreams. Tell you what, since we're friends, I'll give you a deal. Nine hundred."

"Shit, Cal. You're killing me. Five hundred."

"Nope. Say, is Lucy a redhead? I always did like redheads."

"She's blonde. Six hundred."

"Nope. You sure she's a real blonde? Can't always trust 'em you know."

Lucy teased back the waist of her bikini bottom, exposing once again the blonde curls within, and raised an eyebrow at Marshall.

"Quite sure. Seven hundred."

"You're wasting my time, buddy. Look I've got a few more

20

potential clients to meet with – going to need to cut this short."

"Eight hundred."

"Tell you what. Let's split the difference. You're at eight hundred and I'm at nine. How about eight-fifty? That feels fair. Don't you think?"

"Fine. Eight-fifty."

"Wonderful. Glad we could reach an agreement. I'll email you the engagement letter and wire transfer instructions this afternoon – just need to get back to the office. I'll deduct the eight-fifty as soon as the funds hit the account. Will give you an invoice for 'Services Rendered' – I'm sure you'll figure out a way to claim it as a legitimate business expense. You're getting a deal here, Marshall. I'm awfully glad we could reach an arrangement; I do like to be of service. It's why I got into this business, after all."

"Right. That's exactly what I think of with you, Cal. Client service."

Calvin laughed. "You take care of yourself, buddy. And you know, if you find yourself in any kind of trouble with Lucy, just remember I do criminal defense work too. Not that you're going to need it. I'm sure she's a lovely young lady. Just lovely."

Marshall ended the call and began to pull *The MaryJane* into the marina. Looking over at Lucy he was gratified to see that she had put on some shorts and a loose-fitting sweatshirt and was now sitting at the rail on the bow of the boat. As the boat approached its slip a seal bobbed up from beneath the water and thrust its head up in curiosity. Lucy squealed with delight and, as she turned to face Marshall up on the flybridge and point it out to him, he caught sight of the front of her sweatshirt: "Bainbridge High School Girls' Lacrosse."

"Jesus," muttered Marshall to himself, "dodged a bullet there."

Chapter 3

Sometimes, late at night and when all was still, Lilith could still hear the sound of the turkeys. It wasn't the gobble that bothered her. No, it was the incessant scratching in the dirt - the tortured sound of several thousand scaly toed birds wandering aimlessly and awaiting death. And whether it was this aural apparition or her half-hearted conviction of the sentience of all living creatures, Lilith had turned vegan at an early age. In fact, she'd stopped eating animals before she started being Lilith.

Formerly, and still legally, known as Bernadine Montgomery, Lilith was born the only child of an industrial turkey farmer in the Midwest. Her father was a poultry magnate. He had invented a particularly efficient, and especially unpleasant, way of artificially inseminating turkeys, which allowed his firm to breed them to have ever larger and larger breasts – past the point at which reproduction by traditional means had become a physiological impossibility. With this invention, quite a bit of hard work and more than a handful of hard-nosed business dealings, Mr. Montgomery had managed to grow from his beginnings as a two-bit turkey farmer with just a handful of birds to the largest single provider of turkeys in fifteen states – with over thirty million birds awaiting execution at his command.

Bernadine hated her father. Sure, it had started out well enough. He was a doting and attentive man, tender with his wife and young daughter. But things went downhill quickly when Mr. Montgomery's secretary convinced him that his company should begin to observe Take Your Child to Work Day. It seemed like a good idea at the time. But on the first observance, when Montgomery found his daughter staring wide-eyed at the elaborate turkey slaughtering apparatus in action, surrounded by feathers, blood and gore, he knew it had been a mistake. Never again did Bernadine speak to her father with love in her eyes.

Several years after that fateful afternoon, while in her third year at an all-female college, Bernadine became Lilith. It was an entirely organic transition. She'd been sitting in class, attending to a professor's lecture on the subjugation of women in early western Europe when the epiphany occurred. As she saw it, her entire upbringing – indeed even her excellent and quite progressive education – was predicated on the demand by a patriarchy-led society for ever larger and larger female breasts. She had to put an end to it – to do her part to end the oppression of women – whether avian or human – to satisfy the hunger of men. It was of little consequence that women too found their hunger satisfied by the juicy and succulent white meat of the turkey's breast; they were themselves the victims of oppression – brainwashed by a society that tells them what to feel, see and think, and all from the perspective of the male gaze. For Bernadine the world would never be the same. The veil had been lifted from her eyes. She had been awakened. She assumed the name of Lilith – synonymous with female strength and power, and only coincidentally the occasional infanticide – and vowed never again to allow any man to control her actions. Going forward, she would be the aggressor. She would take command. And she would bend men to her will.

Following her enlightenment that fateful November afternoon, Lilith arrived back at the family home in Missouri for winter break with a classmate on her arm and a ring in her nose.

Mr. and Mrs. Montgomery were shocked at the sudden change in their daughter's name, appearance, demeanor and sexual orientation. Mrs. Montgomery assured her husband that this was likely just a phase and that Bernadine would be back to her usual self before long. Lilith and her then partner, Chrysalis, hearing this, concluded that Mrs. Montgomery must be suffering from Stockholm Syndrome and began an earnest attempt to help her achieve her own epiphany. And it was just a few days later that Lilith and Chrysalis found themselves standing in the Montgomery's driveway being informed by the local police that Lilith's father had determined she was no longer welcome and that if she persisted on the property she would be arrested for trespass.

That was seven years ago. Seven years since Lilith had started binding her breasts and stopped speaking with her father – seven years since she had dropped out of college after that same man had refused to pay any additional tuition to the obviously leftist institution that he insisted had brainwashed his daughter. She had kept in touch with her mother through letters and the occasional phone call, but their relationship too had become strained. And it was six years since Chrysalis had suddenly decided that she was not, in fact, a lesbian and started dating a man who was now an investment banker working on Wall Street. That man became Chrysalis' husband, and Lilith's former lover was now a stay-at-home mother with a nanny, two small children, a German station wagon and a preference for being called by her given name of Monica.

Lilith had made her way out west, spending time first in Oregon and then moving up the coast to Washington – intending to settle eventually on an organic farm commune in a remote part of Alaska. But money was in short supply. A stopover in Seattle to earn enough money to complete the trip north stretched from days to weeks to months and, eventually, she realized that the Pacific Northwest was her new home. She had friends there. Whether it was because of her weekly attendance at a feminist activism group or her regular participation in the vegan poetry slam at a local coffeehouse, she was surprised to realize that she'd put down roots. And so, Alaska was off the table.

Eventually, she met Barry. He was a friend of a friend and had access to some excellent weed. She knew instantly that he was in love with her – or at least in lust. She felt his eyes linger on her figure. She watched him puff himself up whenever she was around, strutting and preening in front of her – desperate for her attention. He reminded her of one of her father's turkeys. It was an embarrassment. But she learned quickly that if she feigned even the slightest bit of interest in him then he could be quite generous. She fretted over whether this meant that she was manipulating him or he was manipulating her. If this was a Skinner box, was she the pigeon or the scientist? In the end, she found she didn't care. If she smiled at him and batted her eyelashes even a bit, she received weed and cash. And that was enough, at least for the time being.

When Barry learned that Washington was in the process of legalizing recreational cannabis, it was Lilith who told him. And it was Lilith who suggested he should submit an application and try to get a license. She considered it self-preservation. After all, if Barry got caught selling illegally, then she'd lose both her weed supplier and her primary financial support all in one motion. But if she could get him to go legit and he ended up with a successful business as a result, she would almost certainly benefit. She just had to keep stringing him along.

Her plan worked. In fact, it worked much better than she anticipated. Shortly after Barry and Marshall opened *Herbvana* she found herself working there and earning a steady paycheck. That, plus Barry's continued generosity, meant that she'd carved out a good living for herself. Nothing extravagant, but a clean apartment and a job where she could basically come and go as she pleased while earning enough to eat, put gas in her Volkswagen and keep her tattoo artist engaged. Which, of course, was exactly what Lilith was doing this morning.

"Feel like taking a break?"

"Sure," Lilith replied.

The hum of the tattoo gun stopped and its operator, a woman of approximately seventy – give or take ten years – with a shock of fuchsia running through her otherwise white hair, straightened up from her position of bending over Lilith's bare back. She grabbed a paper towel from a nearby roll, daubed away some blood and ink from just below Lilith's left shoulder blade, and stepped away from the table. Madame Mara was an institution in the Seattle tattoo community, having opened her first shop in Pioneer Square in the late sixties. Rumor had it that she'd plied her trade on Jimmy Hendrix once – a suggestion she strongly denied with a sparkle in her eye that gave her refusals the air of admission. Now, several decades later, she'd relocated her storefront to a back alley near the Pike Place Market.

"You still selling weed over near Poulsbo?"

"Yeah."

"That new stuff's too strong for me. I'll stick with the stuff in my garden." The old woman grinned. She'd tended a series of marijuana plants, each specimen having been grown from a cutting of the previous plant in an unbroken string dating back decades, all starting with seeds she claimed she'd received from a shaman from the Tlingit tribe. The Mother Plant, she called it. "But I'm guessing it's pretty good business."

"Really good. We can't keep it on the shelves. And with all the taxes the stuff's not cheap. Costs about twice as much as weed on the street."

"So why buy it from you?"

"Not everyone does. But your average housewife isn't going to buy from a guy on the street. She wants something a bit more upscale. Wants to feel like she's not about to end up in the local paper after a bust. Funny thing is, we sell more Bainbridge customers than we do Poulsbo – and there's a really nice weed shop on the Island. But Mr. and Mrs. Bainbridge don't want any of their neighbors to see them pulling out of the parking lot of the shop on the Island so they tend to stock their pantry while they're out of town."

"So, they want to get high but don't want people to know. People are funny."

"Yeah. Fastest moving stuff right now, though, doesn't even get you high. It's all that CBD stuff – creams, lotions, oils – you name it. They're putting it in everything."

"CBD?"

"Yeah, some chemical compound. Barry talks about it all the

28

time. Anyway, you strip the THC – that's the stuff that gets you high – out of weed and leave the CBD and you end up with something that nobody knows for sure whether it does anything or not. But people swear by it. Say it cures everything from baldness to hairiness and everything in between. Had one guy come in who claimed it cured impotence because he rubbed some of the cream on his balls and his cock got hard. I had to bite my tongue to keep from telling him I thought I could probably get the same result with a tablespoon of peanut butter. I mean creamy peanut butter – crunchy might be a challenge – but you get the idea."

The old woman laughed. "Men and their willies. Some things never change. So do you see this turning into a long-term thing, or are you just playing it out day to day?"

Lilith lifted her upper body up onto her elbows, her ample breasts, unbound so that Madame Mara could have full access to her back as she worked to complete the elaborate Earth mother goddess and tree of life tattoo begun several sessions before, hung – pendulous – from her chest. "Both, really. Barry and Marshall – they're the owners. I just work there. But Barry's a stoner and Marshall's so uptight I'm sure he's going to force Barry out at some point. I'm day-to-day, but if the string plays out the way I think it will, then maybe Marshall and I will end up owning it. The guy's an asshole. But he's good with the details and the shop is making a shitload of money. So, yeah, I wouldn't mind owning a piece."

"How are you going to make that work with Barry?"

"What do you mean?"

"You think he'll just give you his part of the business?"

"Well, yeah. I think he will. I mean right now he thinks I'm his girlfriend. If I can convince him of that, then yeah I think I can convince him to give me his stake – or at least sell it to me on the cheap. He's completely spineless."

"Wow. You know, my girl, that's pretty mercenary."

"They're men, Mara. They've been holding us down since we first climbed out of trees and walked on two legs. Probably longer. We don't owe them anything." She let herself lie back down on her stomach. "Plus, if I play my cards right he'll be glad to give it to me. Won't even know that anything's up."

Madame Mara leaned over Lilith's back and continued her work. "You said Marshall's sharp. Won't he know if you rip off Barry?"

"Yeah. But I don't think he'll interfere. He's always complaining to me about Barry. My guess is he'd rather have me as a partner than Barry nine times out of ten. The real trick isn't going to be getting Marshall to look the other way while I work Barry – the real trick is going to be finding a way to get Marshall's stake in the business as well. I don't have a plan for that bit yet. But I'm working on it – keeping my eyes open for an opportunity. There's something going on between Marshall and our LCB cop. I haven't figured out what it is, exactly. But something isn't right. If I can just learn what's going on there, it might be an avenue. I don't know. I don't have to do anything quickly – I'm playing the long game here. Don't need to do anything immediate. But I'll own the whole damn thing by the time I'm done, Mara. Just you watch."

"Sounds great, my girl. But you watch yourself. They're not always as dumb as they seem."

As the two women talked, the tattoo gun resumed its metallic hum and the tree on Lilith's back continued to grow. Finally, a few hours later, it was Madame Mara who said that she could do no more for the day. Lilith, in a state of euphoria brought on by the endorphins released while her skin was punctured several thousand times per minute for the better part of the day, wasn't eager to stop. But the old woman was adamant, and Lilith acquiesced. After Mara applied a salve to Lilith's back and then draped it extensively in plastic wrap, Lilith dressed. The two women made an appointment for Lilith's next session and Lilith exited the shop out onto the Seattle street.

It was mid-afternoon and the sidewalks in and around the market were clogged with tourists. Fishmongers threw salmon past a delighted audience and held up lethargic crustaceans – pincers flailing like the hands of punch-drunk pugilists – in an effort to drum up business. Across the street, a large line trailed outside the door and into the street for customers eager to purchase a cup of coffee at a shop they believed – incorrectly – to be the original store in a worldwide chain of coffee shops. The air was bright and clear. It was a beautiful day.

She walked purposefully from the market down to the waterfront and along the seawall toward the ferry that would take her back to Bainbridge Island, all the while reflecting on her position at *Herbvana*. Notwithstanding her bluster to Madame Mara, she didn't exactly know how she would convince Barry to give up his stake. And her confidence that she might gain

31

Marshall's share of the business was even more remote. But her conviction remained strong; she would not accept a life in which her actions were dictated by men. And so, to be true to herself, by her estimation she had two choices – either she would own at least a majority of *Herbvana,* or she would move on and find another opportunity. And since she liked this opportunity, she did not want to move on.

"I will control my own destiny," she said to herself. "I will let nothing interfere with my happiness."

She fixed these statements in her mind, using her footsteps along the waterfront to direct and focus her attention on them. And by the time she had reached the ferry terminal she had added another phrase to her mantra: "I will own *Herbvana.*"

Chapter 4

Sarah Strickland stood at the counter, waiting for her afternoon latte and looking over the headlines on the stack of newspapers near the register. One in particular caught her eye:

"HUMAN FOOT WASHES ASHORE IN PORT TOWNSEND."

"Interesting," Sarah said to herself – picking the paper out of the rack. She scanned the article, up until the reader was directed back to page A12, at which point the barista called her name and she fished around in his pockets for change to purchase the paper.

"Don't worry about it, Sarah," said Elizabeth – the manager of the store. Sarah and her fellow officers of the Bainbridge Island Police Department were fixtures at this, the Island's only free-standing chain coffee shop. Giving an officer a copy of the day's paper – late in the afternoon no less – seemed like the least she could do for one of her better customers. "Did you see that thing about the foot?"

"Was just reading it. Weird, huh?"

"Weird and gross. Apparently, it happens quite a bit up in Canada – especially Vancouver Island. Guess this time the tides just swept it to the US side of the border rather than the Canadian side. I remember a few years ago they had three feet wash up on the beaches up there in a span of just a few weeks. Three. One of them was even still in a sneaker."

Sarah chuckled. "Three is a very odd number of feet."

"Literally."

"Did they ever figure out what was going on?"

"I don't think so – there was a big mystery around it. But I remember the news saying that they thought it might be related to human trafficking. People paying money to get over here from China. This was around the same time they found those bodies in the shipping container."

While she only vaguely remembered the story about the feet, Sarah remembered all too well this second story. Seemed that someone in Asia – Sarah wasn't sure it was China but thought it might have been – had extracted several thousand dollars each from a group of would-be illegal immigrants, sealed them up in a shipping container and loaded aboard a trans-Pacific cargo ship. By the time the container was unloaded in Seattle, the ship's third port of call, every last one of them was dead. Messy business. "A person would have to be pretty desperate to get over here to be willing to pay to come across that way."

"It was just horrible."

"Yeah. So, this foot – the new one up in Port Townsend – what do you think's going on there?"

"That's your game, Sarah – the whole whodunit bit – I just make the coffee," Elizabeth laughed.

"And you do it well! Thanks for the paper. See you tomorrow."

Sarah waived goodbye to Elizabeth as she exited the store and got into her police cruiser parked outside. As she sipped her latte, she opened the newspaper and finished reading the article that had captured her attention. This time, it seemed, the foot wasn't in a shoe. But – as the author explained – this was at least the tenth foot that washed ashore in the Pacific Northwest over the past five years. Since no one had come forward indicating that they'd lost a foot – which is after all the kind of thing that you might notice missing – police on both the Canadian and the U.S. sides of the border didn't have much to go on. But they apparently did not suspect foul play. Rather, the consensus seemed to be that the rogue feet were the remains of unlucky boaters – a remarkable number of whom seemed to go missing in the frigid waters of the Salish Sea every year.

* * * * *

The next morning, and some thirty miles away, Marshall pulled off the highway and into the line at a drive-through coffee kiosk, the nose of his sedan pointing uphill toward the window several cars ahead. Immediately in front of him idled a huge Dodge pickup sporting a lift kit that elevated it nearly a foot above the stock height of the vehicle. An enormous pair of fake testicles hung from the trailer hitch on its bumper.

Exxxpresso Coffee was neither conveniently located nor particularly good. And it was ludicrously expensive. But it had something that the more legitimate coffee shops simply didn't have – and that was nearly naked baristas. As a consequence of that simple fact, it had become a coffee juggernaut in Kitsap County – with eager customers from around the area making the pilgrimage every day to overpay for lousy coffee with a side of

35

titillation.

As the line began to move forward, the driver of the Dodge took his foot off the brake - allowing the truck to roll back very slightly – momentarily allowing the truck to the rest its pseudo-manhood on Marshall's hood. Marshall seethed.

Some ten minutes passed before it was finally Marshall's turn to order. He rolled down his window and a face appeared at the kiosk. But only a face. Marshall's sports sedan was too low to the ground to afford him a clear view of the waitstaff. But no matter, this was a professional establishment – prepared for any potential customer. The barista, whose hair was a shade of red not found in nature, climbed onto a stepstool behind the counter making herself visible from the knees up.

And she was quite visible. Melinda stepped with authority to the top of the stepstool wearing something Marshall guessed was intended to be a nurse's costume. Clad in stockings, garters, and a lacy bodysuit, with a stethoscope fighting to escape her ample cleavage and strategically placed red adhesive tape covering her nipples, she towered over Marshall, making him feel even shorter than he was accustomed to feeling with his five-foot eight-inch frame. On this occasion, however, he found that he didn't particularly mind.

"Good morning, Baby," Melinda purred. "What can I get for you?"

"Quad Americano, please."

"Cream and sugar?"

"No, thanks."

"Sure thing, Baby. Coming right up."

Melinda stepped off the stepstool and disappeared downward back into the kiosk.

"Is Cindy here this morning?" Marshall asked toward the open window.

Melinda, bounding up onto the stool again, popped back into his field of vision. "No, Baby. We gave her the morning off." She again stepped off the stool and disappeared from view.

"Ok. Can I leave something for her?"

"Depends on what it is, Baby." Melinda's disembodied voice rose above the sound of the espresso machine. "Navy kid came through here a few days back and tried to give one of the girls something… well let's just say it was something the girl didn't want – don't want to spoil your day with the details – anyway, if its gross I'm not taking it."

"It's not gross – just an envelope for her – stuff for the business."

"Then yeah, Baby. You can leave it for her. She should be here this afternoon. I'll make sure she gets it." Melinda bounced back up on the stool, the kiosk window once again framing her figure. With the constant popping up and down in the window, she gave Marshall less the appearance of a sexy nurse than a bawdy prairie dog. But this was the pattern whenever he visited *Exxxpresso Coffee*; Marshall had begun to fear that if his visits continued, he would need to either purchase a higher vehicle or prepare to experience physical arousal around ground-dwelling rodents in some sort of pavlovian response.

"Here's your coffee, Baby. Quad Americano – that'll be twelve-fifty. Hope you've got a busy day in front of you, you're going to need to find a way to burn off all that caffeine."

"I'm sure I'll find a way," Marshall said as he paid for his coffee and craned his arm up to the windowsill of the kiosk to drop a few coins into the tip jar perched there. Marshall pulled a large, sealed manila envelope from his bag in the floorboard on the passenger side of the car. "This is for Cindy," he said as he handed it up and into the window.

"What's your name, Baby?"

"I'm sorry?"

"What's your name? So, I can tell her who dropped it off."

"Marshall. She'll know what it is – I'm, uhh, I'm the lawyer for the business," Marshall replied. This wasn't actually true. He had helped her form the business several years ago and apply for the necessary permits to operate the combination gentlemen's club and espresso stand. But he hadn't represented Cindy or *Exxxpresso Coffee* at all since starting *Herbvana* with Barry.

"Ooh, you're a lawyer?" "Yeah."

"I'm studying to be a nurse myself."

Marshall pondered this for a moment, wondering if she was pulling his leg or if her costume was intended to be ironic; most of the nurses he'd known had worn significantly less exciting attire. "Nursing's a good field – lots of demand. We'll always need nurses."

"That's what I'm thinking. Anyway, I'll need to find something to do after a while. These beauties aren't going to

38

improve with age." She cupped her hands to her breasts and gave them a gentle jiggle. Marshall was reasonably certain this wasn't the first time they had been used as a prop – perhaps not even the first time this morning.

"Well, they're looking pretty healthy right now." He once again craned his arm out of the window and dropped a couple bills in the tip jar. Melinda looked down on him with smug satisfaction.

"Oh, Baby. Thank you." Melinda gave him a wink. "I'll make sure this gets to Cindy. You have a great day now, Baby. Ok?"

"You too," Marshall replied. He put the car into gear and pulled forward, circling *Exxxpresso Coffee* and returning to the freeway.

Back in the kiosk, Melinda looked out the window. The drive-through was briefly empty, and she took the opportunity to kick off her platform heels and dab a paper towel at her armpits.

"It's a goddamned oven in here, Lucy. I'm sweating my ass off."

Lucy was seated along the back wall of the shop, perched comfortably on a stool near the door. "It's pretty bad."

"Like hot yoga with itchy lace and creepy dudes. Three months out of the year we bake in this thing and the other nine months we freeze. Mom's got to find a way to make it better or I'm heading over to *The Coffee Grind*."

"Wouldn't recommend it. Cindy's cheap but she's at least working the joint same as you."

"I guess."

In fact, Melinda had no intention of going over to *Exxxpresso Coffee's* nearest lingerie coffee competitor. *The Coffee Grind*, just a couple of miles down the highway, was already under investigation by local police for offering a somewhat more interactive customer experience than the community felt was appropriate. Things really heated up when a local man concealed himself in the bushes nearby with a telephoto lens. While the police were fairly certain that the gentleman's interest in photography was for his own personal enjoyment, the man had gotten lucky with the timing of his lechery – snapping a series of candid shots of one of *The Coffee Grind's* baristas allowing a local politician to lick whipped cream from the cleft at the top of her exposed buttocks, which she'd been kind and flexible enough to thrust through the window of the kiosk. This particular politician had campaigned on a platform of seeking to exclude retail marijuana sales from within the city limits of a municipality a few miles down the highway – all on the pretense of trying to protect family values. So, naturally, when the photos were passed to the press, the Seattle paper was delighted to publish them in full color, above the fold on the front page.

"Hey, what did that guy say his name was?"

"Marshall. Why?"

"And he said he was a lawyer?"

"So he claimed. You know the guy?"

"Sure do. Nearly fucked him on his boat a few weeks ago."

"Lucy!"

Lucy laughed. She loved shocking her older cousin.

"And I would have too. It's a really nice boat. But he got some stupid business call on his phone and we ended up having to come in early. He's loaded. But he's not a lawyer – or at least that's not his day job."

"No?"

"Nope. He owns *Herbvana*."

"The weed shop outside of Poulsbo?"

"Yeah. Even named his boat *The MaryJane*."

"Let me guess, that's how you met him…"

"Don't judge, Mel. You jiggle your tits for tips. I just like to have a little fun every now and then. Anyway, what'd he want with your mom?"

"Gave me an envelope for her. Said it was stuff for the business." Melinda retrieved the envelope from where she'd placed it on the counter and handed it to Lucy.

"It feels lumpy. What do you suppose it is?"

"Wanna find out?" Without waiting for a response, Melinda took the envelope back from Lucy and fired up the steam wand on the espresso machine. Carefully aiming a jet of screeching steam, she loosened the glue on the envelope, peeled open the flap, and peered inside. "Holy shit!"

"What is it?"

Melinda reached into the envelope and removed ten stacks of bills, each bound with a rubber band. "Lucy – you weren't kidding about him being loaded." She thumbed through one of the stacks. "There's twenty – twenty hundreds. That's…"

"Two thousand," Lucy replied.

"Ten stacks? You're holding twenty grand, Mel."

"Sweet Jesus that's a lot of cash." Lucy and Melinda stared at each other for a moment.

Eventually, Melinda broke the silence. "On his boat, huh?"

"Yes," giggled Lucy.

"Get me out on that boat? I'd have fucked him for sure."

Lucy snickered. At that moment, a pickup truck pulled into the drive-through. Melinda put her game face back on and flirted with the visibly nervous and acne-riddled teenager behind the wheel. After she'd extracted twenty dollars from the kid for a hot cocoa and a peek at her left areola, she blew him a kiss goodbye and turned back to Lucy. "So what's your dude want with my mom?"

Lucy shrugged. "I don't know. So far, our relationship hasn't really been about conversation.

Think she's in some kind of trouble?"

"Not sure why he'd be paying her if she was. Feels like maybe he's the one in trouble. But why pay Mom? And why in cash? It doesn't make any sense."

"The cash piece – I remember something about that. Remember I said when we were on the boat business got in the way of things? He took a call on speaker. I wasn't really listening too closely, but I did hear him say that they were having trouble with their bank. He had to move a bunch of money or it was going to be… what did he say…frozen. That was it. The account was going to be frozen and if they didn't move the money they'd lose it."

"Did he say how much?"

"It was a lot. Something like four million bucks."

"Shit."

"Yeah."

Melinda thought for a moment. "I'd still be fucking him." The two women howled with laughter.

"So, what are we going to do," asked Lucy.

"Do?"

"Well, twenty thousand is a lot of money but it's not like it's enough to retire on. We're not going to take the cash and head to Costa Rica, right?"

"Yeah. This would pay a lot of bills, but if he dropped it off for Mom she probably knows it's coming. And I'm guessing he's going to remember me – I did my best to make a lasting impression," Melinda said as she struck a pose. "Damn near stuck my snatch in his face. I can't see a good way for us to keep it."

"Right. We can't keep it. But still, I'd like to know what's going on."

"Me too."

"Want to ask your mom?"

"I don't know. Mom doesn't like it if we get too involved with customers. She's trying to have us keep a relatively low profile – doesn't want to end up in the paper."

"Sure."

"So maybe I just watch and listen? I'll let you know what I learn. In the meantime, let's seal this back up. No use in her finding out that we opened her mail."

"Fair enough." Lucy looked at her phone. It was almost 9:00 a.m. "Ugh. I've got to go. My shift starts in a half hour."

"You still with the evil empire?"

"Yeah. We've got better coffee."

"No doubt. But when you want to start making some decent tips come back here and we'll put you to work."

"I can't see Dad being ok with that."

In point of fact, Lucy's father would hardly have noticed. Since two years earlier, when Jerry came home early one day and caught his wife, Brynn – Cindy's sister – in a mid-afternoon romp with their landscaper – Jesus – Jerry had become even more emotionally distant than was his normal state and poured himself fully into his work. Which was ironic since his emotional unavailability had materially contributed to Brynn beginning to feel neglected and ultimately seeking comfort in the landscaper's embrace.

For weeks, Brynn had agonized over her feelings as she sipped chamomile tea in the kitchen and watched Jesus through the window while he tended her rhododendrons. Shirtless, sweating, dark-skinned, seemingly uninterested in kale and

44

almost certainly in the country illegally, Jesus was everything that Jerry was not. And then one day, when Jesus nipped his finger while pruning and asked if he might come inside to clean out the shallow wound, Brynn gave in to her deepest desires. She launched herself at Jesus with a fervor she'd almost forgotten she possessed. Jerry, entering through the open garage door, walked into the house just in time to see Jesus lying on his back completely naked on the family's dining room table, one leg dangling haphazardly over the side. Brynn was bent over his midsection. "Hola Señor," said Jesus. Brynn shrieked in surprise. It was the muted scream of someone with her mouth full.

Shortly after that fateful evening, Brynn realized being married to an emotionally distant accountant in the Pacific Northwest simply wasn't for her, and Jerry decided that he'd never liked that dining room table. She moved to an artist's commune in New Mexico; he cut the table into small pieces with a chainsaw. Life continued.

"No, probably not. But it would be fun to see the look on his face when you told him," Melinda replied.

Lucy shrugged. "Hey, let me know what you learn about Marshall and the cash, ok?"

"You got it."

Lucy exited and drove away, leaving her cousin to continue selling coffee with a wink and a tease while sweating away in the kiosk. After a few more hours, Cindy arrived, ready to start her shift and give her daughter a much-needed break.

"How's business?"

"Pretty good, Mom. Decent traffic and tips. Have a good morning?"

"Yeah. Got some errands run, picked up some dry cleaning. Nothing special but feels good to get it done." Cindy slipped off her sneakers and velour tracksuit and revealed her choice of work attire for the day – a fluorescent pink corset trimmed with black marabou around the breasts and a matching thong. From her backpack she pulled an aggressively high pair of heels. "Ready for me to take over?"

"Yep. I've got class at 1:00 and want to grab a burger before that. Want me to bring you anything?" Melinda pulled on a pair of sweatpants, a loose-fitting shirt and some sandals.

"I'm good – had a bagel on the way over."

"Ok. Oh – I almost forgot. Some guy named Marshall stopped by. Kind of handsome in a greasy kind of way. Anyway, he asked for you and when I said you weren't here he gave me to give you this." She pulled the envelope from the counter and handed it to Cindy.

"Ok. Thanks."

Melinda cocked her head to the side and looked at her mother. "Everything OK? He said it was legal stuff. Said he was the lawyer for the business."

"He said that? He's full of shit. I mean, he did help me set up the business a few years back. But we haven't used him for a long time. No this isn't for me. He's just dropping it off here for one of the other guys to pick up."

"Another customer?"

"Yeah. Guy named Earl. Real slimeball that one. Does something for the government – our tax dollars at work."

"So why is he dropping it off here?"

"I don't know. Just know that Earl asked me if it would be all right if people occasionally dropped things off for him here and then he picked them up. That was a few weeks back. Ever since, Marshall's come by about once a week with an envelope for Earl. And then Earl comes by like clockwork. 'Course Earl has come by like clockwork damned near every day since we opened. I think he likes the coffee." Cindy winked.

"So, every week Marshall brings by an envelope just like this one?"

"Yeah – for at least a month now."

"And there are others?"

"A few."

"And you don't know what it's about?"

"Don't think I want to know, really. Not sure it's any of my business. Plus, if there's something – I don't know – shady, going on? Well, it might be tricky if I knew too much about it. All I know is that they drop them off and Earl picks 'em up. For all I know, they're writing each other love notes. I sure as hell don't want to know anything about that."

"They're not writing love notes. No way a group of guys pass love notes back and forth to each other while staring at our tits."

Cindy laughed again. "I suppose not. But don't be so

suspicious. Ever since you started taking those classes you've been jumping at every shadow. I'm sure there's nothing to the envelopes. Just idiot guy stuff."

In fact, Melinda's educational endeavors had been making an impact on her. Although she'd told Marshall she was studying nursing – that was a lie. And she hadn't lied simply to match her outfit. She'd lied because she had found that when she told customers that she was studying criminal justice – with an eye toward going to law school after graduation – they tended to look nervous, tip poorly or not at all, and occasionally drive off without their coffee. Possibly some of them had warrants or thought she was working for the police when she wasn't strutting around in her unmentionables. She'd learned to keep her actual course of study and career objectives to herself. But as a practical matter, she knew that Cindy was right. The farther into her studies she got the more she tended to see crime and suspicious behavior around every corner. An occupational hazard, she told herself – it wasn't that she was seeing things that weren't there it was simply that she was finally able to see what was there. All around her, she saw evidence of malfeasance. And her mother receiving an envelope with twenty thousand dollars in cash from one customer, to be picked up by another customer? That had malfeasance written all over it.

"Maybe so, Mom. But it's weird. Do me a favor, ok? When Earl comes around the next time, I want you to try to focus on him and try to remember everything you can about his visit. Maybe even write it down. There's something going on and I'm worried it could be a problem for us. Maybe if we know what it is then we can avoid trouble. Will you do that?"

Cindy hugged her daughter and kissed her on the forehead. "You worry too much."

"Promise me, Mom. Ok?"

"Ok. Now get going before you're late for class."

Melinda left by the back door, getting into her car and driving away. Inside *Exxxpresso Coffee*, Cindy prepared for the afternoon shift. With the warmth inside the kiosk, the marabou fringe on her corset was beginning to stick to the sweat in her cleavage. It was going to be a long afternoon.

Chapter 5

Marshall approached the door and the weather-worn sign that read "BRANDEIS & ASSOCIATES." In a prior life, he'd been one of those associates. In fact, he was confident he'd been the only associate the firm had ever employed – unless you counted the part-time bookkeeper Cal had retained to help him keep the books of the firm just to the legal side of the line between business and fraud.

Opening the door, he found things hadn't changed much in the years since he'd left the firm. The waiting room consisted of an empty desk with a sign suggesting that the non-existent receptionist had stepped away and would momentarily return, along with a collection of desperate looking plants, outdated magazines and shabby furniture. It was not the sort of place where a sophisticated consumer of legal services would find comfort. But then again Cal's typical clients weren't especially sophisticated.

Marshall glanced at his watch. He was just a few minutes early for his appointment, so he sat down to wait – secure in the knowledge that when he'd opened the front door a light had gone off on Cal's desk to alert him that someone had entered the office. Moments later, Cal appeared in the hallway. He was escorting a middle-aged woman carrying a neck brace and a cane.

"Now, Mrs. Henderson, you're going to want to use these whenever you're outside, ok? If the insurance company sees you walking around without the cane or the collar, they're going to think you're not hurt. And these insurance companies and their lawyers – they're bad people Mrs. Henderson. They've even been known to send private investigators out to follow around people who've made a claim. It's important that you use them. Do you understand?"

"Oh, yes," the woman said – nodding vigorously and without obvious neck discomfort.

"Good. As soon as I hear back from the insurance company, I'll be reaching back out to you. Now sometimes they don't respond for weeks at a time – they like to go slowly and drag things out because they think you'll get frustrated and go away. I'm not going to let them do that, Mrs. Henderson. I'm going to be pestering them every day until we get you the money you deserve. Understand? But they may not respond to me quickly. So don't you worry a bit if you don't hear from me for a while. Understand? That just means they haven't gotten back to me yet but rest assured that I'm still working the case. Still working to get you your money. Got it?"

The woman nodded again – the vigorousness only slightly hampered by the cervical collar that Calvin had helped to fasten around her neck.

"Ok. Good. Well, thanks for your time, Mrs. Henderson – and your trust. I'll get back to you as soon as I have some news to report. Have a good day now."

Calvin shooed the woman out the office and onto the sidewalk beyond, closing the door behind her.

"Nicely done, Counselor."

Cal looked back at Marshall, sitting in the chair opposite the door, and began to laugh. "I'm getting too old for this, Marshall. Too damn old."

"You don't look like you've lost your touch."

"Not saying I've lost a step. Just saying it feels like harder work now than it was a few years back."

Marshall sized him up. Cal looked essentially the same as he had the last time they'd crossed paths. Possibly his comb-over was more pronounced and his jowls were slightly more pendulous than before – but the overall impression was the same. "You look like shit, Cal."

Cal laughed. "So, what's this all about, Marshall? What's so important that you didn't want to talk about it on the phone and had to drag your sorry ass all the way down here?"

"I need to talk. Need a sounding board – trying to work some things out."

Cal raised an eyebrow. "Ok. Come on back. I'll start the meter." He locked the front door before leading Marshall out of the waiting room and down the hallway and into his office. "Have a seat," he said – gesturing to a small chair.

Cal's office was a masterpiece of stagecraft. His desk was enormous – subtly elevated, along with his overstuffed leather chair, so as to cause Cal to appear larger than he actually was to anyone who might be sitting opposite it. Behind the desk and on the adjacent walls were large bookshelves containing impressively bound leather volumes – physical manifestations of legal knowledge which betrayed no trace of either the fact that they had been purchased at a thrift shop following the death of a local attorney and the subsequent liquidation of his personal effects, or that they were wholly inapplicable to any knowledge Cal might reasonably be expected to wield on behalf of a client since they reflected an outdated version of the laws of a jurisdiction several thousand miles away. In total, the room had the effect of providing Cal's clients with the impression – wholly unwarranted and inaccurate – that their choice of attorney would serve them well.

"So, what's this all about?"

"I've got a problem – a regulatory problem."

"Yeah?"

"Attorney/client privilege, and all that?"

"Of course."

"Here's the deal - our primary inspector from the LCB? He's a real piece of work. Even before we opened our doors he was all over my ass."

"Isn't that his job?"

"Sure. But he wasn't pushing us to toe the line. Asshole's got his hand out."

"Really?" Cal raised an eyebrow and cocked his head to the side. "A dirty regulator? I'm shocked."

"Yeah, I know. But the guy's a serious problem."

"What'd you do? Oh, shit. You paid him, didn't you?"

"Well, what else could I do."

Cal leaned back in his enormous, overstuffed chair, put his feet on the desk and began to laugh. "The dirty weed cop shook you down and you decided to pay up? You're an easy mark, Marshall. Too easy. So you paid him off – big deal. It's a rookie mistake. Chalk it up to the cost of doing business and a lesson learned."

"Yeah – but we keep learning it. That's the problem."

"He's still got his hand out?"

"He does. Constantly. Expects a payment every week. Says if we don't pay then he reports all our violations and we get shut down."

"Interesting. How deep are you in at this point?"

"Twenty grand a week. It's manageable from a cash flow standpoint, but I'd really like to cut him off. Would love to be out of the business of paying the guy. Trick is, how do I stop?"

"An excellent question. Can't really report him to the LCB without admitting you've been paying off one of their agents, right? And unless I've forgotten everything I learned in law school, paying cash to law enforcement to keep them from doing their jobs is a bit taboo. Not something you want to make a habit of. But you, my friend? You've done just that. Been paying this guy every week since you opened the shop?"

"Before. Almost five years now – every week like clockwork."

"And always twenty grand?"

"Yeah."

Calvin paused, doing some mental arithmetic. "You, Counselor, have now paid a member of our state's illustrious regulatory and law enforcement system bribes totaling about five million dollars?"

"No. I've been extorted in that amount."

"Oh, but that's not the way they'll spin it. You've got a duty to stay on the straight and narrow. Should've reported, him. That's what they'll say. Should have called up the director of the agency – called your sheriff – called your local prosecutor. Done something helpful. But instead, you – the dope peddler who can't keep his hands off underage girls – you decided to just pay off the agent so that he didn't make it hard for you to sell your poison to the men, women and children of Kitsap County. You know what you are? You, my friend, are fucked. That would be the technical legal term. Fucked in the first degree."

"Tell me something that I don't already know. Tell me how to solve the problem."

"It's very difficult to become un-fucked, Marshall. Maybe impossible." Cal paused, staring at the ceiling for a moment, and then took his feet from the desk and leaned forward in his chair. "Seems to me you've really only got one option."

"And that is?"

"Well, you need the pig to stop feeding at the trough. But pigs don't do that. He's not going to stop voluntarily, and you need him to back off without your getting slaughtered along with him. Sounds to me like you need him to go away. Permanently."

"You're not suggesting…"

"Oh, I'm not suggesting anything. As an officer of the court, I would, of course, never suggest that anyone engage in any form of criminal behavior. Even, for example, suggesting that a client grow, process or sell a Schedule I substance – like marijuana, say – in violation of federal law. Some lawyers might be comfortable giving that kind of advice, but I've got scruples, unlike one of my former associates." Cal winked at Marshall and continued. "No, I'm simply pointing out that if the fellow were out of the picture, then he couldn't come around with his hand out and he couldn't make trouble. So, it seems to me that – in a perfect world – your antagonist would simply disappear one day and not come back. Now, wouldn't that be nice?"

"I couldn't do that, Cal."

"Of course not. You don't have the stones. Neither do I. No, you and I are not the type," Cal sighed – seemingly wistful at the thought. "But there are those who are, Marshall. More of them than you know. And you might be interested to learn that the pricing can be quite reasonable. Economical, even. Wouldn't cost you more than a few months of your current payment arrangement."

"You're talking out of your ass, Cal."

"Oh, but I'm not, my boy. I've got a client or two with some expertise in this area. One is quite accomplished, really. Now I, of course, would never reveal a client confidence. But if you were looking for someone to help with this matter, I'm sure I could make a referral. Could make a call to someone with the right mindset – and the aforementioned stones – to get the job done."

Marshall stared at Cal, reclining once again in his chair with his good eye fixed on Marshall and the other lazily lolling to the left. "You've lost your mind. If I'm fucked for having paid bribes, how do I improve my hand having the man killed?"

"Think it through, Counselor. If it works, as it should, then you get to stop paying the bribes. So that's a positive. And, again, if you use a professional, then you should have some comfort that the deed will not come back to haunt you."

"And if the professional gets nabbed – first thing he'll do is to point the finger at me."

"First of all, the professional I'm thinking of isn't a 'he.' Far from it, in fact. She's quite the woman. Second, I'm confident she wouldn't point the finger if her lawyer told her not to. Her lawyer's gotten her out of quite a few close scrapes before. See no reason why she'd stop listening to legal advice now. After all, she wouldn't want to do anything that might waive the privilege. Plus, she wouldn't even know who ordered the job."

"You're her lawyer."

"Of course I am. And I'm yours. Now if she has a conversation with me – well, that's privileged, isn't it? I'm not telling her to commit a crime. I'm just telling her of certain opportunities and advising her of the legal consequences of taking advantage of them. She's not going to want to tell anyone that I did that, because if she did then she'd be waiving her attorney/client privilege and I might be compelled to share all sorts of things that I might know about her. And if you're talking to me about the legal challenges facing your business, well that's a

57

privileged communication as well, isn't it? You wouldn't want to tell anyone about our discussion since that would waive the very same all-important and constitutionally protected – almost sacred – privilege, and free me up to share all sorts of other information you might have given me... for example the fact that you've paid a few million in bribes to a member of law enforcement and used your lawyer's trust account to defraud our nation's banking system. So, neither one of you can be compelled to tell the cops what you've shared with me and each of you would be likely to suffer some pretty serious harm if you did share the information. And of course I certainly can't be compelled to testify against a client unless they've waived the privilege... Quite the interesting scenario, don't you think? Almost feels like a law school exam. You remember law school, don't you? It's that thing you almost failed."

"I... I need to think about this."

"Of course you do. Of course. Shouldn't rush into anything. Besides, your current situation is only costing you twenty grand a week. Small change for a big shot like you, right? Just because you could solve the problem quickly and easily for a hundred – plus my eminently reasonable fee for services rendered in connecting the dots – why wouldn't you want to take a good long time and think about it. After all, you're already fucked. How much worse could it get? Jesus you're gutless. Always were."

"Ok. I get it. Look, I'm not saying yes. But I'm not saying no either. I just don't want to know anything about it. I don't want to touch it – or have it touch me."

"Makes perfect sense. And may I say you're not the first to

express similar concerns. So, here's how this goes down. You put the name of the offending party on a piece of paper and put it in an envelope. I give that envelope to my client. Simple as that. Now of course there is the matter of payment. Cash is usually king. But in this case, I seem to recall that you've got a modest retainer in place. At your direction, I can release some of those funds to pay whomever you think appropriate. Just another business transaction. You don't even need to know the name of the payee. In fact, it's probably better if you don't. So what's it going to be Marshall? Shall we put an end to the matter or would you prefer to maintain the status quo and continue to hemorrhage cash?"

Cal fell silent and stared at Marshall. Seconds ticked by, marked by the ticking of an ostentatious clock sitting on the side of Cal's desk.

"What's your fee?"

"For you, buddy, since you were so generous with your retainer, only fifty grand. Special deal. That means for one-fifty you're out of the business of being extorted. Just think, in only a few weeks you'd be in the black on the whole deal."

"Ok."

"I thought you'd come to your senses. Now I'm going to leave the room for a moment. Going to walk down the hall and take a leak." Cal pulled a notepad and an envelope out of his desk drawer and placed them, along with an ornate fountain pen, on his desk. "While I'm gone, I'm going to leave you with these. You feel free to write down whatever information comes to mind. Seal it up and leave it on my desk before you let yourself out. Got it? With your permission, I'll then provide that envelope to my client. Do I have your permission?"

"Yes," said Marshall quietly.

"Excellent. Nice talking with you this evening. Now you take care of yourself and let's talk soon. Ok?"

Cal rose from his chair and exited the room, humming to himself. Marshall, taking the pen and the notepad wrote 'EARL McALLISTER' on the page, tore it from the notepad and sealed the paper in the envelope. He dropped the envelope on the desk, pocketed the pen, and walked out of the office and into the light of the early evening.

Hearing the front door shut, Cal walked back down the hall toward his office, sat down at his desk and began dialing his phone while turning the envelope over and over in his hands.

"Hello?"

"Angel it's me, Cal. I've got a client that could use your services. Straight job. Nothing fancy. Pays fifty grand."

"Don't waste my time. One hundred."

"I don't think I can squeeze the full hundred out of him. Seventy-five?"

"Squeeze harder."

"I can probably get him to eighty-five."

"Getting closer."

"Ninety? Should be an easy job."

"They're all easy. That's not the point. You want me to stick my neck out, the neck of one of my boys, it's a hundred or nothing."

"I've to make some cash on the deal too. You take a hundred and I'll end up with nothing."

"First of all, that's not my problem. Second, you're lying. Cocksucker like you, no chance you haven't already told the job it'll cost double what you're telling me. Probably said your fee was extra too."

"Angel, I'm shocked. Shocked that you would accuse me of such a thing. After all we've gone through together. All the times I've been there for you and your family."

"Yeah. But you didn't deny it, did you? Look, be straight with me and I'll be straight with you. The job costs a hundred. Whatever you cut on the back end? Not my concern. But I get a hundred. That's the deal. Those are the terms. You can always take your job elsewhere, maybe do the job yourself and keep all the cash. Ever done a job before? You might like it. Might like getting your hands dirty once for a change – instead of just being the little prick that sets it up. Anyway, I don't got all night. Got stuff to do around the house, you know? You going to keep wasting my time or we going to reach an agreement?"

"Fine. One hundred. Same arrangement as before?"

"Works for me. Stop by tomorrow?"

"Yeah."

Cal hung up the phone. Seeing the notepad still on his desk, he picked it up and put it back into the drawer with a chuckle.

"Fucker stole my pen. Can't trust anybody these days."

Chapter 6

Angel Prince spent her first night in jail at sixteen – a late bloomer by some standards – after she held up a gas station attendant. Held a box cutter to his neck while the guy pissed his pants and emptied the contents of the cash drawer, all twenty-three dollars of it, into her bag. She didn't know he'd managed to hit the alarm button under the counter until it was too late and the cops picked her up three blocks away from the scene.

She'd never been in trouble before – had no record of any kind other than one of lousy attendance at school. But she had no real family to speak of – at least not any that she would acknowledge or that would claim her. At her arraignment, the public defender assigned to represent her – a young, underpaid and overconfident lawyer named Calvin Brandeis – had argued that she should be released into his custody pending trial. It was highly unusual, but the prosecutor didn't have many alternative suggestions and it was really either that or keep her in jail pending trial. The judge wasn't inclined to have the young woman stay in jail that long when he suspected that even if she were convicted of the offense, she'd probably be sentenced to less time than she'd spend in lockup awaiting trial. And that's how the two of them, Angel and Cal, first got acquainted.

Some months later, after enjoying fully and frequently the company of the girl while she awaited trial, the thirty-year-old Cal convinced the prosecutor to drop the matter entirely. It wasn't ever clear exactly how Cal managed this, although the astute observer might rightfully wonder if it had anything to do with the fact that the prosecutor was subsequently disbarred for unspecified acts of corruption. In any event, Angel was free and grateful. And while she and Cal didn't maintain their romantic entanglement – such as it was – for long, over time their romance developed into a business arrangement. Angel would need a favor, and Cal would oblige. And when Cal needed a favor, as he often did, Angel could usually find a way to help.

This arrangement, though beneficial for both parties, hit a rough patch a few years later when Angel found herself in a new romance. Instead of a lawyer, this time the object of her considerable affection was stocky ex-con Louis Eldridge. Louis had done fifteen years for shooting a guy after an argument one hot night in Walla Walla while Louis and a few of his buddies who rode around on Harleys and called themselves the Hornets were shooting pool. Louis couldn't exactly remember what the argument was about but he was sure that his anger had been righteous. And Angel was sure that when she saw Louis ride by wearing a black leather vest with the bright yellow Hornets insignia he was the sexiest thing she'd ever laid eyes on. She hopped on the back of that bike and didn't look back.

But then Louis popped another guy. And he started smacking Angel around a bit when he got agitated. It was after he bloodied her nose one night that Angel realized she wasn't attracted to the man so much as the vest and the bike. So, while he slept off the substantial majority of a bottle of cheap whiskey, she took his pistol and put a couple of holes through him. Louis never woke up from that nap, and just like that Angel found herself the leader of the Hornets.

She hadn't realized it at the time, but this particular

community was something of a direct meritocracy. If you killed the leader you quickly found yourself installed as the new leader. Learning this didn't exactly make her feel safe and secure, but as it turned out the other members of the organization were scared shitless of Angel so she had little cause for anxiety.

With Angel installed as the new chief executive, the Hornets entered a renaissance. Membership expanded and Angel found herself something of a natural leader. Under her direction they launched an aggressive expansion – from what had been basically a social club for the low-level criminal element in central Washington to a well-run enterprise with business interests throughout the state. Some were legitimate. Some less so. But all were controlled by Angel from her home base: a dry-cleaning storefront in Port Orchard. For reasons she couldn't articulate, she'd loved the town ever since being brought there in cuffs following the incident with the box cutter and the incontinent clerk. Plus, she enjoyed doing the occasional ironing and pressing. It made her feel domestic.

Throughout it all, Angel had enjoyed having Cal available to bail her and other members of the Hornets out of trouble – literally and figuratively. Cal, on the other hand, had enjoyed having access to the services of the Hornets on an as-needed basis, both for himself and his clients. It was a mutually beneficial arrangement – symbiotic in the way of the dung beetle and the ungulates of the Serengeti although precisely who was who in that metaphor was occasionally difficult to determine.

The next day, just before noon, Cal walked through the door of Angel's Dry Cleaning carrying a bag of dirty shirts and a manila envelope. Angel was behind the counter, trying to explain to some smart-mouthed Navy kid that they didn't accept any responsibility for broken buttons – it said so right on his receipt. He asked to speak to the manager. She told him she was the manager, and the owner, and that he was free to take his business elsewhere. He kept pushing, arguing his case – but it wasn't going well.

When the kid finally lost his cool he let fly with an especially vulgar volley, culminating in a particularly offensive word for that most delicate part of the female reproductive anatomy. Cal winced – worried he was going to end up with blood on his shirts. The kid's blood. It would probably stain the shirts. Angel was good at cleaning things, but Cal knew blood was a tough assignment. To Cal's surprise, and the kid's confused discomfort, Angel just sat down on the stool behind the counter, casually picked up a wicked looking knife and began using it to clean under her fingernails. She stared at the kid – picking the dirt from under her nails with the point of the blade.

"Now where'd a nice little boy like you learn such an ugly word? Tell you what, I'm in a good mood so I'm going to do you a favor. I'm going to forget that I heard you just now. Going to forget that I heard you call me that. And that's good for you. That's real good. 'Cause if I had heard you call me that, you wouldn't be making it back to base any time soon. Now here's what we're going to do. You're going to take your cheap-ass laundry and you're going to leave. Carry it back home to your momma or your girlfriend or whoever you've conned into putting up with your shit. I ever so much as see you in the parking lot of my place again, I'm going to have a little fun with you. Slowly."

"You threatening me? You can't talk to me like that."

"I just did, Sweetie. And you're lucky I did. Lucky I gave you the chance to walk away."

The kid turned to Cal. "Did you hear her threaten me? You're a witness to this, right?"

"Sorry, my friend. I don't hear too well. I'm pretty sure the only thing I heard was you verbally abusing this poor woman. Didn't hear too much after that. Maybe you should just go." Cal looked at the kid and the kid looked from Cal to Angel and back to Cal again. "Now would be a good time. Before she changes her mind."

The kid picked up his shirts – broken buttons and all – and stormed out of Angel's Dry Cleaning – the cheerful sounding bell on the door ringing in his wake.

"Have a nice day, motherfucker. Cal, good to see you."

"You too, Angel. Keeping out of trouble, I see."

"These Navy pricks. Doesn't anyone have any manners anymore? What'd you bring me?"

"Five shirts, one envelope." Cal laid the bundle on the countertop.

"Next Wednesday ok on the shirts?"

"Perfect."

"And on the other matter, any particular deadline?"

"No. Sooner is better than later – but that's always the case, isn't it?"

Angel opened the envelope and emptied its contents on the table – stacks of cash and Marshall's envelope from the night before. "Fifty?"

"Yep. Fifty now and the other fifty when the job is complete." "Anything special about the job? Anything we should know?"

"He works for the state – basically an enforcement guy for the LCB – the Liquor and Cannabis Board."

"I know the LCB. We've had dealings. The guy's a cop?"

"A weed cop."

"You should've told me yesterday. I might've given you a discount – feels like I'm doing the public a service."

"Yeah, well, every job's a public service from someone's perspective. Anyway, keep it clean. The guy deserves it but we can't afford a mess."

"Clean it is. I'll have your shirts by next Wednesday. And I'll call you as soon as we're done with the job."

Cal thanked Angel. After he left the shop, Angel opened Marshall's envelope. "Earl McAllister. Well, Earl. Looks like your luck's about to run out." She picked up the phone and began dialing. "Hey, we got a job. Guy's name is McAllister. Earl McAllister. He's a weed cop for the LCB... Yeah, I know – I wouldn't have minded doing this one for free but we're getting paid for it... Find out everything you can find out about him. Want to know where he lives, his habits, what he eats for breakfast. Everything. Don't touch him. At least not yet. The job needs to be really clean – so we'll scope him out for a while first and then make a plan. Got it? Good. Let me know what you find."

* * * * *

"Hey, Earl?"

"Yeah?"

"Do you think fish get depressed?"

Earl mulled Steve Fujimoto's question over in his mind for a moment. He wanted to be sure he'd heard it correctly. He'd gotten used to Steve saying weird shit, but this was weird even for him.

"How would you know? I mean, I've never seen one look especially happy when they're in the net – even less so after you've whacked it. But no. I don't think they get depressed."

"Do you think they've got, like, aches and pains? I mean like backache or something chronic – course, I mean, some fish don't really have backs, exactly. Halibut for example; I'd be hard pressed to say a halibut has a back. But really, aches and pains – you know, like people?"

"What's this about, Steve?"

"It's right here in the paper." Steve pointed to an article in a badly folded copy of the local newspaper. "Says they've found a bunch of drugs in salmon. Antidepressants and opioids, mostly. But also a lot of caffeine."

68

"Fish don't do drugs, Steve."

"I know. Just, you know, thinking it would be kind of convenient if…"

"Seriously." Earl cut him off. He loved a good opportunity to have fun at essentially anyone else's expense and this line of inquiry felt like it had promise. "I mean, what do you think is happening? Big king salmon's heading into the sound from the Pacific – starts feeling kind of moody – figures why not stop for a pick-me-up. After all, he's been swimming for miles…"

"Earl…"

"His fins are worn out – and what's worse he knows he's just going to find a river, head upstream and die. I mean, what's the point of it all? You're an orphan when you hatch and a bunch of your brothers and sisters were eaten before they even got a chance to swim. That's depressing already. If you're lucky enough to make it out of that river and to the ocean, well guess what? There's a bunch of stuff out there waiting to eat you too. Sucks, doesn't it? And then to top it all off, once you get big and fat and happy you start feeling homesick."

"Earl…"

"Homesick and horny, in a fishy kind of way. Feeling like you want to find a nice girl and settle down. Maybe have a few fry of your own…

"Earl, come on…"

"So you head back into the Sound and you know what you find? First, a bunch of asshole fisherman trying to catch you. Maybe even snag you – how sporting is that? Just so you can end up in somebody's smoker. And if you get past those idiots and back to your river then you may be lucky enough to get eaten by a bear. And I do mean lucky." Earl was laughing now – feeling Steve squirm in the seat beside him. "Cause if you don't get eaten by the bear then things are really going to suck. You're going to start changing colors. In fact, while you're heading up that little stream of yours, your whole body is going to change so much your own mother wouldn't recognize you. She wouldn't recognize you anyway since she died before you were born. But you know what I mean."

"Earl, please.."

"So, by the time you make it to the actual spawning grounds you're pretty much shot. You're a wreck. And you know what happens when you get there? You spawn and then you die. You know, Steve, now that I think of it I bet they probably are depressed. Damned depressed. And for good reason. So yeah, I can totally see why salmon would be popping antidepressants like candy."

"I didn't say the fish were taking pills, Earl."

"Didn't you? You said they were on drugs."

"I said they found drugs in their systems."

"Yeah – so they must be taking them, right? Really can't blame them. They've got some sort of existential salmon blues. That's some heavy shit. Just wait until they do that testing again in a few years. I bet those salmon will have started smoking weed by then as well."

"Jesus. Let it go already."

Earl got one last chuckle at Steve's discomfort, pulled into a parking lot and stopped the car. They'd reached their first compliance target of the day – a mom and pop retailer in a two-traffic-light town in the middle of nowhere. The place looked like it had a grand total of five businesses clustered around two blocks and one of those was boarded up. An almost discreet neon sign in the window promised cheap weed.

The men got out of the car and Steve started toward the door.

"Wait a second, Steve. Let them see us coming. Gives 'em time to worry. I love it when they worry – makes everything go nice and easy."

Steve turned around and sauntered back toward the sedan. Earl was leaning against the fender, lighting a cigarette. Steve, judging the direction of the breeze, passed Earl and tried to get upwind.

"You know those things are going to kill you."

"Well, they haven't managed yet." Earl exhaled a long plume of smoke.

Steve fumbled with his phone while Earl smoked. Out on the highway, a steady trickle of cars passed by. Every so often, Steve could see a driver begin to pull into the parking lot only to recognize the logo on the side of their sedan - "Washington State Liquor & Cannabis Board" – and suddenly get religion.

Finally, Earl stamped out the nub of his cigarette and straightened himself up. "That's enough. They should be good and petrified by now. Let's do this."

Chapter 7

"I've got this," Barry said aloud to himself as he pulled the drawstrings on his hoodie. It was black in color. At least it was black in the front. Conspicuously screen-printed on the back in brilliant white lettering, well out of Barry's sight, was the *Herbvana* logo. It featured prominently in precisely the sort of way you might expect if the hoodie was intended to act as an advertisement for the business – which of course it was.

Barry stumbled out of his vehicle and walked toward the door of the shop, taking care to try to stay outside the obvious field of vision of the security cameras but apparently oblivious to the fact that he had parked with his license plate in full view of those same unblinking eyes. He stepped to the front door of the shop, doing his best to stay in the shadows, and unlocked the door. Upon entering, he pivoted quickly and, retrieving the code from the now slightly smudged palm of his hand, he disabled the security alarm.

"Piece of cake."

After crossing the sales floor, he unlocked the door to the storeroom and stepped blissfully into his happy place – his temple of weed. Pausing briefly to congratulate himself on his success as a "legal" cannabis entrepreneur, he then set about stuffing his pockets with a wide assortment of product. Several items he picked out for himself. Being a generous fellow, he made sure also to pilfer samples for his close friends – and more than a few acquaintances. Since Marshall was laying down the law, and he didn't know when he'd have his next opportunity to stock up, he wanted to be sure he grabbed enough to keep his stash full for a while. "What's the point of owning your own weed shop if you can't enjoy the benefits?"

Throughout the entire escapade, Barry did his best to stay out of sight of the ever-watchful cameras. But he was stoned. And so despite his best efforts to emulate the stealth and finesse he'd watched – studied even – on display in a recent big-budget heist film, he was in full view of the well- placed cameras essentially throughout his illicit visit.

Barry, having pocketed his treasures, returned to the sales floor – forgetting to close or lock the door to the storeroom. He walked to the security panel near the front door, set the alarm, and exited out into the night – locking the front door behind him. Crossing the parking lot to the car, he allowed himself a very slight fist pump, in celebration of a job well done, and proceeded to back out of the parking space – in the process allowing the security camera to get one last close up of the license plate on the vehicle and drive out into the night.

Early the next morning, when Marshall arrived to open the shop for the day, the first thing he noticed was a vial containing a joint lying on the ground directly in front of the shop door. The vial was unopened and still bore the tax stamp required by the state. He chuckled to himself, thinking of the despair that must have been felt when that particular customer – whoever it was - got home and figured out that he had misplaced his purchase. But his chuckle turned sour as soon as he opened the door and looked into the shop. Another vial was lying on the showroom floor, and the door to the storeroom was wide open. "Shit!"

He scrambled inside – dropping his briefcase on the floor and rushing into the storeroom to see the extent of any damage when he heard the security system begin to beep. Rushing back to disarm the system before it automatically alerted the authorities, his mind raced to understand how the shop might have been burgled without setting off the alarm.

The beeping silenced, he turned his attention back first to the showroom. As far as he could tell, nothing was out of place. Moving into the storeroom, again, there was no obvious sign of anything missing; the storeroom was continually disorganized – a fact that had contributed to his long-running frustration with Barry – but appeared no more so than usual this morning.

Leaning back against the storeroom desk, he considered his next steps. Should he call the police and report a break-in? Before calling the police, should he alert LCB that they'd had a breach of security? Even if they had the best security in the world – which they didn't – a breach would almost certainly be a mark on their record. And with Earl as their inspecting officer, Barry wasn't eager to self-report a problem. But if the police were called they would almost certainly loop in the LCB.

"First thing – let's figure out what's missing," Barry said to himself. He grabbed his phone from his pocket. Seeing the time – still before 8:00 a.m., he concluded that there was no chance that Barry was awake yet. And so, not wanting to endure a conversation with a half-awake stoner, he decided to send him a text message. "Break-in at shop. Come quickly." He knew Barry wasn't likely to wake for several hours, which was just fine with him since it would give him the process of taking stock of things in peace and quiet before Barry rolled in.

He jiggled the mouse to wake the computer sleeping on the desk and prepared to pull up an inventory spreadsheet so that he could begin the task of figuring out what was missing. As the machine came to life, however, he caught sight of the security camera out of the corner of his eye. "Come on, Counselor. Use your head. The camera probably caught the whole thing. Examine the evidence."

Logging on to the computer, he clicked into the program for the security system and – using the password printed on the note stuck to the computer monitor – accessed the recordings for the prior 24 hours. Marshall sat, staring grimly at the screen as he watched the grainy black and white footage from the camera inside the storeroom. The system was motion activated, making it appear that just as quickly as the door to the storeroom had been closed for the evening, it was immediately opened again by a hooded figure.

From the vantage point of the camera, the intruder's face was obscured by the hood and in the darkened room – illuminated only by the light streaming in from the outside window and the street beyond – it was impossible to see any distinguishing features. The intruder moved oddly among the shelves within the room – a caricature of someone trying to avoid being seen. Throughout the footage, the burglar appeared as if a phantom, with only the dark fabric-covered shoulders and front torso visible – a flash of pale skin occasionally darting from the sleeves as the intruder reached into bins, grabbed product and thrust it into pockets with a flourish.

After moving through the storeroom, the burglar pushed back through the door and into the showroom. Walking directly away from the lens, the captured a flash of white on the back of the intruder's hooded shirt. A logo that Marshall knew quite well.

"Son of a bitch! The bastard's a customer."

Stopping the video at the point where the thief entered the sales floor, Marshall switched the feed from the storeroom camera to the feed from the entrance of the shop. He watched the intruder walk from the storeroom door across the floor – the vial containing the joint falling from the intruder's pocket. After pausing briefly at the security panel adjacent to the door, the intruder exited the shop.

Marshall switched the view again, this time to the feed coming from the camera outside the shop. The camera revealed the intruder closing the door, locking it, and then walking out of frame. In the last few seconds of video, Marshall saw the tail of Lilith's pride and joy, an aging split-window Volkswagen microbus, back directly into the frame – license plate and *Herbvana* bumper sticker clearly visible – and drive away.

Dumbstruck, Marshall sat back in his chair, pressed his fingers into his temples, and stared at the ceiling.

When Barry arrived at the shop – just before it opened at 10:00 a.m. – he found Marshall still sitting at the desk.

"Hey, Man. I got your text. Some kind of trouble here last night?"

"Yes. We were robbed."

"Seriously? That sucks. Anything missing?"

"That's what happens in a robbery, Barry. Stuff goes

missing."

"Don't get testy – I don't know all your legal jargon, that's your territory. Anyway, what got taken?"

"I'm still trying to figure that out. Trying to compare our inventory records with what's actually here. But it's tough, the inventories are a mess."

"Sorry about that. I've been meaning to try to clean it up a bit."

"Well, it's a bit late at this point. So, anyway, that's what I'm trying to do."

"Did you call the cops?"

"No. And I didn't call LCB either. Want to know exactly what happened before we call them – if we call them."

"Probably smart. Earl, especially. He'd bust our asses for sure about this."

"I'm sure that he would. Especially if he saw the footage from the security cameras."

"Pick anything up?"

"Quite a bit, actually."

Barry bristled. "Like what?"

"Well, it looks like the thief tried to hide her appearance."

"*Her* appearance? We got robbed by a chick?" Barry started to chuckle.

"Yes. And not just any chick. Our thief was your chick: Lilith."

Barry's laughter stopped abruptly. "No way, man. Lilith's cool. She wouldn't do that."

"I watched the tape. She's wearing a hoodie and trying to cover her face. But it's her."

Barry glanced through the open door back out into the showroom. Lilith would be arriving for her shift at any minute. "No way, Marshall. I'm telling you; she wouldn't do that."

"Let me show you something." Marshall jostled the computer mouse and the monitor flickered to life. On the screen, Marshall had a saved a still image of the microbus. "That's our burglar pulling out of the parking lot."

Barry stood still. He hadn't factored on the bus appearing in the security camera. And he'd only taken Lilith's vehicle last night because his scooter was low on gas and he didn't want to stop along the way. Now, he had no idea how he was going to explain his way out of this – out of getting Lilith fired or, worse yet getting her jailed, without implicating himself in the robbery.

"Whoa."

"Whoa is right, Barry."

"Hold on a second. Let's not do anything hasty. I mean, we need to handle this the right way, right?"

Marshall wasn't sure where Barry was going with this. "Yeah. We do. What do you have in mind."

"I'm not sure. Not yet anyway. But I don't want to do anything without thinking it through. You know?"

Marshall thought this might actually be the smartest thing

he'd heard come out of Barry's mouth since he walked into the strip mall that day and said he wanted to start *Herbvana*. It appealed to every lawyerly aspect of his personality. "Sure, Barry. We can think about it for a bit. But we do have to make a decision at some point relatively soon. Let's each think about what we think is right – and then talk as we close up shop tonight. That work for you? But if we do that, we each need to watch her really closely today – right? We can't let her out of our sight. We've got a thief working for us. We need to remember that. Ok?"

"Yeah. Watch her close. I can do that. I mean, I kind of do that anyway, you know?" Barry forced a little laugh, hoping to get Marshall to join in, but Marshall didn't take the bait.

For the rest of the day, Marshall and Barry each kept within eyesight of Lilith. But while Marshall watched her intently for any sign of guilt, Barry only stayed near to Lilith for Marshall's benefit – doing his best to appear like he was watching Lilith while in reality he was trying to think of some plan that would allow Lilith to escape the snare he'd inadvertently set. A snare that seemed certain to catch either her, or possibly himself. A snare he wanted to avoid at all costs.

Shortly before closing, Marshall beckoned Barry back into the storeroom. "We need to make a decision about what to do. If we're going to fire her, we need to do it tonight."

"I don't want to fire her, Marshall. I really don't believe she did it."

"You saw the tape, Barry. We both did. The burglar had a key to the front door, had the security code for the alarm, and drove Lilith's car. Lilith's our burglar. You've got to face facts."

"Yeah. I saw the tape. But I didn't see her face. How do we know it wasn't someone else. Somebody pretending to be Lilith."

"Somebody *pretending* to be Lilith?"

"Yeah. I mean – we don't want to fire her if it wasn't her, right? And we never saw her face in the video, right? I mean so we don't really know it was her. It's all circumspectual evidence, man."

"Circumstantial."

"What?"

"You said 'circumspectual' evidence. You meant 'circumstantial'. 'Circumspectual' isn't a thing."

"Whatever, man. My point is, we don't really know it was her. You can't convict somebody on circumcisal evidence!"

Marshall winced at Barry's malapropism. Circumspectual evidence was idiotic. But circumcisal evidence sounded downright painful. In any event, he had no desire to debate legal terminology with a stoner, even if that stoner was his business partner. "People get convicted on the basis of circumstantial evidence all the time. They send people to jail – sometimes even send people to death – on the basis of less evidence than is shown in that video, Barry. She's our burglar."

"Nah, man. I don't believe it. Why don't we just ask her?"

"Ask her?"

"Yeah. Ask her if she robbed the place last night."

80

"And you think she'll admit it if she did?"

"She's never lied to me before, man."

This, too, made Marshall cringe. Not only had Lilith lied to Barry before – it was Marshall's impression that she was making a living out of it. She obviously had no romantic interest in the guy but had managed to convince Barry that she was his girlfriend – all while conspicuously dating a series of attractive young women. It wasn't that Lilith hadn't ever lied to Barry – it was that Barry hadn't managed to realize she was lying most of the time. "Barry, buddy, I know this is hard. But you've got to face facts. She robbed us last night. She stole from us. We've got to fire her."

"I won't do it."

"Ok, then I will. Because even if you're willing to let her steal from you – I'm not willing to let her steal from me."

"It's not right, man."

Marshall turned away from Barry and walked through the doorway into the showroom. "Lilith – I need to see you for a second."

"Yeah," Lilith replied, "what's up?"

"We got robbed last night."

"No shit?"

"Don't play games with me, Lilith. I know it was you."

Lilith stopped polishing the display cases and turned to look at Marshall. "What?"

81

"I've seen the security video. It isn't especially flattering for you – didn't catch your good side."

"Ok – I don't know what you're talking about."

"We've got cameras all over this place. You know that. There's one in the storeroom, one here in the showroom, and one out in the parking lot."

"Yeah?"

"Yes. And we've got you on each of the three cameras."

"Not last night you don't."

"Yes, Lilith. Yes we do."

"No, Marshall. No you don't. I wasn't here last night. Just ask Barry."

Marshall pondered this briefly. Had Barry had a chance to get to her during the day and tell her that this was coming? Had they cooked up an alibi for her? "What?"

"Just ask Barry. You know, Barry? The stoner on your left? Your business partner? Ask him. He'll tell you I wasn't here last night. I was in Portland visiting a girlfriend of mine. Didn't get back until early this morning. Barry picked me up at the ferry terminal."

Marshall's blood froze. Every instinct told him that Lilith was telling the truth. But if Lilith was telling the truth, why hadn't Barry mentioned that she he knew she had an alibi. Just as he turned back around to question Barry, his partner spoke up.

"See, man. I told you she wouldn't do something like that. It must have been someone pretending to be her – or something like that."

"Barry. Her bus is on the video. You saw it yourself."

"What?" Lilith interjected.

"Your bus. That Volkswagen of yours is on the security footage – backing out of the parking lot just after the burglar re-arms the security system and closes and locks the front door."

"But, I was in Portland."

"Ok. Who had your VW?"

Lilith turned to look at Barry. And it was at that exact moment that Lilith and Marshall simultaneously realized that Barry had been the one who had robbed *Herbvana*.

"Barry – I left the bus at your place. Left you with the keys."

"Uh."

"What the fuck?" Marshall interjected. "Why would your rob your own store?"

"Man, I, uh. I just needed some stuff, you know? I mean my stash was getting low and you've been getting all pissy lately about things and I just thought…"

"You thought you'd rob us?"

"Well, not exactly. I just thought I'd take what I needed and since you wouldn't know then you wouldn't get mad and things'd be cool. You know?"

Lilith began to chuckle. Marshall did not. "No, Barry, I don't know. And things definitely are not cool. You thought I wouldn't find out? We've got security – you know that. Of course I was going to find out. And another thing, we've got to account to Earl for every ounce of weed we've got. Any of it goes missing and its our ass, Barry. You know that."

"I'm sorry, man. I just didn't want to piss you off. Didn't want it to become a big hassle."

"Well you fucked up; I am pissed off. You're stealing from us – but more importantly you're stealing from me. Jesus, how could you be so stupid?"

"I just wanted to be near the plant, man. I mean, this plant is beautiful. It's beautiful, Marshall – it makes everything better – everything peaceful. I never wanted this whole business empire thing, man. That's your deal. I just wanted to stay near the plant and be able to go legit. And now it's all jumbled and you're telling me I can't take what I need and always on my case. This completely sucks. I mean, how can you tell me I can't take what's already mine. That's not stealing, Marshall. That's just taking what's mine, man!"

"It doesn't belong to you, Barry. It doesn't belong to me either. It belongs to *Herbvana*."

"Yeah, but I own half of *Herbvana*."

"You sure do. And from where I sit, that looks like a pretty big problem. Maybe the biggest problem facing us today."

Marshall, narrowing his eyes, walked over to the safe that was bolted to the floor and the wall alongside the desk, an enormous black monstrosity that dominated that corner of the room. No traditional business would require such an apparatus, but in the cash-only world of cannabis retailers it was a necessity. The business routinely had several hundred thousand dollars of cash on hand – a situation that presented tremendous risk. He twisted the dial on the safe and opened it – in the process giving Lilith and Barry a glimpse of stacks and stacks of cash inside. From an upper shelf, nearly so high that Marshall couldn't reach it, he retrieved a small, shiny, black revolver.

"Dude?"

"Don't worry, Barry," Marshall replied. "As long as you do what I say I won't need this. You know, it's funny – I always figured Martha here would be my last resort in case we were robbed." Marshall looked at the revolver, his expression a mixture of fear and admiration. "I could go to the safe and pull this baby out to defend myself – defend *Herbvana* – if necessary. Never really thought I'd had to use it on my partner. That's disappointing, Barry. Really disappointing."

"Man, I don't know what you're planning to do. But you can put that that away. I mean, we're friends here, right? Don't need to go inserting firearms into any of this. We're friends."

"Oh, sure we are, Barry. You, me and Lilith – all good friends. But you know what, friends don't rob other friends, do they? I mean, they don't – for example – sneak into each others' businesses in the middle of the night and rip them off. Right? Except you did that, didn't you. You broke in here last night. And you couldn't even do that well. You fucked it up just like you fuck up everything around here. You managed to get your girlfriend implicated in the whole thing even though she was out of town. Some friend you are to her. Some friend you are to me. Now that I think about it, maybe only Lilith and I are friends. Maybe you're the problem. But you know what, I'm good at solving problems. And I think I've got a solution for this one."

Lilith listened intently. Not knowing where Marshall was heading with all of this, she did her best to stay positioned behind him. Thinking he might turn on her next, she wanted to be prepared to do whatever she could to defend herself.

"Here's the solution, Barry. You're going to sell me your stake *Herbvana*." He pulled open the desk drawer, removed a folder and opened it to reveal a form of purchase and sale agreement. "I drafted the papers a while back, just in case this became necessary. Take a look."

He handed the agreement to Barry who stared at him blankly. "You can't do this, Marshall. It isn't right."

"My offer is more than fair. Read it. Or would you rather have me read it to you? I'm offering you the chance to cash out. A million dollars. A million dollars to just walk away. To walk out that door and never come back. You can even take the money and open a new shop – compete with *Herbvana* if you want – you just can't stay here."

"But I don't want to sell. *Herbvana* was my dream, man. You know that. You can't make me sell."

"Oh, I think we can." Marshall tapped the handle of the revolver. "In fact, I'm sure of it."

"You can't threaten me, man! We're partners." Barry was becoming agitated. Angry even – a side of him that neither Lilith nor Marshall had seen before.

"We were partners. That ends tonight. Don't be stupid, Barry. Sign the papers, take the money and just go away. It's simple."

"It's not simple. It's my dream. It wasn't even your idea, Marshall. It was mine. I won't do it! I won't let you steal my dream!"

Marshall stepped forward, the revolver in his hand. He leveled it at Barry. "Sign the fucking papers, Barry."

Barry snapped, lunging forward and grabbing Marshall by the throat. Taller than Marshall and outweighing him by a considerable margin, the force of Barry's attack caused Marshall to stagger backward. The two struggled, Barry with one hand on Marshall's neck and the other holding Marshall's right wrist – Marshall holding the revolver in his right hand and trying to dislodge Barry's grip on his neck with the left.

"You can't steal my dream! *Herbvana* was my idea! Help me, Lilith! Grab the gun! Call the cops! Do something!"

Lilith watched the two men jostle for position, neither willing to give an inch, and assessed the situation. "I can manage Barry," she thought to herself – "I can handle him." Having chosen her desired victor, she scanned the room for a weapon. Seeing none, she brought herself up behind Marshall and kicked.

Lilith channeled all her anger at the world, at her father and at men in general into that single kick, which traveled swiftly up the inside of Marshall's left leg, grazing his thigh before landing with a sickening smack in his groin. The force of her kick lifted Marshall very slightly off the ground and caused him to momentarily forget all about *Herbvana*, his argument with Barry and the gun in his hand. But that nanosecond of forgetfulness was quickly extinguished. In striking her blow, Lilith unsteadied Marshall, and as a consequence the force being applied by Barry to the shorter man's throat prevailed in their struggle.

Marshall's body tumbled backward, the contents of his shirt pocket catapulting across the room. Barry, his force against Marshall no longer being resisted, toppled over on top of Marshall, who dashed his head against the metal shelving unit in the center of the room before landing, with a slight bounce and a sound not unlike the thump of an overripe honeydew, on the hard concrete floor. The gun fell from Marshall's hand, the force causing the cylinder to burst open. Barry rolled away from Marshall, groaning – the wind knocked out of him from the impact of the fall.

Lilith snatched the gun from the floor. There were no bullets in any of the chambers.

Sitting up, Barry looked up at Lilith, who had by now tucked the unloaded gun into a pocket. "What happened?"

"You took him down. Don't know your own strength, I guess."

"Yeah. I guess. I don't know what came over me. Or you, Marshall. I've never seen you be that aggressive before, man. But it's cool. I know you're just trying to do what you think is right for the business, right? I get it. But let's talk it out. Ok? Marshall?"

Chapter 8

Marshall didn't respond. As Barry turned to look at his partner, Marshall's body began convulsing on the floor of the storeroom.

"Oh, man. Oh shit," stammered Barry. "Marshall! Marshall, come on, man!"

Lilith, standing back in the corner, remained silent as Marshall's convulsions stopped and he lay still – lifeless – on the hard cement floor. Barry began to wail – the plaintive blubbering sobs of a child that has become lost. Whatever strength of will Barry had possessed only moments ago – at a time when he believed his life was being threatened by his friend – was now a distant memory.

"Marshall?"

"He's dead, Barry."

"You don't know that! Check his pulse or his breathing or something. You know CPR? Maybe we do CPR. He can't be dead!"

Lilith took a step toward Marshall's body and found that her right leg was throbbing in pain, the lingering effect of the kick she'd delivered moments earlier. She prodded Marshall with her left foot – not another kick exactly but none too gentle either. He didn't move. She leaned down beside him and clasped his wrist in search of a pulse. Finding none, she shifted her weight to kneel down, put her head on his chest and listen for a heartbeat or sounds of breathing, only to slip on the rapidly growing pool of blood that was forming around him and land solidly on Marshall's chest. His body let out a long gurgling sound from the pressure of her weight on his torso, like air and fluid being let out of a balloon.

"Oh, shit. What are we going to do? I killed him, Lilith. I killed him."

"Shut up, Barry."

"I'm sorry, Marshall. I'm sorry, I…"

"Barry, shut your fucking mouth! Get hold of yourself."

"But he's dead. He's dead and it's all my fault. I killed him."

"Don't be stupid. What we've got to do now is think."

"We've got to call the cops or an ambulance or something."

"And tell them what, exactly? Tell them it was an accident? You accidentally tackled him and bashed his head in? You guys got into a fight and he ended up dead. That's not going to look good for you, Barry. They're not going to believe you didn't mean to kill him."

"But that's the truth."

"It doesn't matter if it's the truth. They're not going to believe you. No. We call the cops and we're going to jail. You, for sure, are going to jail. We've got to think."

As Barry continued to whimper, Lilith stood up and took stock of the situation. Barry clearly didn't know that she had played any role in Marshall's death, and she saw no need to share that information. If someone was going to do jail time, Barry was her nominee for the assignment. But even so, if Barry could avoid jail that would be better. And if Barry thought that she could point the finger at him – could put him behind bars by squealing – but that she didn't – well then that might be the best possible outcome. She could dramatically improve her hand – take over *Herbvana* – she just needed to play her cards correctly. In an instant she pictured herself growing the business to a chain of stores throughout the state and then, as other states legalized marijuana, throughout the nation. She could be the nation's first female cannabis billionaire. Wouldn't that be something? If nothing else, it would be something to rub her father's nose in from time to time.

"You've got two problems, Barry."

"Marshall's dead."

"Ok. Make that three problems. Marshall being dead – that's problem number one. But problems two and three are right here in this room too."

Barry stopped blubbering momentarily and looked, wide-eyed, around the room trying to guess her meaning.

"Problem two is that you've got a body to deal with. It isn't just going to go away on its own."

"Yeah?"

"And problem three is that camera over there on the wall." She jerked her head in the direction of the security camera. "That thing recorded the whole thing. Recorded your breaking in here last night, recorded your fight with Marshall, and recorded your killing him."

Barry's eyes widened. "What am I going to do?"

"First thing to do – and I'm going to help you here, Barry – first thing to do is to try to shut off the camera and delete the recording."

"I... I don't know, Lilith. Marshall said the security was really important. Said we could lose our license without it."

"And he was right – but be realistic. What risk do you want to take – risk that you lose your license or risk that you go to jail for the rest of your life for killing a guy?"

"Yeah. Ok. I get it. So, how do we deal with the camera?"

"We've got to access the security system on the computer. Do you know how to do that?"

"No. Marshall managed all that. I just wanted to grow and sell some weed, Lilith. Just wanted to make people happy."

Lilith looked pityingly at Barry. The sad fact was that he was telling the truth. He'd never really wanted *Herbvana* to become a big financial success and hadn't even seemed to benefit much from the growth of the store. He had simply wanted to be able to do what he loved – what he had been doing already – but not worry about whether or not he was doing something illegal. He'd wanted to go legitimate.

"Well, Marshall's not going to help you with it now. So we're going to need to figure it out." She walked over to the desk. As she looked down at the computer, she began to chuckle. "Some security. He's written his login ID and password on a sticky note and stuck it to the monitor."

She sat at the desk, logged in to the computer, and set about disabling the camera system and deleting the most recent video files on the computer's hard drive. In a few short minutes, she was done.

"Ok," Lilith muttered, "so much for video from the storeroom tonight." She breathed a heavy sigh of relief, confident that by deleting the video footage on the desktop no one would ever know the role she had played in Marshall's death. "Now there's just the matter of cleaning up this place and figuring out what to do with the body."

Barry sat on the floor, his arms clasped round his knees, and rocked back and forth while silently weeping. All the while, Lilith moved around the storeroom muttering to herself. At long last, she spoke. "Ok. I don't know yet exactly what to do with the body. Long-term that is. We've got to find a place to get rid of it where it won't get discovered. But in the meantime, I've got an idea. See those totes in the back?" She pointed to a series of plastic bins – airtight containers they used for storage. "If we empty out one of those totes we can store him in there for a day or two while I work something out. I'm going to need your help moving him."

Barry didn't respond.

"Seriously, Barry. I can't lift him by myself. You've got to pull yourself together."

"I just wanted to be near the plants... such beautiful plants... I didn't want any of this."

"Barry!" Lilith shouted. "Get up and help me!"

He looked up at her, hopelessness in his eyes.

"Look," she said, "we can't bring Marshall back. But there's no reason that you have to give up now. You can still run *Herbvana*. We can run it together. In fact, it will be more fun without Marshall around. You know how he was always busting your ass about things. Now that's over. Right? I'll handle all the details – you don't need to worry about any of it. Just hang out here, talk with customers and be near the plants. That's what you wanted, isn't it?"

"Yeah. But now…"

"But nothing. Now you can actually do that. It's going to be great. We just need to take care of this little detail. And you don't even need to worry about that. I'll handle it. I'll figure out what to do. But I can't lift him, Barry. I need your help to lift him. If you can help me get him into the tote, then I'll take care of the rest. Ok?"

"Ok" Barry said under his breath.

As Lilith opened the lid to the tote, Barry squatted down next to Marshall's body and scooped him up in his arms. "I'm sorry, man. I didn't mean to hurt you. Didn't mean for it to end this way." His voice quavered.

He carried Marshall's body over to the tote, gently placing it inside, and walked somberly back to the other side of the room where he leant against a wall. Lilith could hear him continuing to quietly sob.

She looked down at Marshall's figure in the bin. Despite her best estimation, placing him inside had revealed that the container wasn't large enough to hold Marshall without some manipulation. Glancing over at Barry to ensure he wasn't watching, she grasped Marshall's by the ears and pulled his head toward his feet, folding him not quite neatly in half. While not a gymnast, he was surprisingly limber and pliable. As his body assumed a pike position, she looked down upon the back of his head. Whether the result of the impact with the shelving unit or the floor itself, or both, the back of Marshall's skull was crushed. Bits of flesh hung from it – separated from the bone by the force of the blow.

Lilith closed the tote and clamped it shut. Walking back toward Barry, she noted that the puddle of blood on the floor was beginning to dry and congeal. Barry had walked through this puddle – tracking Marshall's blood toward the entrance to the store. A small piece of Marshall's scalp, long stringy brown hair still attached, hung from the shelf where he'd struck his head. "This place is a mess," she muttered to herself.

"Barry, we've got to get this place cleaned up before we open the store tomorrow."

"Yeah?"

"Yes. But I'm going to go ahead and do it."

"I can help."

"No. I don't want your help. I've got another job for you."

"Ok. What's that?"

"I want you to go home and get completely wasted."

"What?"

"I'm serious, Barry. I want you to get higher than you've ever been before. Completely trashed. Can you do that for me?"

"Well, yeah. I guess. But, why?"

"A fresh start. Tonight's been rough on both of us, right? And we've got to get up in the morning and start all over. Run the shop like nothing's changed. Nothing's different. Just Barry and Lilith running the shop."

"I'd like that."

"I'd like that too, Barry. So, I want you to hit the reset button. Go home, get good and stoned, and sleep in tomorrow morning. Don't worry about opening the shop. I'll be here to do that. Ok?"

"Yeah, sure."

"But here's the thing – nobody can ever know what happened here tonight. Nobody can know that Marshall tried to kill you. Nobody can know that he ended up dead. We just say he left town and keep running the business like nothing's changed. Got it? 'Cause if we let on that he's gone then people are going to ask questions and it's going to come out – and that will mean no more *Herbvana* and a lot of trouble, right? So everything that happened here tonight? It's like it never happened. I'll clean the place up and tomorrow we'll be back in the shop like normal and nothing happened. Deal?"

"Deal. Thanks, Lilith. Thanks for looking out for me. You're the best."

"I love you, Barry. I'll take care of things. You just leave it up to me. Now go home."

She embraced Barry – the most physical contact she'd ever allowed herself to offer him – and he left for home buoyed about the prospect of this fresh start for *Herbvana* with Lilith by his side.

After she heard him drive away, Lilith went to the cabinet where they kept the cleaning supplies for the shop, got out a mop and a bucket, and began the process of scrubbing Marshall's blood from the floor.

Chapter 9

"So if you had to get rid of a body, how would you do it?"

"Bury it vertically – with the head up – in a chicken yard. Why?"

Lilith, slightly taken aback by the speed and declarative nature of Madame Mara's response, craned her head back and made eye contact. "Just wondering. What's the deal with it being head up?"

The tattoo machine resumed its work. "Well, actually it wouldn't necessarily need to be chickens. Could be any kind of poultry. Didn't you mention your family did something with chickens? Anyway, burying it head up makes it harder for the cops to find it."

"Ok. What's with the poultry?"

"Sometimes when you dig a hole you're left with something that's visible from above – even if you try to fill it in really well. If you do it in a chicken yard then anyone looking from above – like from a plane – they'll just think they're seeing another chicken, or where a chicken's been roosting. Anyway, it works pretty well."

"Huh. No, my family wasn't into chickens. But my father's in the turkey business. Honestly, I really can't stand poultry."

"I don't mind it fried. 'Course I'll eat just about anything fried."

"Head up sounds tricky."

98

"Well a lot easier than head down. Legs would be flopping every which way."

"Sure," said Lilith – laughing at the mental image. "But that's not really what I meant. Head up – or head down – you'd need to dig a really narrow but deep hole. I mean unless the person you were burying was really short you'd need to dig – I don't know – a six-foot deep hole that was only a few feet around. That sounds really tricky – like you'd need special equipment or something."

"Nah. Just dig a really deep hole – doesn't matter if it is too big around just can't be too narrow. Then stand 'em up in it and start burying. Pretty quick really. Especially if you've got access to a backhoe or something like that. But can be done with shovels, believe me."

Lilith did believe her. In fact, Lilith was prepared to believe that Mara had done this on more than one occasion.

"If you can't get access to poultry, I'd go pigs all the way. They'll eat just about anything. But what's this about, anyway? You up to no good?"

"Always. You know that."

"I'm being serious, my girl. If you're in some kind of trouble you better let me know."

"I'm not in any trouble – least no trouble I can't handle. But some folks at the shop were talking about this just the other day and it got me thinking. How would you do it if you needed to? Personally, I was thinking the ferry might be a good choice. They get the occasional jumper every so often, you know? So you somehow get the body onto the ferry – maybe on the car deck on one of the sides – and then just a little help getting over the rail and you're done."

"Bad idea."

"Yeah?"

"Yeah. First, there's security all over the boat. Anything that happens – especially on the car deck – is seen. Got a girlfriend who found this out the hard way when she got a bit too affectionate with her man in the back of a pickup on the Bremerton route. It was late at night and the ferry was almost completely empty so she figured why not – kind of sexy, right? Anyway, they'd barely started going at it before they had a deck hand interrupt the whole thing and threaten to turn them in to the cops."

"Shit. What'd she do?"

"Gave the deck hand a deck hand-job in the john. Got her out of a tight spot – she had warrants and if they'd called the cops she'd have gone away for a while. Didn't do her any favors with her fella, though. They weren't together much longer after that."

"Sounds like the car deck is out."

"Yep. You'd be seen. But even if you weren't, the water could be a problem."

"How so?"

"You don't want to end up with a floater. I mean if you're trying to get rid of the body that's not going to help. So you'd need to weight it down some way."

"Like the old stories about the mafia – cement galoshes."

"Exactly."

Lilith pondered this for a moment. She'd done some scuba diving in the Caribbean a few years into her wanderings and remembered needing to wear a weighted dive belt in order to actually make it to a meaningful depth.

"So," Mara continued, "if you can't get a dead guy over the rail without the cameras seeing you you're sure as hell not going to get a dead guy with a bunch of weights strapped to him over the rail. Plus, if he's got a bunch of weights strapped to him then you'll probably have a hard time convincing anybody that he jumped."

The two sat in silence for a few moments while Mara continued to work on Lilith's back. Finally, Mara spoke again. "It's a shame though, if you think about it. You manage to get the body down to the bottom and I'm guessing the critters would do a decent job of cleaning up the mess. Not too deep, mind you – but like down with the shrimp and the crabs and all the other little scavengers. Wouldn't be much left when they were done. Might even be better than the pigs 'cause with them I think you've still got the bones to deal with – don't think they eat those but I could be wrong. But you manage to get a body down deep – say a hundred feet or so – and keep it there, I'm guessing nobody ever finds it. But still, my go-to is going to be the chickens. How's this looking so far?" Mara stopped the tattoo machine, wiped away the excess ink and blood, and allowed Lilith to sit up and admire the progress of her work. Now nearly finished, the design covered substantially all of Lilith's back. "Kinda' weird I guess – talking about ditching a body while you're getting a symbol of life on your back."

Lilith laughed. "Yep. But it's all part of the cycle, right? I mean like with the pigs or the crabs or whatever – you're dealing with a corpse but they're benefitting from the body. Can't have life without death – that's the way it works. 'Course that's also the reason I haven't eaten meat in years – just creeps me out to know that something had to die so that I could have lunch."

Mara, who had just taken a bite of a large sandwich on the other side of the shop, looked over at Lilith with a grin. "Never been a major problem for me. Take this roast beef. If I wasn't eating this cow, somebody or something else would be. So why not me. Plus, it's delicious." She took another bite – larger than the one before now that she knew it made Lilith squirm – something she enjoyed immensely. "What do you think?"

"I think it's wrong. Too much suffering already. And it's bad for the environment – all the methane plus the water and fertilizer needed to grow the food to feed the cows."

"I'm talking about the tree. What do you think?"

"Oh," Lilith said as she looked into the mirror in front of her, reflecting her exposed back in the mirror behind her. "Looks nice. I really like how gnarled you've made the branches. Really beautiful and a bit sinister all at once. I love it."

"Good. You good to get back to work?"

"Just a second."

Lilith hopped off the table and ran to the bathroom in the back of the shop, clutching her t-shirt to her exposed breasts. She'd needed to pee for the last half hour or so, but hadn't

102

wanted to interrupt Mara's work. When she returned, Mara was just finishing the last bite of her sandwich. She hopped back up onto the table and lay down on her stomach.

Mara leaned over Lilith's bare back and resumed her work. "So how are things in the weed business?"

"They're good. Lots of customers every day – the shop is busy."

"Sounds like the business is on fire." Mara chuckled at her own joke. Lilith let it go by without comment – she'd become so accustomed to people making marijuana puns that she was numb to the humor of it.

"Barry's been flaky lately – but that's nothing new. Marshall's been really quiet – keeping to himself back in the storeroom – but basically out of my hair. So I've been able to get a lot done. I'm telling you what, I'm going to own that place one day. I'll be like you with your shop – an institution."

"Could be. I hope it happens. But isn't it still illegal? Heard on the news just the other day that the FBI raided some joint down south."

Lilith had heard this news as well. A shop in Oregon had been the subject of a major bust. "I saw that. From the news – and the rumors, everybody knows everybody else in this business – it sounds like the shop sold weed to the underage kid of a federal judge. Selling to kids is a problem – I was in Marshall's face about just that a while back – he likes 'em young and seems to have a problem turning down high school girls looking to buy and willing to flirt."

"Sounds like a prince."

"You've got no idea. Guy's a world-class prick. Anyway – you can't go selling to minors and expect to get away with it for long. And you sure as hell can't sell to a kid whose mother is a judge. Apparently she went completely apeshit at the kid when she found his stash and by the time she'd finished he'd fingered the shop that sold him the weed. She made a phone call and the FBI swarmed the place that same day. Don't ever fuck with a judge – or her kid."

"Good advice. So how are you going to keep your shop out of the papers long enough to take over and rule the world of weed?"

"Gotta keep the boys from doing anything too stupid. I think I've got Barry handled. And I'm working on a plan for Marshall." Lilith put her head down, closed her eyes and focused on the feeling of the tattoo needle while reflecting on her options for just that plan. Where was she going to get access to pigs or chickens? These and similar questions weighed on her mind.

Later that evening, after finishing at Madame Mara's and making her way back to Poulsbo, she stopped back by *Herbvana*. The parking lot was empty except for Marshall's car – the windshield covered with pollen and dust from disuse for the past several days. Lilith let herself into the shop, went into the storeroom and sat at the desk. Leaning back in the chair to prop her feet up on the desk, she felt the tender skin on her back – Mara's handiwork – and decided against it.

"So, Marshall," Lilith said out loud, "what am I going to do with you? I've got no pigs and I don't plan on hanging out with poultry any time soon. So what, exactly, am I supposed to do with your sorry ass. You're such a prick. You always were. You were a pain in the ass when you were alive and you're still a pain in the ass to deal with now that you're dead."

She rocked slightly back and forward in the chair, clenching her jaw in time with the oscillation of the chair.

"… too much to do. Too fucking much, Marshall! It's not enough that I've got to deal with your body – got to figure out what to do with that piece of shit car too. Looks like something a German pimp would drive and now it's collecting dust in the parking lot. People are going to notice. Going to ask questions…

It's almost a shame you're not here, you know? I mean if there was any one fucker who could figure out what to do with a dead guy and his shit, it would be my buddy Marshall. Teach you that in law school? Disposing of corpses? You'd get an A in that shit. Yep – you were here I'd just ask you and I bet you'd have a plan. But now what good are you? Sitting there in your box. Prick."

Lilith spun the chair around – away from the back of the storeroom and Marshall's makeshift coffin. She put her elbows on the desk and her head in her hands.

"Fuck."

She rubbed her temples and opened her eyes. In front of her, in the corner of the computer monitor, sat a small picture of Marshall. He was grinning from ear to ear, wearing a captain's hat and standing at the wheel of *The MaryJane*. A young brunette was hanging on his arm – through the miracles of modern undergarments her breasts were pushed nearly up to her chin. Seeing him in a happier time did not immediately improve her mood. As she stared at the photo, however, she began to chuckle. "You son of a bitch... it just might work."

She reached up to the wall behind the monitor, took Marshall's keys off of the hook and left the shop. Ignoring her Volkswagen, she strode purposefully over to Marshall's BMW and hopped inside. As she started the engine, the radio came to life and Lilith noted for the first time the comfort of the interior. "Ok – maybe I was a bit harsh with the German pimp bit. This is pretty nice."

She struggled with the controls – finding the headlights and blinkers before managing to find the windshield washer and wiper controls. After cleaning the windshield of the detritus from the last several days, she drove away from the shop – the car lurching as she adjusted to the feel of the clutch.

She arrived at Marshall's house some minutes later and, using the garage door opener clipped to the sun visor, opened the garage, drove inside and closed the door. The garage was spotless and well- organized – exactly the opposite of the *Herbvana* storeroom. On two sides were shelving units. Some of the shelves were empty. Those which were not empty had labels affixed to the shelves identifying the intended contents of the space. Straight ahead was a workbench with a pegboard behind it to hold tools. On the pegboard was stenciled the outline of the tool intended to hang from each hook.

"Jesus... you really were uptight."

106

Lilith let herself into the house. As soon as she opened the door from the garage, a bedraggled cat greeted her, rubbing against her legs.

"I'm sorry! I didn't know he had a cat. Sorry about that little one. You must have been lonely, huh?"

She bent down to pet the cat, who obligingly allowed itself to be picked up - loud purring was interrupted by the occasional loud meow.

Forgetting for a moment the purpose of her visit, she stepped into the kitchen and began throwing open cabinets in a search for cat food. In what was obviously the pantry, she found a large stack of cat food tins. Opening one, she put it on the kitchen counter and set the cat down next to it. She stroked the cat as it ate the tinned shredded fish – a gelatinous and foul-smelling meal. As she scratched it behind the ears, she noted it was wearing a collar with a tag.

"Pussy," she read aloud. "Classy, Marshall. Very classy."

Seeing that the cat's water dish on the floor was completely dry, she filled it at the tap and set it down on the counter. "Been drinking from the toilet? I'm guessing your dad was a lid-up kind of guy. I don't exactly approve – but it worked out for you, didn't it?"

Lilith continued to stroke the cat while Pussy finished her meal. When she'd finished the last of the tin, she rubbed her cheeks on Lilith's hands in apparent gratitude. "How about you come home with me tonight? Wouldn't be the first time I brought a little pussy back to my place – you should feel right at home. One thing I've got to do first, though – need to find some keys. Where do you suppose your dad kept the keys to the boat, huh? Wish you could tell me that."

But Pussy did not tell her that, and so Lilith proceeded to scour the house. Coming up empty in the kitchen, she looked next in the living room and then Marshall's bedroom. As with the garage, both were immaculate. Unlike the garage, however, each room had the distinctive impression of a lair – a place where Marshall had undoubtedly committed as many acts of debauchery as he'd been able to arrange. Although the rooms were almost sterile in their appearance, she cringed as she touched each surface – thinking with distaste at the times she'd witnessed his lechery. But the keys were not visible in either room – and she couldn't bring herself to go through his nightstands or dresser drawers in the bedroom for fear of what she might find. And so she walked back into the living room when she saw his captain's hat – the same one from the photo at *Herbvana* – hanging on a hook by the front door. She pulled the hat from the hook – revealing a set of keys underneath. On the ring was a floating keychain bearing the name "Winslow Marina" along with a black piece of plastic and two individual keys. "There you are."

Lilith pocketed the keys and replaced the captain's hat on the hook. Turning back to the living room, she returned her attention to Pussy, who was stretching on the back of Marshall's slate gray suede sofa. "Want to come home with me? Let's find your litter box."

As it happened this was the easiest task Lilith undertook that day, as her nose led her directly to Pussy's box – overflowing with the waste left there since the last time Marshall cleaned it.

Lilith didn't know how long ago that was – but she knew it was at least three days. Squinting her eyes and holding her breath to avoid the ammonia emanating from the box, she emptied it in the kitchen trash – itself relatively ripe – and then set that bag into the trash bin outside the house.

The litter box now empty, she gathered it – along with a bag of litter and a stack of cat food tins, and put them in the trunk of Marshall's car. Finally, she picked Pussy up and placed her in the back seat of the car, closed the door to the house, backed out of the garage and drove to her apartment. As soon as she arrived, she set Pussy up in her new home and then left again – driving to Winslow Marina and *The MaryJane*.

Marshall had invited her onto his boat on many occasions – each time with a greasy smile that, even if Lilith had been interested in him, would have made her think twice about going. And so although she knew the location of the marina from the keychain, she wasn't entirely sure where to find the boat itself. And, being from a landlocked state, her knowledge of how to pilot it once she found it was somewhat limited. But she was confident she could learn – or at least find someone who would help her or some video instruction on the Internet.

The sun was setting by the time she arrived at the marina – a shimmer of orange light reflecting on the still waters in the harbor. She wandered down toward the entrance. From a bench nearby, she watched couples stroll arm in arm along the waterfront. Finally, she saw an elderly and grizzled man walk toward the entrance of the marina. He waved a set of keys in front of a black box at the entrance and the electromagnet in the entrance released its hold on the metal gate. The man passed over the threshold and the gate clanged shut, followed by a loud click as the electromagnet reenergized and held the gate tightly closed.

Lilith looked at the keys in her hand, and focused on the black piece of plastic. "It's a fob." She walked over to the gate and waved the plastic in front of the sensor. It worked, and she stepped onto the wooden walkway down to the boats beyond.

But there were a lot of boats. As she stood on the walkway she realized that this was a bigger task than she'd expected. At least five hundred vessels of all descriptions lay in front of her, bobbing gently in the evening. The soft lapping of water against hull and clinking of halyards on the masts of sailboats carried across the water and up the walkway to greet her.

Slowly walking down the ramp toward the water, she tried to remember everything she could about *The MaryJane* – wishing she'd paid more attention when Marshall had been blathering on about the boat as he did on a regular basis. Noting that the boats were generally arranged among the piers by size, she made an educated guess and chose one to walk down where the vessels looked like they might be the size of Marshall's boat. As she walked along the pier, noting the names of the boats in the slips, she heard a voice from behind her.

"Can I help you?"

Lilith turned to see an older but quite nimble woman clambering down from the deck of ancient sailboat onto the pier. She wore paint-splattered jeans and a fleece jacket – her grey hair tied back in a messy bun.

"I'm looking for a friend, or, rather, a friend's boat. He's out of town and asked me to check on it."

"You're not a member?"

"I'm sorry, what?"

"You're not a member of the marina?"

"Uh. No. Like I said, my friend asked me to check on his boat."

"Well he shouldn't have done that. That's against the rules. Non-members aren't supposed to be here without someone accompanying them."

"Uh. Ok. I guess I'll leave. I don't want to get him in trouble." Lilith turned to head back up the pier toward the parking lot.

"Just a minute, young lady. I'm not going to turn him in. Or you. But if the harbormaster knows someone's down here without a chaperone there'll be trouble. And you look lost so if you just go wandering around down here he's going to figure it out even though he's not that bright. Now who's your friend – or what's the name of the boat – I know all the boats here. I can help."

"Ok. Thank you. My friend's name is Marshall. His boat is *The MaryJane*."

The older woman laughed. "The weed boat!"

"Yeah… That's the one."

"Oh, I hope I didn't offend you, dear – I just think it's a funny name. I know the boat, but you're on the wrong pier. Come with me." The old woman set off down the pier, with

111

Lilith following close behind.

The two arrived at *The MaryJane* after a brisk five-minute walk along the maze of finger-like piers, during which time Lilith learned everything she might have ever wanted to know about her guide, Beatrice. Throughout her brisk chatter, interrupted only long enough to ask Lilith her name, Beatrice gave Lilith a high-level overview of her entire life story from her birth in California many decades before to her meeting Lilith that very evening, with multiple plot twists and more than a few *non sequiturs* along the way.

"Here it is. *The MaryJane*. She's a handsome boat. Miniature trawler, you know. Looks to be about twenty-five feet. Very capable."

"Yeah," said Lilith, unsure how to end her interaction with the talkative Beatrice. "Well, I should probably go inside and check things out for Marshall. Thanks for the help."

"Oh, dear don't worry about it. Delightful to have met you, young lady. You know we really do need to have more young women involved in boating. This place is normally just filled with men and old women like me. Nice to have young lady like you around here instead of a shriveled old crone. But you watch yourself. I dare say you'll turn some heads around here. Any one of these crusty old liveaboards tries to get too close, you tell 'em they'll have Beatrice to deal with. I'll gut 'em like a fish and they know it."

Lilith laughed. "Thanks. I'll do that." She said good night to Beatrice and climbed aboard *The MaryJane*, unlocked the door to the cabin and descended the stairs into the interior of the boat.

Inside, it was almost completely dark – the only available light being the fading rays of sunlight entering the cabin from the marina outside, much of which was obscured by the curtains covering the windows.

She pulled out her phone to use it as a flashlight. The cabin was comfortable and snug, although spartan in appearance. In the center of the gangway between the door and the pilot station were several buoys and coiled ropes – each buoy bearing Marshall's name and phone number. To the left of the equipment, a cozy booth – a couple of crab pots stacked on top. To the right, a simple kitchen with sink, stove and what appeared to be a small refrigerator. Ahead toward the bow – past the equipment and the pilot station – she could make out a V-shaped berth.

Lilith sat down in the booth, only to jump up in pain. Reaching behind her, she felt a length of fishing line, leading from the seat of the booth to the back of her left thigh, which was punctuated by a fishing hook now embedded deeply into her leg.

"Fuck, that hurts." Lilith seethed at the indignity. Marshall wasn't even alive anymore and yet in her mind – if not her leg itself – he was still causing pain. She gingerly worked the hook free from her flesh. With each painful twist of the metal, she found her resolve in her plan strengthened; she would use the occasion of Marshall's death to bring about some positive change in the world – for herself and for other creatures.

Chapter 10

Lilith picked up the knife. The blade was long, thin and flexible – made to fillet seafood. "But," thought Lilith, "if it's good enough for a halibut it should be good enough for Marshall." As she held it in her hands, gently bending the blade between her fingers, she felt the weight of the task in front of her – the enormity of it. Not since that fateful day at her father's factory farm had she been able to stomach meat, let alone butcher it. And yet here she was, preparing to dissect a human being. "Better get two," she muttered, "he's pretty big."

She placed the two blades in her shopping cart and continued down the aisle. *The Sportsman's Attic* – filled with taxidermy, men and animal jerky – was as close to her idea of hell as she could imagine. It disgusted her. But the disgust was also exhilarating. As she wandered the aisles she found herself drawn to display after display showing what were to her, new and interesting ways to kill. She lingered for a time within the archery section, noting the sharpness of the broadhead arrows, some of which were designed with springs to cause the blades to splay outward when striking their target. "Nasty."

Finally, she came to the gun counter, behind which stood an older man with a graying beard and a bald head. She disliked him instantly.

"Good afternoon, Miss. My name's Lou. Can I help you?"

"I'm looking for some bullets for my gun."

"Well, we've got quite a selection of ammunition. What are

you carrying?"

Lilith fumbled in her satchel and clasped the revolver. As she began to pull it from the bag, the man behind the counter intervened. "Miss – I'm going to need to ask you to keep that in the bag. Store policy. Customers are asked not to carry guns on the premises. Now, if it stays concealed in the bag then I don't have any problem with it. Don't even know it's there, right? But if you take it out then I've got to call security. So please leave it in the bag."

Lilith looked past the clerk at the row upon row of shotguns and rifles immediately behind him. Glancing down, she saw handguns of all descriptions in the glass case between herself and the clerk. She was almost surrounded by weapons – one more didn't seem to make that much difference. But she was out of her element and decided not to argue.

"Ok." She released her grip on the revolver and let it remain in the bag.

"Thank you, Miss. So, what kind of ammunition do you need?"

"Uhh, something to go in my gun."

"Yes. What caliber is the weapon?"

"Caliber?"

"Yes, Miss."

"I don't know what that means. What is 'caliber?'"

"Ah, I'm sorry, Miss. I saw you and took you for a seasoned gun owner. You look like you're quite comfortable around firearms." This was an absolute lie; Lilith looked significantly less comfortable in *The Sportsman's Attic* than did the taxidermy jackalope affixed to the wall. But Lou knew better than to suggest that any customer didn't know what they were doing with a gun unless it was patently clear that was the case – over his years at the store he'd managed to engage in shouting matches with many an enraged but uninformed sportsman over the finer aspects of firearms. Once he even had to draw his own sidearm – holstered on his belt – to defend himself. But – on balance – he found it best if he didn't say things that might insult the customers. "Maybe I can help point you in the right direction in terms of your weapon. Now, this pistol – how did you come by it?"

"A guy gave it to me. He wasn't using it anymore, and I thought I could probably benefit from having some protection. I work in kind of a rough place."

"I see. Well, self-protection is what these are made for. And as I'm sure you know, you've got a God-given Constitutional right to bear arms. Now Miss, I want to personally thank you for being a patriot and exercising that right. There are folks who want to take that right away from us – it makes me proud to see a young woman like yourself educating herself about firearms and their use – their responsible use, that is – and exercising her rights. Good for you, Miss. And good for us as Americans."

"Uh. Yeah. Anyway, I'm just hoping to get some bullets for it."

"And I'm going to help you with that. Now, I hope you'll excuse me for pointing out something you may already know – but firearms – handguns included – come in a range of sizes. I mean, bore sizes. Bore – that's the inside diameter of the chamber of the weapon. We call that measurement the caliber of the weapon. So, to find the perfect ammunition for you – for that handgun of yours, the first thing we need to know is the caliber of the weapon. Do you happen to know its caliber, Miss?"

"Please, call me Lilith." Lou's calling her 'Miss' every several sentences was like nails on a chalkboard. "I don't think I know the caliber. How can I tell?"

"Well, Lilith – the caliber is usually stamped on the barrel of the weapon."

Lilith looked down into her satchel. The revolver was resting, barrel pointing downward, between a half-eaten bag of granola and her wallet – the barrel completely obscured.

"I... I can't see the barrel. I can't take it out of the bag?"

"The store would prefer that you didn't."

"Can you take it out?"

"Miss?"

"Lilith. Can you take it out of the bag for me? I mean, you're obviously allowed to handle all the other guns in the store – you're surrounded by them – can you reach into my bag and pull it out?"

"You know, I don't see any reason why not. If you're comfortable with that I'll be happy to assist you. Here's what we'll do. If you'll just set your bag on the counter, I can handle it from there."

After Lilith placed her satchel on the counter, Lou approached it carefully – looking for all the world as if he was a member of a bomb disposal unit. Gingerly, he loosened the drawstring at the top of the bag to its widest aperture, and then stood over the bag and peered inside.

"Is there anything in there that's going to hurt me?"

"Well – you're reaching in for my gun."

"Yes, Miss. I mean anything sharp or anything like that."

"No – you should be clear on that front."

Lou reached into the bag and pulled out the revolver. Freeing it from the satchel, he inspected the weapon – the cylinder to which was still open after the gun had fallen out of Marshall's hand. After confirming it was unloaded, Lou carefully placed the revolver on a felt mat on the countertop.

"Very nice. Very nice indeed, Lilith. You've got yourself a beautiful little revolver. It's a Smith & Wesson – that's a good quality, American-made, firearm. An excellent piece for self-defense. Small enough for concealed carry – you're going to want a concealed carry permit if you don't already have one – otherwise keeping it in your bag there is a bit of a no-no – but still big enough to get you out of a tough spot should one arise. Very nice little piece."

"Thanks. So – you were going to look at the caliber…"

"Indeed I was. Sorry – got carried away." He rotated the gun on the mat so that the handle was facing Lilith, and pointed to the side of the barrel. "It's stamped right here: '.22 LR'"

"So it's a twenty-two?"

"Twenty-two long rifle. There are a couple kinds of twenty-two. This is the most common kind."

"Ok. So – that's the ammunition I need. Where can I find it?"

"Well, I'm afraid that's going to be a problem. There's a shortage on at the moment. We get it in stock about once every couple of weeks and we're usually sold out within a few hours of unloading the trucks."

"There's a shortage on ammunition?" Lilith looked around the store, incredulous. Everywhere she looked she seemed to see boxes of bullets.

"Not all kinds. But .22LR has been out of stock for a long time. Our government – those idiots back in the other Washington – they've been stockpiling it. Buying almost everything that gets produced. Now, you won't hear about this on your evening network news – but they're starting to arm employees in the postal service and the IRS. Some people think that's not a big deal, I guess. But I do. What are they preparing for, exactly? I tell you, Lilith, I'm worried. Feels to me like they're gearing up for a fight. Now I don't want to fight. But if they're going to come after our guns – well, I guess they're going to get a fight out of even an old guy like myself."

Lilith looked at Lou. He seemed genuinely fearful. "If the federal government wanted a fight, why wouldn't they just use the military? Why would they use the post office or the IRS?"

"They'll use both. Use 'em all. That's why we've got to be ready."

"But if they use the military… I mean let's just say they decide they want to take me out, right? They want to take me out and they've got the army. They've got tanks and helicopters and all that. And I've got this little revolver. I don't stand much of a chance, do I?"

"Probably not, Miss. Probably not. But maybe you'll have taken one or two of them out before they get you."

"But if they come at me with a tank…" Lilith looked at Lou, who was nodding gravely. As she watched him, she realized that he was just as obsessed with guns and with protecting himself against the overbearing authority of the state that Barry was about the wonders of cannabis and that Marshall had been about money and underage women. The fervor was the same – only the object was different. She decided to let drop the issue of the questionable efficacy of a handgun for someone who is being confronted by the full might of the U.S. military. "So, it sounds like you don't have any of my ammunition in stock. Is that right?"

"Unfortunately, that is correct. We're supposed to get some in next Thursday. If you want to stock up, I'd recommend you get here early. There's usually a line of patriots waiting at the door as soon as we open."

"Ok. Wow. Thanks. Maybe I'll see you then." Lilith reached for the revolver on the mat. But before she could grasp it and place it back in her satchel, Lou grabbed it first.

"Allow me," he said. He placed it back in her satchel and then handed her the bag. "Thank you for coming in. Have a nice day."

Lilith put her bag over her shoulder and made her way to the front of the store. As she approached the registers, she passed by an aisle containing supplies for butchering deer and elk: a wide array of knives, a gambrel for hanging the animal while skinning the hide from the carcass, bags for transporting meat and some sort of contraption that, as best as Lilith could determine, appeared to facilitate the removal of the rectum from the animal. In the middle of the display, a bone saw hung on a rack. "Could be handy," Lilith muttered to herself as she dropped it into her shopping cart.

Turning around, she saw the store's display for the upcoming crabbing season. Marshall had already outfitted *The MaryJane* with a full complement of pots and buoys, but she had a strong suspicion that there were not enough crab pots on the boat to complete the task ahead of her. She loaded two additional pots into her cart and pushed it toward the register.

She did her best to avoid small talk with the cashier ringing up her purchases, thumbing instead through a complimentary hard copy of the fish and game regulations in the rack at the cash register. After paying, she made her way out to the parking lot and dialed Barry on her cell phone.

"Hey, Lilith, what's up?"

"I've got a plan. Figured out what to do, you know, to clean things up."

"Uh, ok."

"Yeah. So, I'm going to need you to clear out of the shop tonight. I mean, unless you want to help."

"I don't think that's such a good idea, Lilith. I mean, I'm getting a bit queasy just thinking about it. Don't really even want to know what you're planning, to be honest."

"Didn't think you would, just thought I'd give you a chance to man up."

"You're more man than I am, I think," Barry chuckled.

"Apparently. Anyway, just be out of the shop as soon as you close up, ok?"

"Sounds good. Hey, when can we go out next? Dinner or something?"

"Don't know, Barry. Too busy cleaning up your mess at the moment to think about that. Let's talk about it later."

Lilith hung up the phone. "Useless. Fucking useless," she said to herself. She drove home to her apartment and poured herself a gin and tonic. Sitting on her futon and petting Pussy, she opened an Internet browser on her laptop and began paging through websites on human anatomy. Several hours and several cocktails later she shut down the laptop and staggered back toward her Volkswagen, ready to get to work.

She arrived at *Herbvana* well and truly drunk. The sun was setting crimson in the west behind the cedars and firs. Happy families sat at outside tables in front of the Poulsbo Creamery across the street. Lilith grabbed her bag of knives and entered the store, disabled the alarm and went into the storeroom. From there, she logged into the computer and disabled the security cameras and then switched on the storeroom lights.

"Ok, lawyer-boy, let's get this done."

She unlatched the lid to the tote but was not at all prepared for what she found. Having spent the last four days in the container, Marshall's body had already begun to decay. The microbes in his gut and on his skin hadn't needed to devise a plan or purchase tools to start their work. And they had begun it in earnest. Inside the tote, Marshall appeared to be marinating in the contents of his stomach, although whether they had forced their way out through their entrance or their customary exit she couldn't determine. The visual was challenging, but the smell was almost unbearable. Lilith gagged and turned away.

Once she had collected herself, she turned back toward the tote and – remembering that she could not move the body alone even if she had wanted to shoulder what was now a festering mass – realized she needed to make room for her work. So she unlatched the tote sitting to the right of Marshall's resting place and removed from it several paper grocery bags filled with marijuana flower – untaxed and illicit – the product of Barry's insistence on keeping up his horticultural skills. That task complete, she stripped off her flannel shirt – revealing the white tank top beneath, put on some latex gloves, and got to work.

"Might as well start at the top of the pile," she said to herself. Grasping Marshall's head she pulled back hard in an effort to get him to straighten. But the body was now rigid and unbending. Lilith shrugged and sliced through the flesh at the back of his neck with the fileting knife. Reaching his spine with the blade, she angled the tip in between two vertebrae and slowly but surely sliced through the spinal column. Freed from its attachment to the spine, she carved through the rest of his neck, separated fully Marshall's head from his body, and casually tossed it into the empty tote to her right.

As she looked down at the now headless body, she found that her nausea, so prevalent before, was gone – replaced by an energy and exhilaration. And so, whether spurred on by necessity or the heady rush of the task, Lilith continued her dissection. She paused briefly to debate whether to attempt to save Marshall's clothes – after all they could be donated to a local charity. Ultimately, she decided against this act of generosity as she seriously questioned whether the stains they bore could be removed. It would perhaps be insult enough to give someone a lawyer's clothes – giving them clothing previously saturated with the festering contents of a dead lawyer's gut felt, to her, like it might actually be cruel. So she cut away his shirt. And then she used her knives to slice into his shoulders – separating the arms from the torso and tossing them into the tote alongside his head.

Using knife and saw, she set about sectioning his torso into multiple pieces. As she worked, Marshall's body gradually oozed ever greater amounts of fluid – some partly congealed – to the point that it began to interfere with her ability to gain access to the remainder of the corpse. And so she periodically scooped out the more viscous secretions with a coffee mug – Marshall's own mug from his desk – pouring them into a bucket and then dumping the bucket down the toilet.

Lilith toiled this way, humming to herself as she worked, until she had completed the dissection of Marshall's torso and arrived at his waist. To provide herself with greater access for her work, she pulled his legs and waist out of the tote and let them fall to the floor – a sickly, damp slap of flesh on concrete. She removed his shoes and cut off his pants. To her amusement, he was wearing a pair of boxer shorts with what appeared to be a floral pattern printed on them. She cut those off too and stood back to look at his naked lower half. Where once before she'd found enjoyment in her task, she now found herself filled by a rage she could not explain or express.

Reaching down with her left hand, she grasped his penis at the tip and, stretching it to length sliced it cleanly off in her hand. Her rage unquenched, she took similar action against his scrotum and testicles and, throwing all external evidence of Marshall's sex to the floor she fell upon them in fury – slicing them into ever and ever smaller pieces until she'd worn her blade dull against the concrete beneath.

"Take that, you fuck."

With relish, she scooped up what was left of his manhood and threw it, unceremoniously, into the tote. As she worked next to separate ankles from shins, shins from knees and femurs from hips, she congratulated herself on having sensibly acquired a second fileting knife for the task. Her dissection complete, she deposited all remaining parts of the body into the second tote.

Standing back and catching her breath from the last flurry of activity, she realized she'd been working nonstop. Her throat was parched and her hands were sore from her labors. Also, her bladder ached. Taking a long drink of water, she concluded that she needed one more act – one more opportunity to strike a blow for women – one last chance to humiliate Marshall and her father and the men in her life that she felt had so many times humiliated her. She walked over to the tote containing Marshall's now dismembered remains and, standing with one leg on either side of the bin, squatted over it and urinated.

Having satisfied her bladder if not her anger, she latched shut the bin containing the body and went about the shop cleaning up the mess she'd created during the evening. Marshall's clothes she bundled in a plastic garbage bag along with her own tank top – now fouled beyond cleaning. She used a mop and some water with bleach to clean the sites of dissection – the original tote and the floor. Satisfied that all was in order, she donned her flannel shirt, grabbed the bag containing the clothes, turned out the lights and exited the store. She threw the bag into her bus and drove across the street to the Poulsbo Creamery, where she ordered a vegan milkshake and tossed the bag into the dumpster.

Chapter 11

"So how long have you known Marshall?"

"Quite a while. I hired him when he was fresh out of law school and couldn't find work. Seemed like a nice enough guy – maybe not the smartest legal mind – not law review or Supreme Court material – but a decent guy."

Lilith did her best not to react to Cal's description of Marshall, who in her mind was anything but a nice guy. Barry spoke up.

"That's where I met him – I mean, here in your office. I came in looking for legal advice and the next thing I knew the two of us were in business together."

"That so? Probably an ethics violation. Like I said, maybe not the sharpest legal mind. But hey, that was a few years ago so it must have worked out well for you guys, right?"

"Worked out great for me. Don't have too many complaints."

"Well that's good. So how can I help you?"

Barry sat stone-faced – looked over at Lilith, who was more than happy to lead the discussion. "We're actually here because of Marshall," she replied. "He's taken off for somewhere. Not sure where. And anyway we need to keep running the business, keep things going without him – at least until he comes back."

"Took off?"

"Yeah. Haven't seen him in a couple of days. Just left. Probably off with one of his girls."

Cal thought Lilith said this last bit with a tone consisting of equal parts envy and disgust. Something was going on here. Something more than what the two sitting in his office were letting on. Could he use this somehow? Marshall was a friend of sorts, but business came first. "Funny. I saw him just maybe a week ago. He was here in the office. He didn't mention anything about going away. But then again he did seem a bit agitated."

"Agitated. What about?" Lilith asked.

"Well, I unfortunately can't tell you that – my ethical obligations to him as a client prevent me from sharing what we discussed. In fact, I probably shouldn't have even mentioned that he was here. But I'm worried about the fellow. Did he say anything to you before he disappeared?"

"Not specifically. But he did seem upset about something. I could tell it had something to do with the shop but didn't understand exactly what."

"Gutless."

"I'm sorry?"

"I said he's gutless. The thing the two of us talked about? I'm not going to tell you what it was and you don't actually want to know. But I'm not surprised to hear that he's disappeared. Gutless, spineless, call it whatever you want. He never had the balls to deal with anything challenging."

Cal's words brought forward a parade of images in Lilith's

mind. She knew from personal experience only a few hours before that Marshall hadn't, in fact, been either gutless or spineless. To the contrary, he seemed to have had a disturbingly large amount of intestine and his spine had been rather difficult to section into pieces. As for his testes, they'd at least been present – though her experience with external human genitalia was insufficient to allow her to make any meaningful assessment of their relative size. "Yeah. I wouldn't call him gutless, exactly," said Lilith. "But he isn't around – and that's a problem. Barry and I need to be able to keep running the business, pay vendors, pay *Herbvana*'s taxes – all that. But even though Barry owns half the place, Marshall is the only guy who ever did any of that. In his files we found a copy of your engagement letter – you represent the business – so we're hoping you might be able to help point us in the right direction. Help us understand what we need to do in order to keep things going for as long as he's gone."

"Interesting. I'm sure I can help. And you're right – I do represent the business, rather than Marshall personally. That's a good clarification. Marshall reached out to me when the bank pulled the *Herbvana* account a few weeks back. Asked me to represent the business as it sorted out its banking situation. He wired some of the cash that was on deposit at the bank into my trust account so that it wouldn't get frozen when the bank pulled the plug. But in the meantime, he was supposed to be looking for a new account to hold the funds."

Barry spoke up. "Is the money still here?"

"Yeah. Well, not here – but in my firm's account. It probably needs to be moved out of there fairly soon. The state bar doesn't take kindly to lawyers just holding client funds indefinitely. Not sure why they care if the client doesn't care – but I don't need them poking around my account asking questions."

"How much?"

"I don't have the exact figure – but it was a lot. Over two million." In fact, Cal knew precisely the amount that was in the account, and that it was substantially closer to three million than to two, but these two clearly didn't know exactly how much was in play and he wasn't going to pass up another bite at Marshall's apple.

"So how do we get access to the funds?" Lilith asked. The business is spinning off a lot of cash. But we've still got expenses. Plus, we need to understand what we need to do to pay taxes. You probably know this, but the tax bite from the state is pretty huge."

"Well, first thing is you need another bank account. I can't just go down to mine and easily withdraw two million in cash and hand it to you. You'd need an armored truck and even if you had one, they wouldn't have that much cash on hand. You're going to need to find another account and get it set up for the business first – then I can have the funds wired to the new business account."

"Got it. What does the business need to do to open a new account?"

"First thing is to find a bank that's willing to do it – a lot of 'em are too scared. That's why the last bank pulled the account. Since weed is still illegal according to the feds, and the banks are regulated by the feds, most of them are steering clear. Your best bet is probably a credit union, or to just open a new account without telling them exactly what the business is. But with a name like *Herbvana* they're going to figure it out and end up just shutting down the account like the last one."

"Ok," said Lilith. "Suppose we find a bank that's willing to open the account. What then?"

"You need to have one of your corporate officers open the account. The bank's going to want *Herbvana*'s formation docs – articles, bylaws, all that – and some board resolutions showing who has authority to sign on the account. That should do it."

"So we give them something that we've signed, that says we're authorized to sign. Isn't that kind of stupid?"

"Very. But you're going to be working with the front line of the bank here – basic customer service personnel. Smarter than Marshall but that's about it. They'll have a checklist of things they need to see. You help them check off the boxes and you'll get your account."

"Cool," said Lilith. "So, we'll get the account open and then you can wire the cash into it. I'll get started on that."

"Anything else we should know while Marshall's gone?" Barry continued, "I mean, he handled all the legal stuff – this is all new to us."

"Well, it kind of depends on how long you think he's going to be gone. If he comes back soon then I think you're good. But if he doesn't show for months or years – or ever – then you've probably got a problem with your license. The LCB tracks ownership of licensees closely. If he's out of the picture, the

State will want need to know that. And if someone's going to replace him on the license they're going to want to know that too."

"Huh," said Lilith. "Would be really nice if we knew when he was coming back. But I guess we'll have to play it by ear for a bit."

"Sounds like it. You've called him, checked his place, all that?"

"We have. Nothing. Even his cat's gone."

"He has a cat?"

"He does indeed. But it isn't in his place. His car was left at the shop. But he's nowhere to be found."

"Weird."

"Yeah. But then again he's kind of a different dude."

"That he is." A light on Cal's desk illuminated, letting him know that someone had come in the front door. "Well, I'm afraid our time this morning is up. I hope this has been helpful, but if there's anything more I can do to assist please let me know. I'll go ahead and bill for our time this morning against the *Herbvana* retainer. You get me the details on the new bank account is set up and I'll initiate the wire from the trust account."

Cal stood up from his elevated desk – towering over Barry and Lilith – and escorted them out of his office and into the waiting room. In the corner of the room sat an ancient woman wearing a tremendous amount of jewelry, being escorted by a handsome and well-dressed man who appeared to be in his late twenties. "Ah, Mr. and Mrs. Jones. Here to discuss your estate planning? I'll be right with you." Cal turned back to look at Lilith and Barry. "Please keep me informed. And if I hear from him, I'll be sure to let you know as well."

Barry and Lilith exited the waiting room out onto the sidewalk and climbed into Lilith's Volkswagen parked outside.

"He knows something's up."

"Don't be stupid, Barry. He doesn't know anything. How could he? And even if he did, what proof would he have? He wasn't there. I don't think he's ever even been to the shop. You worry too much. I've got this completely under control. Just need to tie up a few loose ends and everything will be fine."

"I hope you're right."

"I know I'm right. Here's what we're going to do. We'll dig into Marshall's files and find whatever he wrote up and gave the bank when he got the last account. Quick copy and paste of that with our names – dropping Marshall's – and we get the new bank account. That gives us access to two million dollars. Two million. That kind of money will buy a lot of piece of mind. Worse comes to worse we could disappear too – somewhere tropical, maybe."

"I don't want to disappear. Certainly not the way Marshall disappeared. I just want to stay here and keep *Herbvana* going. It's my dream, Lilith."

"Of course not. And I don't either. But it won't come to that. It's going to be fine. We've just got to keep on script, you know? Anybody asks about Marshall and where he is, we don't know. He just left. Maybe he went to visit a sick relative or something. But the point is we don't know exactly where he is and we don't know when he's coming back. And while he's gone we're just doing our best to keep things going and run the shop until he's back. Simple as that."

"Yeah. Simple. Easy for you. But I get nervous, Lilith. And then things get all jumbled and confused."

"Time to grow up a bit. You've got to step up. We've got to be on the same page here. You understand?"

Barry nodded. "How did you know he had a cat?"

"I went over to his place to straighten a few things up. Part of tying up the loose ends I mentioned. His cat was there – pretty pissed that she'd been left alone for as long as she had. I brought her back to my place. Gave her a new home. She's pretty sweet, actually. Didn't even know I liked cats until I had her around for a bit."

"Yeah. Cats are awesome. You should, like, film her doing silly stuff and put it online. There's a bunch of cat videos on there, you know? They crack me up."

"Maybe when we get a break from everything else. For now, though, let's keep focused on what we've got to do."

The two rode in silence – Lilith driving and Barry in the passenger seat staring out the window – until they arrived at *Herbvana*. After arriving, Barry set about opening the shop up for the day's business and Lilith busied herself at the computer in the storeroom.

Over the next several hours, she brought Barry a series of

papers to sign and by the end of the day she'd created a paper trail that she hoped would be sufficient to convince a bank clerk that she and Barry were the actual owners, directors and officers of *Herbvana* – and that they should have exclusive signing authority on any bank account that might be opened in its name. Figuring that if she was going to all the trouble of setting it up she might as well improve her position, she named herself *Herbvana's* President – knowing full well that Barry wouldn't read the documents she gave him to sign let alone question her decision to claim that title.

When it came time to close up the shop, Lilith suggested to Barry that he head home. She would lock up. And so he hopped on his scooter and rode away into the twilight of a northwestern July evening.

As soon as Barry was out of sight of the parking lot, Lilith switched off the video cameras, went into the parking lot and retrieved a large cooler from the back of her bus. Bringing it back inside, she opened Marshall's bin and began the task of transferring pieces of the corpse into the cooler, filling it fully. Slightly disappointed that her cooler apparently had a one-half of a lawyer capacity, she resealed the tote, dragged the cooler back outside and into the bus.

Driving into Bainbridge, she could hear a sloshing noise coming from the cooler directly behind her seat. She turned up the radio.

It was almost dark when she arrived at Winslow Marina. After parking the bus, she commandeered a dock cart and used it to transport the cooler through the gate, down the gangway and to *The MaryJane*. She heaved the cooler over the side of the boat

135

and slid it across the deck, adjacent to the waiting crabbing equipment. After returning the dock cart she untied *The MaryJane* and set off through Eagle Harbor and toward the open waters of the Puget Sound beyond.

The lights of Seattle glittered in the night across the water. She motored the boat out into the forest of buoys off the eastern side of the Island and cut the engine, allowing the boat to drift. After clambering down the ladder from the flybridge to the deck below, she opened the first crab pot. Discarding the bait canister from inside, she grabbed some zip ties and secured the doors to the trap completely open. "No use having anybody get trapped in there," she muttered – allowing herself to be briefly concerned for the fate of crabs that might get stuck inside the trap while they did her the favor she would ask of them.

Opening the cooler, she stuffed as much of Marshall's remains into the trap as she could while still allowing the top of the pot to close – an odd jumble of parts including a hand, a portion of his midsection and various other pieces that she couldn't quite identify following his dissection. Lilith took a quick look around to make sure no-one was watching her work and dropped the pot over the side of the boat. The pot hit the water with a splash and then sank out of sight, bubbles trailing to the surface as it descended to the depths below.

She allowed the boat to drift south on the incoming tide for a few moments before repeating this process a second time. To her frustration, this time she found that she'd failed to section Marshall's torso into small enough pieces to allow each of them to fit within the pot. But she found a fileting knife among

Marshall's fishing gear which was sharp enough to allow her to divide the offending piece in two. Once again she tossed the pot over the side.

Her cooler nearly empty now, she readied her third and final pot of the evening. By now the tide had pushed *The MaryJane* almost to Port Blakely and the wind had pushed the craft slightly closer to Bainbridge – but she was still within the forest of buoys and felt secure in her location. Working to fit the remaining contents of the cooler into the pot, she struggled with the upper part of his leg – which was simply too long to allow it to enter the pot from the door at the top and then close the lid. After some consideration, Lilith inserted the piece – knee first, into the pot from the side and through the door intended to allow crab to enter the trap – with the hip end of the limb sticking out the side of the pot.

She dropped this last pot into the water just as the ferry passed by, tourists and commuters alike standing on the upper deck and enjoying the evening air. Conscious of being observed, she quickly tossed a buoy over the side as well so that she might simply appear to be crabbing while at the same time smug in the knowledge that the buoy was not attached to the pot and would simply float away on the tide. As the line attached to the buoy slowly slid over the side of the boat – pulled only by the differential between the speed of *The MaryJane*'s drift and the drift of the buoy itself, she cut the line with the fileting knife – hoping to make it appear that the line had been sliced by the propeller of a passing vessel.

Her work done, she restarted the *MaryJane*'s engine and enjoyed a leisurely cruise back into Eagle Harbor and Winslow

Marina, where she tied up *The MaryJane*, rinsed her cooler with sea water, and headed for home.

Chapter 12

"Good morning, Sweetie. The usual?"

"Yes, Ma'am. And may I say you're looking awfully nice this morning?"

"Aw, Earl. You're always so sweet. I bet you say that to all the girls. Let me get your coffee started."

As a matter of fact, Earl did say this – or something like it – to all the girls at *Exxxpresso Coffee*. Earl found that his day was just a little bit better if he started it with coffee served to him by a nearly naked woman who was many years his junior. And this morning, as he watched Cindy standing in the roadside coffee kiosk and pouring a touch of cream into his coffee while wearing nothing more than spike heels, a lace thong and a well-secured apron? Well he was just about positive he was going to have a good day - the wings tattooed from her lower back down past the lilac lace and terminating on each cheek at the widest point of her bottom all but guaranteed it.

"Here you go, Sweetie. That'll be seven-fifty." Cindy leaned slightly out of the window of the kiosk and toward the window of Earl's truck. Her ample breasts – with heart stickers strategically placed on her nipples – threatened to escape the constraint of her apron and knock the tip jar from the windowsill of the kiosk.

Earl handed her a ten dollar bill. "Here you go, Gorgeous," said Earl while admiring the scenery. Don't worry about the change."

139

"Thanks, Earl," Cindy cooed.

"Seen Marshall lately?"

"Nope. Haven't seen him around at all."

"Huh. Any chance he's dropped by when you weren't here? He said he was going to drop another package off for me here. Said he was going to give it to you, but maybe he got confused."

"I don't think so, Sugar. I've been here every day and we've actually been short staffed. Melinda had trouble with her kid's daycare yesterday, so she couldn't make it in. And Becky – you know Becky, right? Tall blonde – real cute – likes to wear the cheerleader outfits? – anyway, Becky had an accident with the steam wand on the machine in here and damn near scalded her lady bits off – still not sure what she was doing on the counter – anyway she's home recuperating. Doc says she's got to apply a cream to the burns for a few days – bet you'd be willing to help with that, wouldn't you?"

"You know, Ma'am, I am always looking to be of service.'

"You're bad, Earl!"

"I am sorry, Ma'am. I will try to be better. But really, you don't think that Marshall might have given something to one of the other girls?"

"I don't think so, Sweetie. Like I said, I've been here every day, and almost the whole day every day – and I haven't seen him. But I tell you what, when I see him next, I'll tell him you asked about him. Ok?"

"That would be mighty kind of you, Ma'am. Mighty kind."

140

"Ok, Earl. Now, Sweetie I'm going to need to help out some of other customers. Looks like a lot of boys need coffee this morning. Can I get you to move along?"

Earl looked in his rearview mirror. Behind him, a mix of construction workers, yard crews, Navy kids and one enormous, bearded guy on a motorcycle were filing in behind him in the drive-through – all eagerly awaiting their opportunity to ogle.

"Yes, Ma'am. Now you have a good day."

"You too, Sweetie. See you tomorrow."

Earl started his pickup and pulled back out onto the highway. He fumed as he sipped his coffee. He trusted Cindy more than Marshall. That much was certain. She might be selling coffee and a quick thrill on the side of the road, bus she wasn't a lawyer-turned dope peddler. If Cindy hadn't seen him then Marshall hadn't paid, and that was a problem. "Who does this little prick think he's dealing with?" Earl muttered to himself as he drove toward the office. "I'll tear him a new asshole – that's what I'll do. Snap the leash a bit. And I'll do it nice and official. Feels like it is time for *Herbvana* to have a very thorough inspection."

Arriving at the LCB office, Earl parked his pickup and walked inside. His clenched jaw and purposeful step were completely out of character for the typically jovial persona he tried to assume among colleagues. Steve Fujimoto, looking up from some paperwork, called out to him. "Earl, everything ok?"

"Just dandy."

"Uh. Ok. I only ask 'cause you don't seem like yourself this morning."

"Nope I'm good. Just didn't get to enjoy my coffee this morning, that's all."

"Oh, man. I hate that. Just the other day I was making myself a latte at home and realized we were out of milk. So I'm sitting there with the espresso shots pulled and an empty frothing pitcher. Had to have an Americano instead. Put me off my game the whole day."

Earl couldn't tell whether Steve was being serious or was mocking him. But since he had one fight on his hands that day already – and it wasn't even 9:00 a.m. yet – he didn't feel like finding out. He grunted in response to Steve's comments, sat down at his desk, and looked at his calendar for the day. He had a series of committed appointments with retailers, processers and grow operations – none of which were within an easy drive of *Herbvana*. The last site visit was scheduled for 2:30, and if he made that one brief he could manage to pay a visit to Marshall with enough time to blister his hide before getting back to the office just after 5:00. But first, before he could even begin to get his work done, he saw one appointment that he couldn't miss.

"Goddam it," Earl muttered.

"What's up?" Steve replied from the adjacent desk.

"Goddammed piss test's been scheduled."

"Yeah? They got me last week. Seems like they're getting more frequent."

Steve was right in his assessment. Earlier that year an LCB agent had crashed his official vehicle into the front of a daycare center over in Spokane during broad daylight. When the cops got there, the fellow appeared to be strung out on methamphetamine and had a couple of bottles of oxycodone in his pockets and an open beer in the vehicle. An investigative reporter for the local paper, the editorial board of which had been a vocal opponent of the move to legalize recreational weed in the first place, had jumped all over the story, ultimately learning that in the officer's most recent random drug test the man had tested positive for pregnancy, leading some to speculate that it was just possible that the State's testing system was ineffective. There was talk of a possible Pulitzer for this fine work of journalism.

"Governor's embarrassed. Hard to be taken seriously as an elected official when you've got meth heads in your weed police. Shit rolls downhill, Steve. It rolls downhill. Ok. Guess I'll go and let somebody watch me take a piss. Maybe I'll get lucky and it'll be that new lady nurse. Who knows, might impress her with the equipment and get a date out of it."

"Good luck with that."

"We've got a full schedule, plus I need to make one more stop at the end – surprise inspection over in Poulsbo. Why don't you stay here and get caught up on your paperwork. I'll go piss in the cup. When I'm done I'll come back here and we can head out."

"Sounds good."

Earl got up from his chair, walked back out of the building and drove away in his assigned sedan. No sooner had he left the building, however, that Steve's desk phone rang and he was summoned to the office of his boss, LCB Director Salvatore Svensson.

"You called for me, Sir?"

"Come in, and please close the door behind you." Svensson sat at a desk in the small private office. He was a striking man, with the lean and lanky appearance of his Swedish father melding uneasily with the swarthiness and large nose of his mother's southern Italian lineage. Seated in a chair immediately opposite Svensson was a young woman in a business suit. "Please, Fujimoto, have a seat." Svensson gestured to the empty chair beside the young woman.

Steve sat as directed. "How may I be of assistance, sir?"

"I want you to meet Eleanor Fritzell. Eleanor is with our internal affairs department."

Steve's heart sank. He had never interacted with anyone in internal affairs – and in fact his entire understanding of internal affairs issues came from detective shows on television – but he had a general sense that you didn't engage with IA unless something was wrong.

"It's nice to meet you, Ms. Fritzell."

"Nice to meet you too, Steve. Please, call me Eleanor."

"Fritzell has been looking into some things. And I want to make it clear to you up front Fujimoto that we don't know that anything is wrong. But we must be certain. Do you understand?"

Steve did not understand, but he nodded.

"The trouble," Svensson continued, "is that we've had some complaints. Now here at LCB we have an obligation to take complaints seriously, even if we think they're without merit. Understand? We don't get to ignore a complaint just because we think it might be false or just because we don't have faith in the integrity of the person who complains. Understand?"

Steve kept nodding, wondering where this was going. He'd only been on his current assignment for a few weeks and wasn't sure how it was possible that anyone had complained about him yet. He searched his mind for any interaction that might have been problematic.

"And so, Fujimoto, that's why Fritzell is here. She's helping us look into these things – and you're going to help too. Have I made myself clear?"

Eleanor, perhaps sensing the confusion in Steve's eyes, jumped in. "Mr. Fujimoto – may I call you Steve?"

Steve nodded. Since he'd entered the room, this was the first question he'd been asked to which he was certain he knew the correct answer.

"Good. Thank you, Steve. Steve, it pains me to say it but we've heard some disturbing complaints about your partner, Mr. McAllister."

"Earl?"

"Yes. In fact, we arranged for Earl to have a drug test this morning because we wanted to have an opportunity to speak with you alone."

"Alone?"

145

"Yes, alone. Or, more succinctly, without Earl. We don't actually think he is using any illegal substances. But like you he is subject to random testing and so we thought that would be an easy way to get him out of the office for a few minutes without arousing suspicion."

"Yeah. Pretty clever."

"Thank you, Steve. Anyway, we probably don't have that much time before he finishes his test and comes back, so I'm going to need to keep this brief. Ok?"

Steve nodded.

"We need you to watch Earl for us, Steve. We need you to watch him and report back to us on what you see. Can you do that, Steve?"

"Yeah. But, what am I watching for? What are these complaints?"

Fritzell looked over at Svensson, who shrugged his shoulders and gestured toward her with an open palm. "Your call, Fritzell. You share what you think you can."

"Steve, we received an anonymous tip on our whistleblower hotline. The caller said that Earl was taking cash from some of our cannabis licensees."

"I haven't seen anything like that."

"And it may be entirely false, Steve. That's the thing. It could just be sour grapes from a licensee who got written up for a violation, or an angry ex-girlfriend, or who knows what. But the fact is that we're obligated to investigate these things when we get these calls. And when we looked closely at Earl's circumstances we found a few... anomalies: things we couldn't quite explain about Earl and his situation. And that's why we need your help."

"Ok. So what do you need me to do?"

"Well, first, we need you to keep this conversation – and the fact that Earl's being investigated – entirely confidential. We don't want Earl to know that we're looking into his behavior because if he knows that and is actually guilty of something, then we won't be able to catch him in the act. Right? But at the same time, we don't want anyone else to know that we're investigating him because it will make people think he's guilty of something even if he's completely innocent – and that's not fair to Earl. So keeping this quiet is essential. Do you understand?"

"I understand."

"Ok. Good. So the second thing we need you to do is to just keep your eyes open. You go on inspections with him. We need you to watch for anything that you think is unusual and report it back."

"Anything that I think is unusual?"

"Yes, Steve."

"You know we're talking about weed businesses, right?"

"Cannabis licensees, yes."

"Yeah – so essentially everything about a weed business is unusual. What do you want me to report."

Eleanor laughed. It was a friendly laugh – somewhat

dissonant in the context of her businesslike appearance. "Good point. I should be clearer. We don't need you to report things that are unusual about the shops. We're really just wanting you to report anything that you think is unusual about Earl's behavior. Anything that seems inconsistent with LCB policy or your training. For example, if you accompany him to a shop that has a bunch of violations and he doesn't write any of them up – that might be unusual. If you see a licensee give Earl anything of value – that would be a violation of LCB rules – and so unusual. We would want you to report that sort of thing as well. Make sense?"

"Yeah. So, basically, you want me to spy on Earl."

"People sometimes put it that way, Steve. But, really, what I'm hoping is that by keeping your eye on him you'll be able to help clear his name."

"Fujimoto," Svensson cut in, "here's the deal. If I've got a dirty agent, I've got a problem with my boss. So, I can't afford to keep anyone that I can't trust. That means that if Earl's bent he's gone. And if Earl's bent and you know it and don't tell us, you're gone too. Do I make myself clear?"

"Yes, Sir."

Eleanor looked at her watch. "Earl should be getting back soon. We should wrap this up." Producing a business card from the inside pocket of her jacket, she handed it to Steve. "I want you to write down anything that seems suspicious or out of the ordinary. You can use this number to reach me at any time."

"Any questions, Fujimoto?"

"No, Sir."

"Thank you, Steve," said Eleanor. "Please go ahead and head back to your desk. Earl should be returning any time now."

Steve stood up and exited Svensson's office, closing the door behind him. "What do we know about the whistleblower," Svensson asked.

"Not much, really. I've listened to the call probably twenty times. The caller is a woman. There's a lot of strange noise in the background on the recording. You can hear traffic, but also some kind of screeching. We're hoping she'll call back and give more info."

"Ok. Keep me posted."

"I'll share as much as I can, Sal."

When Steve got back to his desk, Earl was leaning against the edge of it and looking disgruntled. "Where've you been?"

"Sorry – was in the bathroom. All that talk of your test made me need to go." "Let's head out. Got a busy day ahead of us."

Steve grabbed his coat and bag and followed Earl out to the sedan, wondering what the day had in store.

Chapter 13

From their office at the LCB, Earl and Steve were almost a hundred miles away from *Herbvana*. And with numerous appointments throughout the day that he couldn't reschedule for fear of drawing suspicion, Earl seethed as he waited his opportunity to pay Marshall a visit. He inflicted his mood on each licensee he met with that day – several retailers, a cannabis processing facility and a couple of grow operations – finding fault with each of them and issuing numerous citations. It was in all actuality one of the most productive days of Earl's recent tenure, and Steve was glad to note that he didn't observe anything particular suspicious at any of the visits.

It was almost 4:30 in the afternoon by the time they finally arrived at *Herbvana* – a visit which Steve knew was unscheduled but which Earl had characterized as a surprise inspection.

"For this last one, I'd like you to stay in the car."

"How's that?" Steve was more than a bit surprised by Earl's request – both the fact that he'd made it and the fact that his tone seemed almost reasonable at the time.

"I've got some history with these guys. Trying to get them to toe the line. You know, encourage them to come forward with concerns, self-report issues and all that. Think they're actually coming along but if we both go in there it'll just freak them out. Could lose all the progress we've made so far – make them clam up. So I'll take this one solo. You just hang out in the car – walk across the street and grab yourself an ice cream even – I shouldn't be long."

Earl pulled the sedan into the *Herbvana* parking lot, exited the vehicle and entered the shop. Lilith greeted him at the door. Barry was perched on a stool behind the counter.

"May I see your ID?"

"Cut the shit, lady. You know who I am."

"Yes, sir. But here at *Herbvana* we card everyone who comes in. It's the rules, after all."

Grudgingly, and with awareness that he was being filmed by the shop's security cameras, Earl fished his wallet out of his pocket and flashed her a copy of his driver's license.

"Thank you, Officer. Please come in."

"Where's Marshall?"

"I'm afraid he's out today. How can I help?"

"Don't believe you can, Missy. Where is he?"

Barry looked over at Lilith and Earl. As he opened his mouth to speak, Lilith replied "He had to go out of town – I think his mom's sick or something."

"Out of town. Hmm. Funny thing is I'm pretty sure I saw his car parked beside the shop – but then I'm a pretty observant guy. For example, I can tell just from standing here that the entrance to the shop, the one I just stepped through and that's intended to keep minors out, isn't quite up to code. And that lock on the storeroom door over there? Boy that doesn't look like it meets the LCB standard for securing your products. Yeah, as I stand here I can already tell we've got a bunch of violations on our hands. Guess I'm going to need to do a full site inspection. It's a shame Marshall isn't here. Shame for you, anyway. He always seemed to be to convince me that things weren't as bad as they seemed around here – help me change my perspective – mighty good lawyer, I guess."

On its face, this was laughable. Marshall hadn't been a mighty lawyer – having never won a case. And he hadn't been a good lawyer either, as evidenced by the fact that he'd cheated almost every client that had suffered the misfortune of retaining him.

"Ok. Guess I'm going to have to do this. Mr. Jones, you're listed as the co-owner on the license. If Marshall's not here then you're next batter up. This is going to be a full site visit. I want to see every last gram of weed you've got in your inventory, your tracking sheets, your excise tax records – all of it. We're about to have ourselves a fun afternoon. Recommend you get eye candy here to close up shop while we do our business. *Herbvana* is officially closed until I'm satisfied that you're in full and total compliance with the law."

Barry stood up, unsteadily, and began to wish he hadn't decided to stop using weed the day after Marshall's death. His interactions with Earl – like those with authority figures in general – had always felt much more manageable when he was stoned.

"Ok, Officer. How would you like to start?"

Glancing around the room, Earl fixed his eyes on the door to the storeroom. He wanted to find a way to separate Barry and Lilith – to get Barry alone and get the real story on Marshall.

"Let's start in the back."

"Uh. Sure. We'll start in the back. Lilith, I'm going to help Officer McAllister with his inspection. Please go ahead and close the till, shut off the sign and lock the front door. We're closed. After you're done out here, you can go ahead and head out if you want."

Lilith nodded at Barry – trying her best to send him encouragement but knowing full well that there was no way she was going to leave the shop while Earl was still there – she didn't trust Barry to deal with Earl alone.

Barry led Earl back into the storeroom, a stinking and disorganized morass of metal shelving units containing product of all descriptions. Against the wall on the right was Marshall's desk and computer. At the back wall sat a series of plastic totes. All throughout the room were bins spilling over with weed. Barry tried his best to appear calm while steering Earl toward the desk.

"Ok, Officer. How would you like to start? I can pull up our inventory records on the computer if you'd like."

"First thing – shut off that damn camera."

"I'm sorry?"

"The security camera. The one filming us right now. Shut it off."

"Ok," said Barry, grateful that he'd begun paying attention to how Lilith had operated the system in the days since Marshall's death. With a few keystrokes on the computer he accessed the program for the camera and shut it off. "All done. So, how

153

would you like to start?"

"Now, Stonerboy, you listen to me and you listen good. I've got business to settle with your partner. You know about business, right? It's how things get done. Only this time, things aren't getting done. And that's not making me too happy. Understand? Now if I were you, I'd want me to be happy. In fact I'd want me to be the happiest guy on earth. Cause when I'm happy, I'm a friendly guy – easygoing even – and you get to go about your business selling weed to the neighborhood. But when I'm unhappy? When I'm unhappy you get shut down. Your life turns into a living hell when I'm unhappy. Understand? So, I'm going to ask you one more time – and no bullshit from you or your little skank out front." Earl leaned in close to Barry and whispered, "where's Marshall?"

Barry swallowed hard and tried his damnedest to focus. "He's out of town. Back east somewhere."

"Right. Your partner – the brains of this outfit – goes out of town and you don't even know where he's gone. You're lying."

"Officer, if I knew exactly where he was I'd tell you. Believe me, I want you to be happy."

"Good thing. So tell me this, when is he coming back?"

Barry opened his mouth to speak, then realized he had no idea what to say. His mouth hung open for just a beat before he closed it; by all appearances he looked like a fish struggling to breathe on dry land. "I'm sorry – I don't know."

"So you don't know where he is. And you don't know when he's coming back. Sounds like you've got yourself a problem, boy. See, the law requires that I be able to talk to the licensees at any time – sorry, let me dumb that down for you, I can see you're struggling with it. The law says that I can talk to you or Marshall any time I want – so long as you two own this little establishment. So, if I can't talk to Marshall, well then you're breaking the law. And if you're breaking the law then I've got to shut you down. See the problem?"

"Uh. Yeah. Maybe we could, I don't know, get him on the phone or something?"

From the other room, Lilith heard Barry and felt her throat turn dry. She knew he wasn't especially bright – but this seemed stupid even for him. As inconspicuously as possible, she moved her way into the storeroom.

"Now that's a dandy idea, boy. You're smarter than you look. Let's do that. Let's give him a call."

"Uh. Ok." Barry pulled his phone out of his pocket and dialed Marshall's number. From the back of the storeroom, the sound of a cell phone could be heard beginning to ring. Earl's head jerked toward the sound and he strode toward the noise. Reaching his hand back into one of the bins – he pulled out Marshall's phone.

"Now isn't that…. curious," said Earl.

"Must've left his phone."

"Nothing gets past you, does it Stonerboy? You're a regular Einstein. But let me ask you this – what makes a guy leave town suddenly and not take his car or his phone? I mean, I could see leaving the car. You might get a ride to the airport, for example, and not want to park out at SeaTac. It's highway robbery what they charge for you to park your car. But your phone? Oh, he's going to need his phone. In fact, I don't think I've ever seen him without it. He wouldn't be caught dead without it."

Barry didn't respond. Lilith, sensing that Barry was about to crack under Earl's gaze and questioning, moved over to the desk and leaned against it. She reached out and clasped Barry's hand.

"Isn't that sweet? A couple of lovebirds in a shitload of trouble. You know," Earl continued, "I'm beginning to think that Marshall didn't leave town after all. In fact, I think he's probably pretty close by – maybe even in this room – and just avoiding me. And that makes me sad. Hurt, even. I'd hate to think that anyone was trying to avoid me – that's downright unfriendly, wouldn't you say? Hey, Marshall! You in here? Come on out, boy!"

Barry squirmed, his eyes darting to the back of the room where the totes stood in a row. Earl, seeing this, turned his head to see what had caught Barry's eye.

"Now what are you looking at, Stonerboy? Something caught your eye back here, didn't it?" He stepped back away from the desk and began to walk slowly past the shelving units toward the back of the storeroom. "I wonder what it was. Marshall? Are you back here?"

Barry held his breath. He was starting to tremble.

"Earl," said Lilith, "Marshall's not back there. You could see if he was."

Earl chuckled. "Miss, I've been doing this a long time. You'd

156

be amazed at the places I've found people trying to hide from me. Oh, I've found people on the roof. People in crawlspaces. So, who's to say that our boy Marshall wouldn't try to hide anywhere he could. Now I dare say these bins of yours back here look pretty small."

"They are, Earl. There's no way he'd fit in one of those things."

"But you know what, Missy, Marshall's a pretty scrawny little shit himself. So maybe he could just fit in one of these." The lid on the rightmost tote was slightly ajar. Earl lifted it, revealing its contents.

"It's just recycling, Earl. Packaging for recycling."

"So why do you care so much? And why did Stonerboy look back here when I called out for Marshall? Oh I think he's back here – or at least there's something back here that Stonerboy doesn't want me to see."

Earl unsnapped the lid on the next tote and threw it open. Inside were several large bags containing marijuana flower.

"Now isn't that interesting. These don't appear to be labeled. Don't have a bar code or anything. You know, if I had to guess I'd say that these may have been produced illegally. Oh, that's a big problem. That what you didn't want me to see?"

"Ok, you found it," said Lilith. "You found it. We've got some stuff that didn't come through a licensed grower. You got us. Just write it up – we'll pay the fine."

"Oh you'll more than pay the fine, Miss. This is black market stuff. Illicit. That's a felony, Stonerboy – we're talking jail time."

Earl turned to look at the two of them. He was inches from the last tote. Walking back toward them with a sneer on his face and a gleam in his eye, he suddenly stopped. "You know what? I've got you on that illicit weed – looks to be a few pounds of the stuff – but I really should be thorough. After all, you may have another few pounds hidden away. Wouldn't want to not find that, now would I?"

He turned and took a step back to the final tote. Opening it, he immediately recoiled, clasping his hand to his mouth. He instinctively clamped his jaw in an effort to stifle the vomit quickly climbing up his throat. Inside the container was a jumble of blood and body parts. His eyes flashed across bits of flesh. Some were recognizable; most were not. An arm, separated at the shoulder, lay on top of the pile. Lower down, Earl spotted a foot partially submerged in gore. Just as he had managed to overcome the shock of the sight, his brain registered the smell emanating from the bin and he lost his battle with nausea – the contents of his stomach joining the putrid mass.

"What the hell is going on?" Earl shouted – vomitus spittle trailing from his lips.

"Oh, shit," wailed Barry. "Oh shit. I didn't. I mean, he did it, man. He came at me. I didn't mean to. It was him. It was him, man!" Barry slumped in the corner, weeping.

"Where's Marshall?" Earl thundered. But as he stared, incredulous, at the scene before him he knew the answer to his question.

"Now Earl," said Lilith – her voice eerily calm, "let's talk about this. You don't need to do anything here. Don't do anything stupid. We can talk this out."

"Are you nuts? Talk this out? Marshall's dead – cut up into little pieces." He vomited again. "How are we, exactly, going to talk this out?"

"Marshall was a snake, Earl. You know that. He was a snake. A slimeball lawyer, ok? I mean, what's one less lawyer, right? Seriously, think this through. Don't do anything stupid. We can make this right."

"Make it right? Lady unless you're a shitload better than humpty-dumpty's men Marshall ain't getting put back together here."

"No – he's not getting put back together. I'm just saying nobody's going to miss him. Nobody's going to go looking for him. And nobody's going to find him either. We've got it handled."

Barry wailed.

"Shut up, Barry!" Lilith bellowed. "Now, listen Earl. I know what's been going on, ok? I mean, Marshall didn't tell me but he didn't have to. You coming in here all the time and finding violations but not writing us up. Not making a case out of it. I get it. Just business. And this is just business too, ok? I'm sure we can find a way to see ourselves out of this."

"Barry!" shouted Earl. "Did you do this?"

Barry continued to sob and, from the appearance of things, he'd now lost control over his bladder.

"Look," she said pointing to Barry, "he's useless. Completely

159

and utterly useless. Stoned half the time and even when he's not high he's still an idiot. Ignore him and talk to me." She took a step toward him – her fingers idly unbuttoning the top button on her blouse. "You don't want to make a big deal out of this, right? You've said it before. You're almost retired. The last thing you want is to fuck that up. And believe me, Earl, this could seriously, seriously fuck that up. So let's just stay calm and figure out how to make this right, ok?"

Earl looked at Lilith, glanced back at Marshall's body – or what was left of it in the bin – and then back to Lilith. She was right. He didn't want this to get in his way. As the shock of the discovery began to wear off, Earl began to feel more like himself and it occurred to him that although this was obviously not a good day for Barry or Lilith – and Marshall had clearly seen better days as well – this might turn out to be a pretty good day for him. He could use this to his advantage.

Earl closed the bin, caught his breath and began to speak. "You know what, little lady? You're right. I am almost retired. But that doesn't mean I'm old. Nope, actually feel pretty young. Spry, even. Especially when I come in here and see a young lady, such as yourself. Yeah. I've noticed you more than once. I'm guessing that a wild child like yourself could probably teach an old guy like me a thing or to."

"You're not my type, Earl."

"Oh, but I am, Ma'am. I certainly am. See right now I'm more your type than anybody else on earth. I'm the type that decides whether you're going to spend a few minutes with your mouth around my cock or a few years in prison. That sounds like your type to me."

160

"Fair enough, but I may not be your type, Earl." Lilith smiled sweetly and let her eyes slowly drift down toward Earl's crotch. She knew she had him beat as soon as he'd taken her bait. "The last cock I came across I sliced clean off with that little knife over there. Of course I had to spend a bit of time sawing at it – the knife's not that sharp at the moment. But I sure had fun doing it – the most fun I've had in a while. And when I finished cutting it off – and the balls – a lady should never ignore the balls, right Earl? – I chopped the whole thing into little, teeny pieces. Can't imagine what I'd do if I managed to get one in my mouth."

Earl watched the arc of Lilith's eyes drift down below his belt and felt himself turn a bit frightened. For the first time in years he felt he had met his match. They stared at each other in an uncomfortable silence.

"You know, Miss. I may have misjudged you. Perhaps we can come to a more businesslike arrangement."

"I'd like that, Earl. What do you have in mind."

"Well, as you've pointed out, I'm almost at retirement. Just a few more months and I've got my pension. But that doesn't go too far. In fact, I'm probably going to need some supplemental income in my advancing years."

"Yeah?"

"So here's what I'm thinking. You and stoner-boy cut me in – make me a silent partner, if you will – and I'll just forget about what I've seen here today."

"How much?"

"Sixty percent of the profits."

"That's a lot, Earl. Too much."

"Oh it is a lot – but it isn't too much. If I recall correctly, Marshall was sucking down fifty percent, plus there were certain… expenses…. that came off the top. Marshall won't be collecting anything anytime soon and some of those expenses are going to go away with this new arrangement. So, you two love birds are actually getting a good deal. Feels like I'm being generous. I recommend you accept before I change my mind and do something… official."

She stepped toward Earl. So close that he could smell her hair and feel her breath on his cheek. Ever so gently, she took one finger and, starting at his belt buckle, began tracing the downward path of his fly – her other hand resting on his chest.

"Fifty percent, Earl," she whispered. "Equal partners. Ok?"

"Fifty-five percent."

"Oh, that's still too much, Earl," she purred. "I want us to be partners. Don't you want to be my partner, Earl?"

"Yes, Ma'am." Earl started to lose his nerve.

Her hand wandered lower still. Cupping his balls in her hand, she cooed "Fifty percent. Who knows, maybe I'll even change my mind about cock. Ok?"

"Yes, Ma'am. Fifty percent."

"Oh I'm so, glad you want to be my partner, Earl. But there's just one problem. One that I think we need your help to solve. One that *I* need your help to solve. Can you do that, Earl? Can

162

you help me solve my problem?"

Earl swallowed hard. Her body pressed close against his. Her fingers alternately stroking and squeezing his balls, his heart had begun pounding and he was starting to sweat. Simultaneously aroused and terrified, he struggled to keep focus. "What do you need?"

"Well, Marshall was on the *Herbvana* license, right? And that license comes up for renewal every year. Now I could be wrong, but I don't think he's going to be able to help us renew next year. So what I'd really like, Earl – what I really need – is to have a way to make sure that Marshall doesn't need to sign. I need to get him off the license, somehow. You know? But if I were to buy him out then there'd be paperwork – lots of paperwork – and background checks and a lot of red tape. You don't like red tape, do you Earl?"

"No, Ma'am."

"I didn't think so. Not a take-charge kind of guy like yourself. So how are we going to fix that, Earl. How are *you* going to fix it for me," she purred. "How are you going to fix it – *for us?*"

"I can make it happen. I'll get it done."

"Oh, I'm so happy to hear that, Earl. That makes me so, so happy. Almost as happy as you seem to be at this very moment. You're going to fix it for us so that I'm on the license and then I'll make sure you have a very, very happy retirement. Might even have to throw a special retirement party to celebrate. Do we have a deal?"

"Yes, Ma'am."

"Good boy. Now do me a favor and let me get back to work, ok? We've got to get our doors back open for our customers. Wouldn't want to keep them waiting, would we? Not with you getting 50% of the profits. Ok?"

Grasping his hand in hers, Lilith led Earl toward the door back into the storefront. Releasing her grip, she turned to him as he opened the door.

"Thank you, Officer," she smiled. "We always appreciate visits and your help keeping us in compliance."

"Have a good day, Ma'am."

Earl desperately tried to regain his composure as he exited the store and back into the light of the afternoon. Approaching the car, he saw Steve in the passenger seat looking at his phone and eating an ice cream cone.

"That took longer than I expected. Everything OK?"

"Yep," said Earl. "Everything's great."

Chapter 14

"You know, Agnes, this is pretty nice. The beach at sunset. It doesn't get much better than this."

Helen Rasmussen listened to the waves gently rolling in - a steady rhythm of quiet crashes. She'd lived on the Island for the better part of thirty years, but it wasn't until just this last year that she'd managed to move to the beach. And that was only after her late husband, Olaf, had passed away.

Olaf had been a bit of a worrier, a fact which happily meant that he'd secured a ridiculously large life insurance policy early in their marriage and then just kept paying the premiums. The kids were grown and moved away. The mortgage was paid on their modest home in the woods. But Olaf kept paying those premiums. And so when Olaf managed to choke to death on a particularly gristly bite of Reindeer Roast at the Sons of Norway Jul Dinner last December, Helen made out pretty well. She was upset, of course. She liked to say publicly that no amount of money was worth losing her beloved Olaf. But deep down, if she was honest to herself at least, she had to admit that a house on the beach at sunset beat the dour stoicism of an aging Norwegian most days of the week.

"Yep, pretty nice."

Agnes wasn't listening. She loped down the beach and began to dig furiously in the wet sand. "No, Agnes! No digging!

Agnes looked briefly at her, stopped her digging and started back toward Helen, tail wagging furiously. Halfway back, she picked up a length of bull kelp in her mouth. Then, her nose working overtime, she dropped the kelp, sniffed the wet sand and began rolling aggressively in the new smell she'd found.

Helen laughed at the clowning dog, listening to the sound of children playing farther down the beach and took a sip of her wine. Hauling herself up out of her Adirondack chair, she pulled a gnarled stick from the unlit fire ring at her feet, whacked it against the rocks a couple of times to knock off the cobwebs, and called to the now-fragrant golden retriever. "Agnes! Want the stick?"

Seeing the stick in Helen's hand, Agnes bounded over, tongue lolling out of her mouth. Just as she reached Helen's feet, Helen gave the stick a heave into the water and Agnes chased after it. Olaf and Agnes had loved playing fetch since Agnes was little more than a ball of blonde fluff. In fact, Helen was never quite sure whether it was Olaf or Agnes who enjoyed it more. Since Olaf's passing, Helen had felt obligated to keep the game going.

As she took another sip of her wine, Helen admired the glittering buildings of Seattle in the distance. In the watery space between her small patch of beach and the skyscrapers some eight miles off, an armada of small sailboats darted back and forth, tacking and jibing in the evening breeze. Closer in, a ferryboat was making the turn into the Island's harbor – seagulls surfing the unseen air currents left in its wake.

Agnes bounded out of the surf, stick in her mouth and ran back over to Helen, who dutifully took it from the dog and threw it back into the waves. Agnes charged after it.

The ferry passed by and Helen could hear tourists' voices carried by the wind. The cruise ships were making their annual summer pilgrimages to Seattle, and with the local hotel concierges recommending their guests take a quick ferry ride over to Bainbridge and back to kill a few hours and see the local scenery while waiting embark on their cruise to Alaska, the ferry was full of eager visitors. Helen never quite understood why you'd want to go on a cruise – it wasn't exactly her and Olaf's style – let alone why you would want to endure a 30-minute ferryboat commute (one way) as something akin to foreplay in advance of a multi-day cruise to go stare at glaciers. But she appreciated the influx of cash the tourists brought to local businesses during the short summer cruising season even if she didn't love the increase in traffic.

As she pondered the idiocy of spending one's free time trapped on a boat with a bunch of strangers, Agnes came bounding back out of the surf carrying her prize. A few tourists on the upper deck of the ferry were waiving to her now. Struggling to waive back to the watching audience without spilling her remaining wine in the glass in her left hand, she absent-mindedly reached down with her right to take the stick from Agnes and give it another throw – as much for the entertainment of the viewing tourists as for Agnes' enjoyment.

Grasping the stick from Agnes' mouth, something felt different in Helen's hand. It was smooth and slick. But this tactile signal from her hand didn't register in her conscious mind. It wasn't until she cocked her arm back, with the stick parallel to her head, that she realized something had changed. And, in reflection later that evening, she wasn't sure whether it was the difference in texture or the bits of flesh hanging off it

167

which had been her first clue.

Helen screamed and dropped the stick. Agnes scrambled to retrieve it again and Helen screamed again. The tourists continued to waive.

Shooing away the eager dog, Helen looked down. What had been a stick was unquestionably now bone. And gristle. A stick-sized length of bone and gristle. Although she'd been retired from nursing for the better part of a quarter century, she knew exactly what it was. It was a femur. And it was human.

She put her foot on the bone to prevent Agnes from carrying it off and briefly considered tossing her wine to the sand. Thinking better of it, she gulped down the last of the chardonnay, fished her phone from her pocket and dialed 911.

"Emergency Services – how can I be of assistance?" a woman's voice answered.

"There's a bone on the beach!"

"Ma'am?"

"A bone. A human bone. A femur. My dog just brought it to me."

"Are you in danger, Ma'am?"

"Danger?"

"Yes, Ma'am. Are you in danger right now?"

"Well, no. I don't think so."

"Is anyone in danger, Ma'am?"

"Well someone obviously was. I mean, somebody's missing a

femur. So yes, I'd say someone *was* in danger – at least at some point."

"But nobody is in danger right now? Is that what I hear you saying?"

"Yes. I guess so. I mean, I think so – I don't really know. Again – somebody's missing a leg!"

"Are you missing a leg, Ma'am?"

"No! I just told you. My dog brought me the bone."

"Ok, Ma'am. I'm going to need you to hang up and dial the police."

"I beg your pardon?"

"The police, Ma'am. You just said nobody was in danger – so this isn't really an emergency."

"But – there's a human femur that's washed up on the beach!"

"I understand that, Ma'am. But if there's no imminent threat to anyone's safety then this is really more of a routine police matter. Also, sometimes it can be difficult to tell the difference between a human bone and one from another animal."

Helen pondered this development while Agnes began to surreptitiously gnaw bits of gristle away from the femur pinned beneath Helen's foot. It hadn't occurred to her that she'd be second-guessed about the source of the bone, that by calling 911 she apparently wasn't actually calling the police, or that her emergency would be so easily dismissed by the 911 operator.

"Well I must say I'm surprised. Here I am minding my own business on the beach at sunset and I find a human bone – a pretty recently lost one if I'm not mistaken, and I call you and you tell me I shouldn't have called…"

"I didn't say that, Ma'am…"

"I would have thought you'd be more concerned. And you can't even transfer me to the police? Pretty lousy customer service if you ask me."

"Ma'am?"

"Customer service, young lady! I pay your salary!"

"Yes, Ma'am." This wasn't the first time a 911 operator, or indeed even this operator – had heard huffiness coming from a caller on Bainbridge. In fact, the residents of the burb – which prided itself on being somehow superior to the other hamlets in the county – were routinely some of the rudest callers and regularly called for things which were clearly not emergencies; although it was perhaps apocryphal, the dispatchers still told the tale of a caller years before who had dialed 911 to complain that the local grocery store had run out of arugula. "I understand, Ma'am. Would it be more helpful if I were to connect you?"

"Fine!"

"Ok, Ma'am. I'm connecting you now. Have a good evening."

Helen fumed while the phone rang.

"Thank you for calling the Bainbridge Island Police Department. If this is an emergency, please hang up and dial 911. Our normal business hours are from 8:00 a.m. to 4:00 p.m.

Monday through Friday. If you have reached this message during our normal business hours, please hold the line and an operator will be with you as soon as possible. If you are calling outside of normal business hours, please leave a message and we will return your call."

Helen, disgusted, hung up the phone. She looked down at Agnes, who continued to happily gnaw the hip-end of the bone.

"Come, Agnes!" she directed as she walked up the beach toward her house. Agnes picked up the bone and dutifully followed at heel. "Drop it!". On command, the dog dropped the bone on the back porch and the two entered the house. Helen grabbed Agnes by the collar and began to drag the now filthy dog to the shower, pausing only briefly to grab the half empty bottle of wine from the kitchen counter.

Helen woke earlier than usual the next morning, trundled into her kitchen and fired up her espresso machine. Agnes trotted in behind her, looking as bleary as is possible for a golden retriever. The clock on the microwave read 4:48. Helen sat in silence. The sun was rising over the Cascades – east of Seattle. Helen loved the spectacle of the rising sun in the picture windows that looked out from her living room toward the beach and the city and mountains beyond.

The sunrise, so consistently glorious in the summer, brought her no joy this morning. Before the sun had a chance to light up the porch and steps leading to the water, revealing Agnes' discovery of the night before, she closed the curtains.

Several cappuccinos and most of the way through the newspaper later, the microwave clock read 8:00. Agnes picked up the phone and dialed the police department.

"Bainbridge Island Police Department. How may I be of assistance?"

"This is Helen Rasmussen – I'm at 1585 Pleasant Cove. I need you to send an officer down here as soon as possible."

"I see. What seems to be the problem?"

"Very upsetting. It's all just very upsetting. And I called last night and the woman with 911 wouldn't help me. Said I needed to call you instead. And I did call you – or she did anyway – and you weren't there. So, I'm calling you now. I need you to send someone. It's all just very upsetting, don't you see?"

"I hear that you're upset, Mrs. Rasmussen. We'll send someone out right away. But to know who to send we need to know a bit more about what is upsetting you. Do you need medical help – is anyone in danger?"

"Well someone was absolutely in danger! You don't just lose a leg, don't you see? A leg!"

"I see. A leg. Yes, Mrs. Rasmussen, that does sound like it could be upsetting. You think someone lost a leg?"

"Think someone lost a leg? I know they did! I had it in my own hand, don't you see. I held it. Ghastly thing, really, to lose a leg. I mean how does something like that happen?"

"I see. Yes, Mrs. Rasmussen." The receptionist couldn't quite understand what the older woman was going on about but she sounded sufficiently distraught that he dispatched a squad car to her home. "I'm sending someone now, Mrs. Rasmussen. You just stay put and they'll be right there. Ok?"

"Well of course it isn't ok!"

"No, Ma'am. I don't mean that someone losing a leg is ok. I'm just asking if it is ok if I send someone out to your home. Is that ok?"

"Well why do you think I called? That's exactly what I asked for!"

"Yes, Ma'am. They're on the way. You just stay there and they'll meet you at your home. Is that ok?"

"Fine!"

Helen hung up the phone, refilled her milk frothing pitcher and ground some additional espresso beans. Several minutes and another cappuccino later, she heard a knock on her front door.

"Finally, you're here!"

"Yes, Ma'am. Are you Mrs. Rasmussen?"

"Of course. Who else would I be?"

The officer ignored the question. The vaguely feral look in the old woman's eyes put him off his nerve.

"I'm John. Officer John Wilkerson. I understand you're having a bit of trouble this morning?"

"John Wilkerson?"

"Yes, Ma'am."

"Your mother's name…. Elizabeth?"

"Yes, Ma'am. Did you know my mother?"

"Yes, I know your mother. And I know you, young man. And your five brothers. There are six of you boys altogether aren't there?"

"Um. Yes, Ma'am. You have me at a disadvantage, I'm afraid. Have we met?"

"Of course we've met. I worked in Dr. McGregor's office for thirty-three years. Young man I've probably seen your backside."

Wilkerson chuckled. "Well, Ma'am hopefully it won't come to that again today." He had a kind- hearted twinkle in his eye that helped to calm the hyper-caffeinated octogenarian. "I didn't get a lot of information from my dispatcher. He said something about a leg – but nothing more than that. How can I help you?"

"It was horrible."

"Yes?"

"I thought it was a stick. Agnes brought it to me."

"Agnes?"

"Yes. We were playing fetch, you see."

"Yes. Fetch. Mrs. Rasmussen, would you mind if I came inside so that you could tell me the whole story? I want to be sure I understand your concerns."

"Oh, my heavens. Where are my manners? Of course. Come inside. Come inside immediately." Helen ushered Wilkerson into the house, through the foyer and into the kitchen. "Can I make you a coffee?"

Wilkerson eyed the espresso machine and the elderly woman

174

in turn – beginning to understand a bit more about her frantic appearance.

"No, Ma'am. I've already had plenty this morning. Please – tell me what's going on."

Helen related to Wilkerson the story of the prior evening's events, taking care to leave out the part about drinking wine on the beach. She didn't know if that sort of thing was permitted, but wasn't about to admit to something that she thought might be illegal. As she talked, Wilkerson took notes, interjecting periodically to ask for clarification.

"And that's when I called the police!" Helen concluded.

"I see, Mrs. Rasmussen. And where is the bone now?"

"Please – call me Helen. Agnes dropped it on the back porch. I didn't have the stomach to deal with it. And besides, I didn't want to tamper with evidence. It's bad enough that Agnes was chewing on it – though I don't suppose you can charge a dog with a crime for chewing on a bone – but still. I'm not getting near it."

"So, the back porch? Would you mind if I took a look?"

"I want you to take a look and to take it away!"

"Ok, Helen. I'll just pop out to the porch and take a look."

Wilkerson rose from his chair. He glanced at the curtains in the living room but decided against taking the direct route. Exiting via the front door, he walked around the house – down toward the beach – and mounted the stairs to the back porch. Finding nothing, he tapped on the French doors leading into the house.

A few moments passed, after which the curtains were drawn back and Helen peered at him through the glass.

"Yes?"

"Helen, where did you say that Agnes dropped the bone?"

Helen looked down at Wilkerson's feet. "Right where you're standing. But I don't see it. Did you take it away?"

"There's nothing here, Ma'am. No bone, I mean. I've looked from the waterline up to this door."

"Well it was there!"

"Yes, Ma'am. I understand. Ma'am, are you sure it was a human bone? You know we've got a lot of deer on the Island and sometimes…"

Helen opened the French door and cut him off. "Young man, I was a nurse. I know a human bone when I see one."

"Yes, Ma'am, er.. Helen. Well, unfortunately there isn't anything out her now."

"Probably those damned otters – or maybe the coyotes. I've been hearing them almost every morning, you know. They trouble Agnes so. One of them must have dragged it off."

"Coyotes. Yes, could be. But it isn't here now, you see. So, I really can't do much more to help you."

"Well, no I suppose you can't."

"Ok, Helen. Please call me if you need any additional help, ok?" Wilkerson handed her his card. "This has my cell phone number on it. You can reach me anytime."

"Thank you, John. Thank you for taking the time to come. Please say hello to your mother for me."

"I would, Helen, but Mom unfortunately passed away a couple of years ago."

"Oh how dreadful."

"Yes, Ma'am."

"I am very sorry to hear that."

"It's quite all right, Helen. She had a wonderful life – six boys as you rightly recalled – and a bunch of grandchildren before she passed." Wilkerson stepped into the house and offered his hand to Helen. "I must be going now. If you need anything else, please give me a call."

Wilkerson patted Agnes on the head, exited the house and walked to his squad car. He wasn't sure what to make of the whole thing. He wasn't positive that Helen Rasmussen wasn't just a lonely elderly woman who might have imagined the whole incident. There were only two things he was reasonably certain of: she needed to cut back on the coffee (or switch to decaf) and she'd seen him naked. And that was just about enough excitement for one summer morning.

Back at the police station, Wilkerson poked his head into the office of the Police Chief: Sandra Glickman. Glickman was a recent transplant, having taken the post as part of a lifestyle change – hoping that serving in the seemingly sleepy island community might offer a better quality of life than she'd previously experienced in her prior role as a senior officer in the force of a large Minneapolis suburb.

"Hey, Chief?"

"What's up, John?"

"I just finished a really odd call – was hoping to get your thoughts."

"Of course. Come. Sit down."

Wilkerson walked over to the chair opposite Sandra at her desk and sat down. "Dispatch got a call this morning from a house over on Pleasant Cove. That's over near Rockaway Beach – beautiful neighborhood – right on the water. Anyway, the call comes in and it's a lady – sounds like she's in a bit of distress. She keeps saying something about a leg, but the dispatcher isn't quite sure what is going on so I head over."

"A leg?"

"Yeah. A leg. Anyway, I get there and sure enough we've got an older lady at the house. She's wound herself around the axle pretty badly. From the look of her, I'm guessing she'd been up all night and probably had about her weight in coffee during that span. She's visibly shaking. Honestly, if I thought it was possible I'd have said she was strung out on cocaine when I got there. Anyway – she tells me the whole story. Says she was playing fetch with her dog on the beach the night before. She's throwing a stick out into the surf and the dog – Agnes..."

"Agnes?"

"Yep," Wilkerson chuckled. "Beautiful golden retriever – doesn't quite live up to her name. Anyway, says that Agnes is retrieving the stick from the surf – can't be all that far out there actually as I don't think the lady's got much of a throwing arm –

178

but anyway retrieving the stick and then she comes back with a femur."

"A femur."

"Yeah."

"Instead of the stick?"

"Yep. Instead of the stick. Now the lady apparently takes the femur out of the dog's mouth – thinking it's the stick mind you – without looking at it. And then freaks out…"

"Like you might…"

"Exactly. Now she's sure this is a human femur. Apparently used to be a longtime nurse on the Island. I don't remember her, but she clearly remembers me, my mom, my brothers – the whole family – so I'm inclined to think she probably can tell the difference between a human femur and the bone of some other animal. Anyway – she freaks out when she figures out she's holding a bone. So she calls 911. But they don't send anyone out."

"Why not?"

"County policy. Unless the dispatch thinks someone is in actual physical harm they don't send a car out."

"They don't?"

"Nope. Budget cuts I think."

"Got it. Completely the wrong answer if we're trying to improve relationships with the community – I'll add it to my list of things to try to fix. So, anyway, is this sorted?"

179

"Not really. I've got her calmed down. But when I got to her house – there was no bone."

"No bone."

"Nope. She said that Agnes dropped it on the back deck."

"Good old Agnes."

"Yeah. Anyway, Agnes was chewing on the bone and she…"

"Agnes was chewing on the femur… the human femur…"

"Yeah."

"And to think I've always liked golden retrievers – never occurred to me that to them we were just walking chew toys."

"Seriously. Anyway, Agnes supposedly dropped the bone on the back porch last night. But when I got there – no bone. So I can write all that down and put it in the log – but without a bone I'm not really sure what to do."

"Do you think the old lady – what's her name?"

"Rasmussen."

"Do you think Rasmussen is crazy? Maybe lonely and wanting some company from a strapping young police officer?"

Wilkerson paused. During their morning together, Helen had mentioned Olaf several times and obviously did seem a bit lonely. "I don't know. She said she was recently widowed – so maybe."

"Look – if there's no bone then we've got no physical evidence to go on. Which means all we're really left with is an elderly widow with a lot of time on her hands and way too much coffee. I'm not saying she imagined the whole thing. But I think it is at least plausible that she did. Or that Agnes really did find something on the beach and she jumped to a conclusion about what it was. We have to consider those as options."

"Yep. That makes sense to me. So what next?"

"Go ahead and fill out your report. Describe the incident just as you described it to me – just a house call with a concerned citizen. In the meantime, call over to the neighboring PDs and see whether anyone's reported a missing kayaker or something. Giving Rasmussen the benefit of the doubt – it is at least possible that we've got a floater out there feeding the fish and Agnes just happened to get lucky. Still – that doesn't explain why the bone wasn't here this morning. Rasmussen have any thoughts about that?"

"Coyotes."

"Coyotes? Like, the wild animal?"

"Yep. Or maybe otters."

Glickman sat back in her chair, stifling a laugh. She'd wanted a change of pace from the gang- related work she'd been doing back in the twin cities. And here she was wondering whether wild animals might be responsible for stealing evidence of a potential crime or, alternatively, that a lonely old lady might just have a really active imagination. She'd gotten her wish.

Chapter 15

Metacarcinus magister or, as it is more commonly known, the Dungeness crab, is native to the waters of the Puget Sound. It has the distinction of being the state crustacean of Oregon, if indeed that is any distinction. But it takes its name from the sleepy port of Dungeness, Washington on the Strait of Juan de Fuca.

Like its very distant cousin, Homo sapiens, the male Dungeness spends the majority of its life in search of two things – food and sex. And not necessarily in that order. When either is scarce, it is prepared to fight to secure its fair share. It is equally ill-tempered in times of plenty.

And as is also often the case with that distant cousin, the male Dungeness is prepared to endure quite a lot from his female counterpart in order to enjoy her affection. Courtship is a relatively simple affair: the male will embrace the female – potentially for several days - while awaiting the opportunity to mate. When she decides the mood is right, she gives him a subtle cue by urinating in the general vicinity of his eyes.

In terms of its pursuit of food, the Dungeness is not a picky eater. Clams are fair game, as are small fish and other crabs. It will chase live food but is also quite content to scavenge.

Most Mammalia of the Puget Sound, and indeed more than a few native Cephalopods and Aves, will readily devour Metacarcinus magister if given the opportunity. It is delicious to a fault.

* * * * *

Leaf Donegan, kneeling on his paddleboard, pushed off from the beach, steadied himself and stood up. The nose of his board pointing toward Seattle and the sun rising over the Cascades range beyond, he paddled purposefully across the calm water. Here and there, baitfish breached the surface – seeking to avoid being eaten by larger predatory fish. Fried egg jellyfish lurked beneath the surface, trailing their tentacles as they drifted along on the tide.

Leaf was happy, although he didn't necessarily want everyone to know that. A thirteen-year-old boy living on Bainbridge Island, he felt obligated to display a certain amount of angst. But in reality, life was pretty good. He was out of school for the summer. His parents were largely occupied with work during the day – keeping them out of his hair and leaving him free to play video games with his friends, practice graffiti techniques on the walls of the abandoned cannery, and chase girls.

Females were not his quarry this morning, however. In fact, if he came across any he'd have to throw them back. He'd set a crab pot the evening before – baiting it with the carcass of a roast chicken made for dinner that night – and was eager to see what was in the pot.

Leaf steered his board through the labyrinth of red and white buoys, each marked with the name and contact information of a hopeful angler. Looking to the shoreline, he did his best to gauge where he had dropped his pot – and from there to make an educated guess as to where he might locate the buoy bearing his name. After some searching, he found it and sank to his knees to get to work. He uncoupled the buoy from the line, stowing it in the milk crate he'd lashed to the back of the board, and began to haul on the line.

As he pulled on the rope, his tugs propelled his board – skipping along the water in the direction of the crab pot some thirty feet beneath the surface. Reaching that spot, Leaf found to his great delight that the line immediately felt much heavier in his hands – offering the promise of a full pot. He gripped the line tightly and began to haul it up, arm over arm, doing his best to keep his balance on the skittish board.

Finally, after one close call in which he almost capsized the board in the wake of an oncoming ferry, he could see the pot itself just below the surface of the water. With one last carefully balanced heave he brought the pot up onto the board and surveyed his catch: six Dungeness crab and two smaller Red Rock crab – now all eagerly seeking to escape the confines of the trap. Leaf beamed.

He opened the top of the trap and gingerly reached inside – ignoring for a moment the crabs themselves and grasping instead a small box affixed to the inside of the pot's innermost column. Releasing the clips holding the box in place, he withdrew the object and placed it inside a plastic pouch attached to a lanyard around his neck.

"Look at you later," Leaf muttered to himself.

Next, Leaf reached back into the pot and carefully extracted, one by one, the two Red Rock crabs and tossed them back into the water. Finally, he retrieved from the milk crate a bright orange plastic measuring gauge and placed it on the board between his knees while he fished the first Dungeness out of the pot. Holding the crab carefully by its rearmost legs so that it couldn't reach his hand with its formidable claws, Leaf flipped the crab onto its backed and examined its abdomen.

"Nope," Leaf said to the crab as he tossed it back into the water.

Reaching back into the pot, he again extracted a crab and flipped it over. Satisfied with what he saw, he measured the width of the crab's carapace – the animal's outer shell – with the plastic gauge and once again tossed the animal back into the water.

"See you next year, buddy. You're a little too small."

He extracted the third crab and flipped it over. "Another female," he remarked as he dropped it over the side – watching the crab slowly sink back into the depths and out of sight.

Continuing this process, Leaf extracted each of the remaining crabs from the pot. At the end of his efforts he was left with only two that were keepers – males above the minimum size and that weren't in the process of molting. "Not awesome – but it'll be dinner."

He stowed the keepers in the milk crate, taking care to strap his makeshift lid to the top so that they wouldn't escape, lashed the pot itself to the front of his board, got to his feet and began to paddle back to the beach. As he approached, he waved at old Mrs. Rasmussen – his neighbor three houses away – who was on the shore playing with her dog.

"Any luck?"

"A couple of good ones – had to throw back four."

"I hear it's a good season so far. People seem to be catching quite a few."

Helen turned to attend to Agnes, who was pestering a seagull intent on eating something lying on the beach, and Leaf continued to paddle his board home. Reaching the beach in front of his parents' home, he dragged the board onto the shore – high enough so that it wouldn't be swept away by the rising tide later that day – detached the milk crate and dragged it back down toward the edge of the water. Reaching the line of the surf, he set the crate down, squatted down and produced a knife from his pocket.

"End of the line for you guys. Who wants to go first?"

Leaf could hear the Dungeness in the crate – clicking noises – and as he pulled the lid off the box one of the two captive crustaceans reached up with pincers extended in a defensive posture.

"We have a volunteer."

Using the blade of his knife, Leaf flipped the crustacean onto its back and reached with his other hand to grasp the rear legs of the flailing animal. In an instant he pinned the crab on its back on the beach next to the crate and thrust the blade of the knife swiftly into the point at which its abdomen joined its thorax. As the crab writhed in pain, frantically searching with its pincers for purchase on its attacker, Leaf twisted the knife downward –

186

cutting through the abdomen until he reached the lowermost part of the crab's shell. The crab convulsed and then grew still, at which point Leaf removed the knife and proceed to disassemble his prey.

Removing first the flap covering the abdomen and then tearing the gonapods – the genitals of the crab – from the animal, Leaf next turned it right side up in his hand, grasped its mandibles and pulled them from their sockets before grasping the carapace and wrenching it free from the crab's body. The internal organs of the crab now exposed, Leaf worked with a combination of his knife and his bare hands to strip the animal of lungs and brain matter before grasping the carcass in both hands and breaking it in half.

"One down," Leaf said happily to himself as he set the two halves of the animal to the side and reached into the crate to extract the second unlucky specimen. "Agh!" Leaf exclaimed as he withdrew his hand from the box.

The second animal, perhaps by instinct or in reaction to having seen his compatriot so unceremoniously dismembered in front of his watery eyes, had sought revenge on the boy. Using its powerful pincer, the crab had attached itself to a finger on Leaf's right hand and was holding on with all its strength. Leaf, wincing in pain, shook his hand but could not loosen the crab's grip, and when he attempted to use his left hand to loosen the animal's hold, the crab tried to attack his left hand with its other pincer. Time seemed to stop for both Leaf and the crab as they danced in hand-to-claw combat on the beach until the boy, spying a reasonably sized rock on the beach, flopped to the ground, grasped the stone and proceeded to smash the carapace of his adversary with a series of sharp blows. His shell crushed, the crab finally loosened its grip enough to allow the boy to use the knife to pry open the claw and remove his finger.

With his finger throbbing from their encounter, Leaf proceeded to dismember this second animal with relish. Whereas before he simply wanted to clean his catch so that it might be cooked, this time it was personal. After he'd broken this second crab in half, he picked up the four halves of the two animals, waded out to his knees in the surf and submerged his prize beneath the waves – giving them a quick shake to rid their carcasses of the final remaining vestiges of their internal organs, and then walked up the beach and into his house.

Leaf walked into the kitchen, collected a large bowl from a cabinet and filled it with ice from the freezer. After placing the crab on the ice, he placed the entire bowl in the refrigerator and then grabbed another few pieces of ice for his finger – by now swelling quite badly from the encounter with the crab. Ice in hand, he walked upstairs into his bedroom, sat at his desk and fired up his laptop. Using his left – clearly non-dominant – hand, he fumbled clumsily with the lanyard around his neck until he had removed it, and then removed from the plastic pouch on the lanyard the plastic object it contained: a waterproof box for a camera. Disassembling the box he freed the camera inside, removed its flash drive and inserted it into his laptop.

"Let's see what we got."

Leaf downloaded the time-lapse video files from the camera and watched in rapt attention as all manner of marine life paraded across the screen. In the dusky depths, the camera captured sea stars, small fish, and a great number of crabs moving in its field of vision. Every so often a crab could be seen skittering into view and feeding on the chicken in the pot. As the frames progressed, the light from the prior evening's setting sun diminished and the footage took on an eerie quality until it went completely black. Leaf clicked the fast-forward button and allowed the recording to clip by at an accelerated pace until the frame began once again to lighten – reflecting the morning's dawn.

As the light of the rising sun began to illuminate the scene, Leaf saw once again the same cast of aquatic characters in the foreground. Close behind his pot, however, he could see something had been added to the scene – something that wasn't visible when the sun had set the night before. An additional crab pot was resting perhaps 3 feet behind his own: the left side of the pot in the background partially obscured by the bait box in his own trap. "Cool! Twice the action."

As Leaf studied the scene, he watched a large Dungeness move into the pot behind his own – navigating the door to the pot with ease. Walking from left to right on the frame, the crab could be seen reaching out to grasp something with its pincers. And then, to Leaf's horror, amazement, and delight, the crab walked back to the right side of the frame – dragging behind it the head of Marshall Owens and feasting on the flesh of his now completely unrecognizable face.

"NO WAY! THAT IS SO COOL!" Leaf jumped out of his chair, his shouting startling the family's cat and causing him to dart from the boy's room. He watched the time lapse intently, amazed at his good fortune. "This is going to get, like, a million hits," he muttered proudly to himself as he downloaded the

189

footage from the camera into editing software on the laptop and proceeded to create a version of the footage that began at daybreak and the appearance of the second pot. Satisfied that he had distilled his film down to its most exciting essence, he then uploaded the footage to his personal channel on an Internet video-sharing site. If he were honest, Leaf would be forced to admit that up until now his channel had been a bit of a disappointment. He had a handful of followers – mostly kids from school. But no real excitement. His attempts to film interesting stunts or challenges had mostly failed. He'd only managed a few hundred views of his attempt to light his own flatulence on fire. Considering that he'd achieved not only ignition of his intended gaseous target but also combustion of some very short and very curly hairs – which he'd only just recently managed to sprout and was quite fond of – the exercise hardly seemed worthwhile.

"This is going to be huge. Ok. Need to figure out what to name it. Think, Leaf, think. Without the right name the search engines won't pick it up. Needs to be something that grabs your attention."

Leaf sat for a moment or two and then let his fingers fly over the keyboard. In his excitement for his discovery, he'd forgotten all about his fight with the crab and the pain in his finger. Now, at this moment, he was possibly the happiest he'd ever been.

"All right – here we go. 'CRAB EATS HUMAN FACE'"

Leaf sat back in a self-congratulatory stupor. Then, on reflection, he realized that his title was still missing a few key elements. He needed to put something in it that would get picked up locally so his classmates – and especially the classmates who didn't already follow his channel – would see it. And he needed to make sure that people knew just how amazing the footage was. With a few keystrokes, the title now read:

"INCREDIBLE FOOTAGE – DUNGENESS EATS HUMAN FACE – MUST WATCH - #BAINBRIDGE #CRAB #AMAZING"

Satisfied with his effort, he finished the uploading process and began to dream of the fame and wealth his newfound footage would undoubtedly provide. Leaf bounced excitedly around his room – periodically refreshing the browser on his laptop in the hopes that he might see the number of views of his footage begin to skyrocket.

But the Internet, though fast, is not fast enough to satisfy the impatience of a thirteen-year-old boy without parental supervision. Leaf took a big breath and tried to stay calm. "It's going to take a bit for people to find it. It's still early." As he tried to catch his breath, he realized that his stomach was growling, so he went back into the kitchen. After grabbing a bag of nacho chips from the pantry, he opened the refrigerator and reached past the bodies of the morning's catch to retrieve a soda, and then retreated back to his room. Much to his disappointment, there were still no hits on his video.

The rest of the morning passed quickly for Leaf in a sugar and caffeine-fueled whirlwind of videogames and electronic dance music, periodically interrupted by his checking the hit counter on the video. Just after noon, his phone lit up with a text from his best friend, a scraggly haired kid named David but who everyone in their grade called Montezuma on account of his once experiencing the sudden onset of food poisoning in the middle of gym class back in fourth grade.

"Just woke up – busy?"

"Nope – come over?" Leaf replied.

"On my way."

Leaf put down his phone and continued the serious business of battling zombies on his computer – doing his best to avoid spilling soda on the keyboard. A few minutes later, he heard Montezuma at the door.

"Dude, you're not going to believe what happened to me this morning. It's like epic."

David raised an eyebrow.

"Seriously, man, it's like the most amazing thing ever."

"Did you defeat the elder-warlock in *Scrolls of Oblivion*?"

"No – seriously man, I'm not talking video game stuff. Talking about real life."

"Yeah?"

"So I went out this morning on my board to pull the crab pot I dropped last night? And the water was really calm and, like, it was a really amazing morning for a paddle? Anyway, when I pulled up the pot I had two keepers?"

"Cool – but, like I got four keepers last week off the Crystal Springs pier. Two's not that many, dude."

"No, seriously, dude – let me finish. Anyway, I had the two keepers and I paddled back to shore and when I looked at the footage?"

"Footage?"

"Yeah. Oh, sorry – left a bit out. When I dropped the pot last night I put a camera in the pot."

"You got a camera?"

"Yeah."

"I just use my phone."

"Sure – but, like I didn't want to put my phone underwater – you know?"

"I get that. So, what were you saying?"

"Oh, yeah. Anyway, I went back and looked at the footage from the camera."

"From under the water?"

"Yeah."

"In the pot?"

"Yeah. I've got this box I can put the camera in that lets it take pictures underwater and it doesn't kill the camera."

"I had one of those when we went to Hawaii with my grandparents last year. Pretty cool. Got lots of pictures of coral and stuff when we were snorkeling. Got one picture that I think's a shark but it's kind of blurry."

"Ok. So, Montezuma, dude, like I was saying I checked the footage and you'll never guess what's on there."

"Uh. Crabs?"

"Yeah. Crabs – but what else?"

David looked perplexed. Leaf didn't wait for an answer. "Some dude's head!"

"What?"

"I'm serious. There's a dude's head in the recording – least I think it's a dude, it's kind of hard to tell."

"So, what, like a guy's swimming and checks out your pot?"

"NO – the dude's head is IN a pot."

David looked at him blankly. "Why'd you put a dude's head in your pot? That's messed up, Leaf."

"Not my pot. Another pot. Somebody else's. Anyway, you can see this other pot and there's a dude's head in it and – wait for it – there are crabs eating the guy's face!"

"Agh! That's seriously messed up! Can I see it?"

"Totally! Come in – I'll show you!"

David followed Leaf to his computer in his room, and Leaf pulled up his video channel. Together, the two of them watched the clip. David, uncomfortable with the idea that an adolescent rival, friend or not, might know he was impressed with what he saw, tried his best to feign ambivalence.

"Dude, that looks totally fake."

"What?"

"How did you make the video?"

"I told you, man. I didn't make it. I just dropped the pot and the camera recorded it."

"So why is the footage all jumpy?"

"I put the camera on time-lapse mode. Otherwise it doesn't have enough memory to record overnight. Probably wouldn't have had enough battery either."

"Huh. Looks like something we did a couple of years back in video production class – back when I was in sixth grade. We made these stop-motion videos. You, like, take a lot of pictures and then string them together to make a film clip. If you do it right then it looks like a movie. If you don't do it right – it looks like your crabs."

"Yeah, well, I didn't do that? I just dropped the pot and the camera did the rest."

"Yeah, whatever. Anyway, want to play *Battlefront Destruction*?"

Leaf was incensed. Not only had his video not managed to go viral, but now his friend didn't even believe it was real. "Dude! You can't tell me that this isn't the most amazing video you've seen."

"Yeah, man – it's cool. So, anyway, do you want to play?"

And so the two sat together on the couch at Leaf's house for the remainder of the afternoon – David trying to hide his envy at Leaf's good fortune and Leaf trying to hide his anger that David didn't acknowledge that same envy, until David's phone lit up with a text from his mom telling him it was time to head home.

Leaf said goodbye to his friend and began to boil some water to cook the crabs. His parents would be home from work in a half hour, and he'd promised his mom that he would have dinner started before they got home.

Chapter 16

David rode his bike home and, upon arrival, dropped it in exactly the center of the driveway in full knowledge that his mother had told him not to leave it there. He couldn't be bothered to put the bike away; he was too angry to comply with domestic niceties. Angry and jealous. Leaf was always showing off his latest toy or gadget. That was bad enough. But now that he had managed to take one of those gadgets and capture footage almost certain to go viral he was going to be insufferable. It was going to be a long summer.

He walked up the steps to his house, ruminating on the unfairness of it all, and entered his house. A modest home, with no particular view of water or mountains, his house was substantially smaller than Leaf's – smaller indeed than the homes of most of his classmates and the guest houses of a few of them. But he was lucky to live there, a fact that he knew and resented.

"How was your day, David?"

"Fine," David replied. His voice was sullen; Sarah Strickland had become accustomated to this tone from her son. She hoped it was a passing phase but it didn't seem to be passing quickly enough for her liking.

"Do anything fun while I was at work?"

"Nope."

"What did you do?"

"Hung out with Leaf."

"Yeah? That sounds like fun. What did you guys do?"

"Played games."

Strickland studied her son with a mixture of worry, frustration and admiration. Like any mother, her worry and frustration stemmed from watching her child go through the challenge of adolescence – in his case perhaps made more difficult since David's father was absent from his life and the boy had no real male role model. As a single parent she worried about trouble that might find her son – or him it – while she was away at work. And as a police officer she knew all too well that there was plenty of trouble around for a boy like David. But it was her profession that spurred also some of her admiration of her son. His ability to answer direct questions without providing so much as a shred of additional information was remarkable. In fact, she often thought that if the men and women she'd occasionally arrested during her time on the force were as skilled as David at avoiding unnecessary admissions of guilt, her job would be much more difficult and not nearly as enjoyable. When she told someone that they had the right to remain silent, they typically seemed to lose the ability to do so. Her son – having no such right when questioned by his mother in the family home – seemed to be in supreme control.

"Cool. How is Leaf?"

"Fine!"

"There's a crack," thought Sarah. What had happened that would make David visibly react? She knew her son was jealous of Leaf; his parents were well-off and Leaf certainly liked to flaunt his good fortune. But even so, something must have happened.

"Did you guys have a fight?"

"No."

"Huh. You seemed like maybe you were angry with him."

David sighed. "He got a new camera – had to show it off to me."

"I'm sorry, babe. I know that's frustrating."

"Yeah. Just sucks. He's kind of a jerk."

"I'm sorry. Anything I can do?"

"No."

"Ok." Sarah hugged her son. "How about some dinner?"

Sarah and David went into the kitchen together. Out of habit, the boy grabbed silverware and some glasses for drinks while his mother got out a couple of plates and began to fill them with food.

"Mom, can I have a soda?"

"How many did you have over at Leaf's? place"

"Uh. Some. I'm not sure."

"Sounds like maybe milk tonight. I'll have some too."

"Ok."

The two sat down to eat at the small table adjacent to the kitchen. "So, Leaf got a new camera, huh?"

"Yeah."

"Pretty cool?"

"Yeah. It can record underwater."

"Wow. That is pretty cool. What's he going to do with it?"

"He put it in a crab pot."

"Wow. I don't think I would have thought of that. Record anything interesting? I know we're supposed to have a lot of octopus, octopi? octopuses? – whatever, a lot of those suckers in the sound."

"It's octopuses. We learned it in school. Has something to do with the fact that the word is Greek."

"Really? That's interesting. Did he get any of them on film?"

"No. He got some crabs but then did a bunch of video editing and now it looks all fake and gross and stupid. He put it on his video channel – thinks its going to go viral. Probably will too. Jerk."

"I'm sorry, sweetie."

"Just doesn't feel fair, Mom. He's not a nice kid. Isn't even a good student. Now he's going to get, like, a million followers for his channel."

"You're right. That doesn't sound fair. But sometimes that's just the way it goes, I guess. I learned a long time ago that I can't worry about other people's success. And I can't judge myself against their accomplishments. All I can do is be the best person I can be. But that's hard, David. It's hard for me today, at forty-three, so I know it's hard for you at thirteen."

"Yeah."

The two continued to eat in silence, each one lost in thought, until David spoke: "He's not even that good at video editing."

"He's not?"

"No. He did this stupid thing where it looks like the crabs are eating some dude's face. Looks completely fake. I could have totally done a better job if he'd asked me."

Sarah stopped, her fork midway between her plate and her mouth, and looked at her son. She felt a tightening in her stomach. "A guy's face?"

"Yeah."

"Being eaten by crabs?"

"Yeah," David laughed. "Gross, right?"

"Gross indeed. So, how did he pull that off?"

"Not very well. He put the action in the background – I mean that makes sense, harder for people to see how fake it is when you don't have it up front. But still, the footage is jerky and grainy and stuff. Plus, the head looks totally fake."

"The head?"

"Yeah. I mean for sure you can tell it's supposed to be a head, but the face is all distorted – like its swollen or something. Plus, there's stringy hair covering a lot of it. Totally fake. I could have done a much better job."

"I'm sure that's true." Sarah moved her food around on her plate. While David continued to eat in the ravenous way of a growing teenager, her appetite had disappeared – replaced by nausea and a growing sense that what the boy thought was fake might actually be all too real. After allowing what she hoped would be a long enough period of time to pass so that her question wouldn't raise suspicion in her son, she spoke: "Remind me again, where does Leaf live? Is he over on the west side of the island?"

"Nope. Down near Rockaway Beach."

Sarah nodded and swallowed hard. This was not the answer she was hoping for; the proximity of Leaf's home to the Rasmussen call a few days ago left her with the uncomfortable feeling that the boy's video and the old woman's complaint might be related.

"That's right. You told me that before. Pretty area."

"I guess."

The two finished their meals and went back into the kitchen. As they shared the tasks of cleaning up after their dinner, Sarah replayed their discussion back in her mind. She needed more information – needed to be able to get access to Leaf's video – but didn't want to let on to her son that anything might be amiss.

"So, you ever think about having your own video channel?" she asked the boy.

"Yeah! I'd love to do that. I mean, I know you don't like me online and everything. Know that you've said it isn't safe. But all my friends have them."

Sarah was sure that this was an overstatement; it was not the case that all of David's friends had channels. But a fair number of them did. She knew this because he was constantly telling her about the content – usually quite insipid – that they'd posted. One of them even had a channel where he did nothing but record himself playing video games. A couple of decades of police work hadn't prepared her to uncover the reason that anyone would watch anyone else play video games in person, let alone online – but the fact was that her own son would watch for hours at a time. It was baffling.

"You know, now that you're thirteen, I think it's legal for you to do that."

"I know! I mean, legal with the government and everything. I know I still need your permission."

"Well, maybe we could work something out. You're getting pretty grown up. And I've noticed you've been pretty responsible lately."

David's mind flashed back to his leaving his bicycle in the center of the driveway, right behind his mother's police cruiser in precisely the sort of place that you wouldn't leave your bike if you were – in fact – being responsible. He made a mental note to try to get outside and move the bike before his mother learned of its exact location. "I'm trying."

"And it shows. I'm not saying 'yes' – but I'd like to know more about how it would work. Like, how do you download stuff? Can people figure out who you are and where you live? Stuff like that."

"So," started David – trying to sound as patient as possible – "you actually don't download anything? You upload stuff to the channel. So, nothing comes into the house or our computer. It all goes the other way around."

"Ok."

"And, I don't really know how anyone would find me or figure out where I live or anything unless I told them. Like, I could post a video that had a link or something to where we live – that would tell them. Or maybe put something in my personal bio that would let people know. But other than that, I don't know how they'd figure it out."

"And you wouldn't do that, right?"

"Not if you didn't want me to. I mean, a lot of my friends do, because they want to have other people at the school find their videos if they're not already following their channels? They usually put something in like 'hashtag-Bainbridge' or something like that."

"What does that do?"

"Helps people find your stuff. If you were searching for something about Bainbridge Island, having 'hashtag-Bainbridge' would make it easier to find."

"Clever."

"Yeah, Mom. The Internet is like that – pretty clever," David laughed.

"So if you had a channel what would you download – sorry, upload – to it?"

"I'd love to make a gamer channel. 'Course I'd need a webcam in order to do that."

"A webcam?"

"Yeah. To film me playing the games."

"So you'd be on camera on the channel?"

"Well, I mean, not if you didn't want me to. That's the way most of the gamers do it – but it could maybe just be aimed at the screen. I wouldn't even have to talk on the recordings if you didn't want me to."

"You wouldn't talk?"

"Not if you didn't want me to."

Sarah snickered. The one time her son was consistently loud and boisterous was when he was playing video games. The thought that he could keep from talking while playing them was absurd. "I'll need to think about that. So, your buddies with channels – do they usually identify their location? Leaf, for example, does he do the 'hashtag-Bainbridge' bit or does he keep a lower profile?"

"Leaf's trying to make money off of his channel. That means he needs as many views as possible. He hashtags everything to try to get people to the channel. He hasn't made any money yet. I mean he hasn't said that he's made any money yet and I know he'd rub my nose in it if he had, so I'm pretty sure he hasn't."

"How do his parents feel about him being public with his channel?"

"I'm not sure they know. They're never home."

"So he's by himself a lot?"

"Yeah."

"Must get lonely."

"I guess."

"What do his parents do?"

"I don't know. Something over in Seattle, I think. So – can I start a channel?"

"Let me think about it, David. I know you're excited about it, and I get that. But I want to be sure that if you do it you do it safely. Tell you what, I'll ask a few people at the station tomorrow. I think one of them may even have his own channel. If there's a way to do it that makes sense, we'll figure it out. Ok?"

"Ok. Thanks, Mom." The kitchen now clean, David hugged his mother and bounded out of the room to go turn on his computer and begin his nightly ritual of playing videogames online with his friends – Leaf included. Sarah leaned against the sink, dissatisfied with herself for being less than completely honest with her son – she thought it extremely unlikely that she would get comfortable with his having a video channel – and turning over again and again in her mind her son's description of Leaf's video.

"It couldn't be connected," she muttered to herself. Sarah made herself a cup of tea, walked into the living room and sat down on the couch. The family's cat – an overweight calico – looked up at her, yawned, and stretched before coming over to sit in her lap. She stroked the cat, who was now purring loudly, and tried to relax. Throughout, however, she was haunted by thoughts and questions about her son's story. Could Leaf really have edited a head into the footage in a way that made it look like the crab was eating it? But it couldn't have been real. If it had been real, how was it staying on the bottom. Bodies float – what about decapitated heads? Was it weighted down somehow?

206

Do crabs even eat people? She actually thought she knew the answer to that last one – recalling a disturbing documentary she'd seen some time ago about Amelia Earhart and the idea that she might have been eaten alive by crabs on a remote island in the Pacific.

Her mind racing, she decided to try to settle the matter once and for all. Relocating the cat, she got up from the sofa, reentered the kitchen and pulled her phone from the counter where it was charging. Going to her browser she searched "Bainbridge Crab." Many thousands of search results popped up. She scrolled through the first few pages and found nothing helpful. Changing tacks, she used her browser to call up the video channel website and ran the same search. A handful of videos came up in the search results.

Sarah sat back on the sofa, stroking the cat and watching videos – one after another – of crabs. There were videos clips of small crabs on the beach picking at bits of food and of large crabs being held up in triumph by anglers, their pincers waiving angrily in the air. There was a video of a toddler dressed in a crab costume at Halloween. Finally, Sarah thought that she'd found the video in question when she ran across a video of crab taken from inside a crab pot – but there was no head to be seen. When she was just about to give up, she thought back to her son's description of Leaf and his efforts at self-promotion. She entered 'Leaf Donegan Bainbridge' in the search bar.

And there it was. The first video under his name.

"INCREDIBLE FOOTAGE – DUNGENESS EATS HUMAN FACE – MUST WATCH - #BAINBRIDGE #CRAB #AMAZING"

"Subtle," Sarah muttered out loud. The cat looked up at her, purring and rubbing her chin against Sarah's arm.

Sarah touched play. The video from her phone reflected, flickering, in her glasses as she watched the footage. Grainy or not, there was no mistaking the images on the screen. She didn't know if it was a fake. But she knew she must find out. Exiting the video, she dialed John Wilkerson's number.

"Hey beautiful, something going on or are you just feeling lonely on a Friday night?" John sounded cheerful. He always sounded cheerful, a trait that endeared him to Sarah but that she thought might annoy their new police chief.

"John, remember your lady who said she'd found a femur on the beach?"

John laughed. "Sure do. Still not sure if she was crazy. That was easily one of the odder calls I've been on in a while."

"I'm – I'm not sure how to say this, John. I don't think she was crazy. I'm thinking she may really have found part of a body."

"Well it certainly could be. I mean we lose kayakers from time to time, and they've had a bunch of feet wash ashore a bit farther north. So, yeah – could certainly be. But what's this about, Sarah? You didn't really call me up in the evening to talk about a crazy lady on the beach, did you?"

"She's not crazy John. Well, I can't say that. She may be crazy. But I don't think she imagined the bone – sometimes even crazy people are right. I think we may have a problem on our hands. A big problem."

John could hear the concern in Sarah's voice. She wasn't the kind to scare easily, and while she didn't sound frightened, exactly, she sounded concerned.

"Ok. How can I help?"

"There's a video I want you to see. One of David's friends posted it today on online. Can I text you a link?"

"Sure."

"Ok. I'll send it to you. Please watch it and then call me right back."

"Will do."

Sarah hung up the phone, texted John a link to the video, and waited for his call. Minutes passed.

To Sarah's mind, too many minutes. When she could wait no longer. She dialed his number.

"Sarah?" The cheer had left John's voice. "Sarah, is that real?"

"I don't know. David thinks that his buddy edited the video to add it in. But if he did, he did one hell of a job."

"Yeah. Plus, where would he get the footage to add into the video? I mean, I've only seen a couple of bodies after they've been in the water for a while, but they look – well, they look like that. The bloating – how's a Bainbridge kid going to know enough about that to fake the video? I don't like, it Sarah. I don't like it at all."

"So you think it might be real too?" "I think we need to know more."

"Yeah. There's one other thing I haven't told you, John."

"Ok. I don't like the sound of that. Shoot."

"The kid that took the video?"

"Yeah?"

"He lives just off Rockaway Beach. He claims to have taken the video from the beach outside his house."

John was quiet. "So, we've got an elderly lady who says she found a femur living down the street from a kid who claims to have footage of a human head in a crab pot just a few days later."

"Yeah. It can't be a coincidence, John."

"It could. And the old lady could be crazy and the kid could be lying. But there's enough here that we're going to need to investigate. How do you want to play the hand?"

"We've got to talk to Sandra. We're going to need to question the kid – but I'm not about to go and start grilling some beachfront teenager without getting her in the loop. Kid's parents would probably squeal anyway and it would be all over the paper before we know it. Probably even end up with some kind of lawsuit. No, we need to do this the right way. So we need to get her involved."

"Makes sense to me. Talk with her in the morning? Know she's supposed to be off tomorrow, but this feels like it's probably worth sharing sooner rather than later."

"Definitely."

"Ok. I'll shoot her a message and see if she's available to

meet in the morning. Thanks for talking this through with me."

"Of course. You'd do the same."

"I would, indeed. But still, appreciate your being there. This whole thing gives me the creeps."

"Me too, honestly. I've seen quite a bit over the years, but that? Well, that's just gross. Ok —we'll talk to Sandra in the morning. In the meantime, go be a mom and try to forget about this until morning, OK? I know that's going to be tough but give it a go. Play a game with David or something – maybe something cheerful – you know, without corpses." John laughed, and the sound of cheerfulness returning to his voice lifted Sarah's mood.

"Will do, John. Talk to you in the morning."

She hung up the phone and walked toward the familiar sound of David talking to his friends online while they played videogames. She leaned against the wall just outside his door, finding comfort in the normalcy of their conversation. Despite their adolescent boasting and their overuse of "dude" in their interactions, they were still children at heart – children who were either unaware or unimpressed by the fact that there seemed to be a killer in their midst.

Chapter 17

Sarah slept fitfully – her dreams filled with visions of crabs and corpses. When she arrived at the police station the next morning, John was already at his desk. From the look of his face, Sarah got the impression that he too had failed to get much rest.

"I've been thinking," he said, "come to a few conclusions and got a lot of questions."

"Yeah?"

"You want conclusions or questions first?"

"Conclusions. I've got plenty of questions of my own."

"Ok." John looked down at a paper on his desk where he'd scrawled a few notes. "Number one. The video appears to contain the head of a man – an adult – with dark hair. The man appears to have some modest facial hair – hard to say for sure with the quality of the footage but it looks like there's some growth. So conclusion number one for me is that *if* the footage is real and I'm not saying it is – and if the thing in the crab pot is an actual human head – and again, no promises there – then our victim is an adult male with a full head of dark hair and possibly a short beard."

"Victim?"

"Well, yeah. I mean he didn't put his own head in the pot. Right?"

"Sure?"

"Exactly. You ever do any crabbing, Sarah?"

"No. And honestly at this point I don't see me doing any in the future. Also, quite possible that crab's off the menu for me permanently."

"I get that. Hard to imagine enjoying crab legs any time soon. But hear me out. The reason I ask is because it gets me to my second conclusion – someone had to put it there. There are doors on a crab pot that let the crabs walk in to get the bait. But they're only big enough to let in crabs. They're not so big that a head could just roll in. I mean – it sounds silly to say it out loud – but one thing I was wondering is if we'd had a floater – could the head become detached and then get washed by the tide or currents or something *into* the pot – or maybe could the head get dragged into the pot by an animal. But the answer to that's got to be 'no.' The doors for the crabs aren't big enough to let an adult human head in. So the only way to get it in would be to open the top of the pot – the part where you put in the bait and take out the crabs you've caught – and drop it in."

"Ok…"

"now the pot on the video appears to be latched shut at the top. So, again, if it's not been faked and if the thing that appears to be in the pot really is a human head, then somebody had to open the trap, put the head in there and then close the trap back up again."

"Got it."

"Now here's conclusion three. The person who put the head in the pot had no intention of catching crabs."

"How do you figure?"

"Well, first of all, just like you said you're not going to be eating crab any time soon, right? But more than that, I looked at the video on my computer – rather than my phone – and with the larger screen you get quite a bit more detail."

"Yeah? Like what?"

"Like the fact that whoever dropped that pot did something to those doors I mentioned – the doors that let the crabs into the pot."

"I'm confused – there was a crab in the pot so it obviously got in somehow."

"Yeah. But again, this is where it helps to have done some crabbing. The way these pots work is that the doors are slightly weighted. You want the doors to stay closed unless a crab is pushing on them to get inside of the pot. Crab pushes in – gets into the pot – and then the door swings shut. And they're one-way entrances; they can't swing open to the outside so the crab can't push its way back out."

"Ok?" Sarah wasn't sure where this was going.

"But these doors? They're not swinging shut. In fact, if you look at the video closely – again on a real monitor, you wouldn't have been able to see this on your phone – if you look at the video closely you can see that the doors are stuck open. Someone has done something to the doors to keep them from swinging shut."

"Sure. So, they didn't want to catch any crabs in the pot. But I'm guessing they weren't going to pull up the pot anyway, right? They're probably not going to want to eat anything that's been eating – well, eating their bait. Right? This doesn't seem like a revelation."

"You're right – they weren't going to pull up the pot. But that's exactly why the doors of the pot are so interesting."

"I don't follow."

"If the doors on the pot were working properly, then crabs would come in to take the bait and then get stuck. Whoever did this didn't want the crabs to get stuck. Our crabber actually cares about making sure that the crabs don't get stuck in the trap and die. And if you don't mind my saying so, someone who cares more about the welfare of crabs than the welfare of the person whose head they've just dropped into the water for the crabs to eat? Well, that's a pretty strange person."

"Fair point."

"But having the doors stay open explains Agnes' bone as well."

"Agnes?"

"Sorry. Agnes is Helen Rasmussen's dog. Agnes is the one who actually found the femur."

"Ah."

"Remember how I said that the doors that let in the crab are too small to fit a head through?"

"Yeah. But I bet they're not too small to let out a leg bone."

"Exactly! In fact, depending on the size of the pot – it's hard to get a sense of scale from the video – it's possible that the femur was sticking out of the pot through the open door when the pot was dropped."

"You think the pot with the head in it may have had the femur in it too?"

"I don't know. It's certainly possible. But regardless, if the door to the pot was stuck open and the bone was sticking out, then I wouldn't be at all surprised if the bone went for a walk – if you'll pardon the expression. You saw how the crab was dragging the head around in the pot. Makes perfect sense that crabs might have done the same thing with the femur and just dragged it out of the pot."

"And once it's out of the pot, then it floats around and washes ashore for Agnes to find."

"Yes. OK – on to conclusion four – our crabber not only wasn't likely to pull the pot back up – it wouldn't have been possible for them to pull it. Again – if you look at the video on a larger screen you can see that the pot isn't actually connected to a line."

Sarah looked at John. From her expression, he could see that she wasn't following him.

"The way you do this – the way you catch crabs – is to drop a pot that's connected to a line and a buoy. Then, when you're ready to pull the pot back to the surface and see what you've caught you go find your buoy and pull the line back in – pulling up the trap in the process. But there's no line attached to the pot. No line means our crabber couldn't even try to retrieve the pot."

"Wow. Pretty good sleuthing, officer. For a handsome guy

you're surprisingly clever. So, we've determined that if there's really a head in that pot, it is a man's head, it was placed there on purpose by some third party, whoever put it there had a soft spot for crabs and didn't want to hurt them, and had no intention of ever pulling up the pot. Any additional insights?"

"I wish. Just left with a lot of questions. For example, how do we know that the kid didn't fake the footage? Some people do a lot of crazy stuff to get famous on the web – how do we know this kid isn't one of them?"

"Well, the fact that Agnes came up with a bone…"

"But I never saw it. Helen could be nuts."

"Right. But if Helen is telling the truth, then I'm inclined to think the kid didn't fake the video."

"Fair enough. But I've got some more questions."

"Yeah?"

"There's usually quite a few people crabbing out in front of Rockaway. Now this pot didn't have a line on it. If someone dropped a pot without a line and buoy, wouldn't somebody notice that? Also, if the femur and the head were the real deal – where's the rest of our victim?"

"That's a very good question. But before we ask any more questions here, I want to come back to your conclusion – what was it? Number four, I think. That the person who dropped the crab pot wasn't going to go back to pick it up."

"Yeah?"

"That means it is still there. And if it is still there, and if your first conclusion is right, then the head is still in it – assuming it wasn't faked."

"You're right."

"Which means, that we need to know exactly where the kid's pot was when his camera recorded the footage – which means that we need to talk to the kid."

"You got his name?"

"Leaf Donegan. David says he's a bit of a jerk – but I'm not sure how much of that is real and how much is just David being jealous of a classmate who lives on the water and has parents with a lot of disposable income."

"Could be both. Sandra's in her office doing paperwork – let's go bring her up to speed. If we're going to talk to the kid we're going to need her buy-in. Leaf's parents could raise hell."

Sarah knew only too well how right John was. Only last year she'd been threatened – along with the entire department – with a lawsuit for breaking up late-night party attended by local high school students. A couple dozen teens were drinking and carrying on at a big house out near the country club. She'd shown up on account of a noise complaint from a neighbor and the next thing she knew the father of one of the little darlings was pounding his chest about filing a civil rights suit – something about how her targeting the kid was evidence of police profiling. The department's attorney assured her that the case had no merit – that it was very difficult to "profile" a rich white kid when you arrest him for underage drinking while he's trying simultaneously to hold onto his beer, vomit, and loudly threaten your job with a lot of "I'm a taxpayer – you work for me!" stuff

218

that sounds ridiculous coming out of the mouth of an adult but even more so when spewing from a teenager. But it had all been a very big hassle and she wasn't eager to repeat the experience – only this time in the higher-stakes context of a potential murder.

Sarah and John made their way down to Sandra's office and Sarah poked her head through the open doorway. "This a good time for a consult?"

"Of course, Sarah. Come in and have a seat."

The two officers entered the office. Upon seeing John trailing behind Sarah, Sandra quipped "Good morning, John. Come across any bones lately?" She winked at him with a cheerful grin.

Sarah and John exchanged a quick glance. Something in their exchange made Sandra realize that something was wrong.

"Uh oh. What's going on, you two?"

The officers sat down and Sarah explained to Sandra the circumstances of her discussion with David and described the video. As Sarah spoke, John chimed in periodically with clarifications, and then his initial conclusions, all the while Sandra leaned back in her chair, listening closely. When they'd finished their explanations, Sandra spoke.

"I know I'm going to regret this. But I need to see the video."

John rose from his chair and moved across the desk to Sandra's computer. "May I?" he said as he opened her browser. With a few keystrokes he'd located the video and set it to play.

She watched intently as the drama played out on the screen.

When it ended, she let out a long sigh, folded her arms and stared down at her desk. Viewing the footage had spurred a tidal wave of memories of crime scenes she'd worked back in Minneapolis, including more than a few where some or all of the victim's body had been consumed by animals. She'd left that world to try to escape those memories, yet here they were – flooding back toward her as if driven by the currents reflected in the video. "It looks real enough to me," she said quietly. "What do we know about our filmmaker?"

"His name is Leaf Donegan. He's one of my son's classmates," Sarah replied. "An eighth grader. He lives over on Pleasant Cove."

"Just down the beach from Helen Rasmussen," John interjected.

"David thinks his parents both work in Seattle," Sarah continued. "Not sure what they do – The boys travel in the same circles at school, but our families aren't close."

"David ever given you any indication that the kid is violent?"

"No. They've had arguments from time to time, but mostly they're friendly enough. Leaf likes to show off – from an outsider's perspective he appears to be pretty spoiled – but I've never heard anything about him being violent."

"You don't think he might actually know anything about how the head got in the trap?"

"I don't know for sure, but I doubt it."

"And suppose he faked the video – what would be the point in that?"

"Bragging rights, mostly. Leaf's a teenage boy. He wants attention. The kid has a video channel for the sole reason of trying to get people to like his posts – trying to get page views. Looking for his fifteen minutes of fame, I guess."

"Ok. So we've got a lonely, spoiled kid, left alone all day and looking for attention. He suddenly – and he says accidentally – comes up with some pretty extreme footage. And instead of reporting that to anyone, he puts it on the Internet in a bid to be famous online. Am I tracking?"

Sarah nodded.

"It looks real – but then again I went to the movies last week and one of the actresses in the film died before they started filming the thing – so what do I know what's real and what's fake. But if it is real and he didn't fake it, then why doesn't he call the police instead of just putting it out there for all his friends to see? Something doesn't add up."

"Remind me, Sandra," Sarah replied. "Do you have sons?"

"Nope. Two girls – both grown and off the payroll."

"So here's the thing. And please don't take this the wrong way – I love my kid – but teenage boys are idiots. I mean sure, some of them will have the occasional moment of clarity, but the typical adolescent male is a knucklehead. Not just humans either – primates in general. Baboon troops kick the adolescent males out – make them strike out on their own until they've grown into adulthood and settled down – otherwise they're likely to endanger the whole troop. Honestly, I barely trust my own – who, again, I love dearly – to remember to breathe. So, yeah, I can totally see how this particular knucklehead could think the

221

footage is real and not decide to call us. In fact, I doubt he's told his own folks about it."

Sandra looked at John. He was making a level effort to keep from laughing at Sarah's description of his gender. "You want to offer a rebuttal, Officer?"

"I wish I did, Sandra. She's pretty much nailed it. The fact is, some of us never get invited back to live with the rest of the troop."

Sandra laughed – a needed release of tension in the context of their discussion – allowing John and Sarah too to laugh briefly before turning their attention back to the seriousness of the matter.

"Ok," Sandra said, "here's how we're going to do this. I want the two of you to learn as much as you can about the kid's parents between now and this evening. Keep me in the loop on what you learn. Tonight, once we think they're home from doing whatever it is that they do all day long – I'm guessing at least one of them is a lawyer; I've never seen so many lawyers in a single zip code as this place – then I want the two of you to pay Leaf and his family a house call. Gently. We don't need to scare them, exactly. But I want you both to be there so that there's no confusion about whether we're serious. And while you're there – parents permitting – you're going to interview the kid and find out everything you can. If they flip out, get out of there. But if they don't, then I want to get him on the record about whether or not he doctored the film. And if he says he didn't fake it, then I want to know exactly where and exactly when it was shot. Got it? Ok, now go find out whatever you can about the parents."

Sarah and John got up and walked to the door. As Sarah turned to exit the room, she observed her police chief turn her attention back to the video on her computer screen and mutter to herself "I'm never eating crab again."

The two officers spent the next several hours trying to learn everything they could about the Donegan household which, thanks to the Internet, was a relatively easy task. Leaf's father, Dave, was indeed an attorney – practicing at a small firm in Seattle where his primary client seemed to be a firm that bought up patents solely for the purpose of suing people over claims of alleged infringement. His mother, Willow, professed to be some sort of psychic healer. After poring over the online profiles of the parents, supplemented by access to the state's criminal justice database, the officers concluded that neither Dave nor Willow Donegan appeared to have any sort of meaningful criminal record although Dave's background check revealed arrests for indecent exposure and criminal mischief – all on the same night almost twenty-five years ago near the University of Washington campus over in Seattle. As best as the officers could determine, alcohol and a fraternity had been involved.

Later that evening, once the officers surmised that the Donegan's might be at home for dinner, Sarah and John drove out to Rockaway Beach to speak with Leaf. Pulling up at the house, however, they saw no cars in the driveway and no evidence that either Mr. or Mrs. Donegan were at home. They debated briefly and half-heartedly about whether to simply go ahead and ring the bell, risking a conversation with the boy without his parents around.

"Could be easier to get him to talk," John said.

"Could be easier to get us sued," Sarah replied.

Ultimately, they decided to wait. And while they waited, John decided to introduce Sarah to Helen Rasmussen just down the street. They parked the patrol car on the street between the two homes and took a walk in the bright early evening light.

As they walked along, completely alone on the road, Sarah spoke up. "I'll never understand why people on Bainbridge don't get out more – get to know their neighbors – you know, be friendly. I mean, you pay a stupid amount of money to buy a house out here. It's beautiful. And then when you get home you shut yourself up in it and don't come out. What do you suppose that's about?"

"I blame the ferry."

"How so?"

"To afford to live down here you probably have to work over in Seattle, right? So, you're on the boat regularly. Every day, probably. That means you're sitting with a couple thousand of your closest friends twice a day whether you like it or not. That's going to wear on you. By the time you come home in the evening and you've probably had just about as much forced friendliness as you can handle – especially if you're not exactly the outgoing type to begin with. You start drinking on the boat on the way home – one of the best ways to catch DUIs around here is to just follow the people driving off the ferry in the evening – and then you shut yourself up in your house and don't come out until the next morning, when you do it all over again. Horrible way to live your life, if you think about it. I wouldn't trade with 'em."

John knocked on Helen's door, a quick percussive tapping greeted immediately by Agnes' loud barking from inside. Moments later, Helen opened the door a crack and peered at the two of them through the gap between the door doorjamb – a security chain purporting to prevent it from opening all the way.

"Good evening, Helen."

"Oh, John, it's you. Nice to see you again."

"Helen, this is my colleague Sarah. We were in the neighborhood and I thought I'd just stop and check in on you. Everything ok?"

The elderly woman closed the door briefly and Sarah and John heard the rustling of the security chain. The door swung wide open and Agnes bounded out, jumping up and putting her front paws on John's chest.

"She remembers you. Agnes. Agnes! You're embarrassing yourself. Don't jump up on the police officer. That's probably a crime – you're going to end up in dog jail."

"It's all good, Helen," John laughed. "You know, I'm not usually greeted with this kind of friendliness when I'm out on patrol. It's a nice change."

Helen looked over at Sarah. "I'm sorry, dear, I didn't catch your name."

"Sarah Strickland, Mrs. Rasmussen. Very nice to meet you."

"Please, Sarah, call me Helen. It's nice to meet you as well. So you work with John here?" – gesturing to John who was still being mugged by Agnes – "that must be nice. He's quite handsome in that uniform, isn't he? I can imagine that makes the day go by quite pleasantly."

Sarah snickered. "You know, Helen, I think the uniform is a bit more flattering for my male colleagues than it is for me. Makes Officer Wilkerson here look nice, but it does nothing for my figure. John, are you finished flirting with our canine citizen?"

John was now seated on Helen's front porch with Agnes fully in his lap. She'd rolled over onto her back and was allowing him to rub her chest and belly, tongue lolling out the side of her mouth – a picture of four-legged contentment. "Almost. I think I missed a spot when I was scratching behind her ears. Agnes, you'll let me know when you want me to stop, right?"

Agnes did not appear to provide any such instruction so John continued to caress the delighted dog.

"Helen, Sarah and I wanted to stop by and just check in on you. Have you had any more excitement out on the beach?"

"None to speak of. I mean the otters have been out quite a lot in the evening; you know they pester Agnes so. But other than that nothing out of the ordinary."

"And that bone that Agnes brought you – the one that wasn't there the next morning – did that ever reappear?"

"It did not, thank heavens. That was a ghastly sight – I hope I never see anything like that again."

"Me too," Sarah chimed in. "John told me all about it. That must have been really frightening."

"No dear. It wasn't frightening. It takes a good deal more than a bit of bone and gristle to frighten me – I was a nurse for thirty years. But it was ghastly – just like I said – very disturbing. And I hope I never see anything like that again."

"Well," said John, "you make sure you give me a call if you do, ok? You promise?"

"Of course. Sarah, he really is handsome. And I don't see a ring on either of you. You would make quite the couple."

"John," said Sarah, "we'd better get out of here before Helen calls a minister."

"Good idea," chuckled John. "Ok, Helen. If I learned anything from my Mom, it was to heed the advice of a strong woman. So I'm going to follow Sarah's lead here and head out before the two of us end up hitched." Standing up, he reached out to shake Helen's hand only to have her lean forward and clasp him in her arms. Returning the embrace, John spoke again, "you be sure to give me a call if you need anything, and I'll be right there."

"I will, John. Sarah, you look out for him for me."

"Will do, Helen." Sarah extended her hand – half expecting Helen to embrace her as well. Helen grasped Sarah's hand in her own and gave it a firm handshake instead.

The two officers walked back down Helen's driveway toward the street – Sarah chuckling the whole way. "Unless I'm mistaken, Helen Rasmussen's got a crush on you, John."

"Yeah. I'm huge with elderly women. That's my key demographic."

"I've got it on good authority that you're popular with some a bit younger as well."

Chapter 18

By the time Sarah and John walked back down the street to the Donegan house, John working the whole time to brush Agnes' hair off of his uniform, two cars had appeared in the driveway: a compact electric car and an enormous sport utility vehicle. "Maybe it's supposed to balance out," John wondered aloud as they approached the door.

Leaf answered their knock. He was slightly more weasel-like in appearance than Sarah remembered from the last time she saw him – reminding her of a ferret in need of a dermatologist – although she wondered whether her current impression might be unfairly informed by her knowledge of the video and the reason for their visit. He didn't give any obvious sign that he recognized her in her uniform and she had no particular desire to let him know that her son had played a critical role in two police officers arriving at his home so she didn't intend to volunteer.

"Are you Leaf Donegan," John asked?

"That's me. What's up?"

"Leaf, my name is Officer Wilkerson. This is my partner, Officer Strickland. We'd like to talk with you briefly. Are your parents at home?"

Leaf turned briefly ashen – an acne-riddled weasel searching his mind in an effort to recall what precisely he might have done that would have brought the police to his door. He turned his head and called over his shoulder. "Mom? Mom, the police are here and want to talk. Is that ok?"

John and Sarah heard the clink of glassware and a startled expression. Moments later, Willow Donegan appeared at the door wearing what appeared to be a designer peasant skirt and a crisp white linen blouse – her brown hair arranged in a messy bun. "Go get your father, Leaf," Willow said as she took the door from her son. Leaf scampered away. "Good evening, Officers. What brings you to our home this evening?"

From the porch outside the door, Sarah could smell the wine on Willow's breath. "Good evening, Mrs. Donegan. I'm Officer Strickland. This is my colleague, Officer Wilkerson. We were hoping to have a few words with Leaf this evening."

"Is he in some sort of trouble?"

"I don't believe so."

"Then why do you want to talk..."

Just as Willow had started her question, Dave Donegan appeared at the door. "Let me handle this, Willow." He inserted himself between his wife and the door frame. "Do you have a warrant?"

"I'm beg your pardon?"

"A warrant. You're not coming in here without a warrant. I know my rights, Officer." Dave Donegan had a wild gleam in his eye. In his legal practice over the better part of the last two decades he'd never had the opportunity to use any of the information he'd learned in his criminal procedure or constitutional law classes in law school and he was finally getting the chance. His memories of those classes – undoubtedly altered by his having watched countless courtroom dramas on prime-time television – came flooding back in a torrent.

Sarah remained calm. "Mr. Donegan, I'm afraid we've gotten off on the wrong foot. We're not here to search anything. In fact, we don't necessarily even need – or want – to come inside. After all, it's a beautiful evening. We're just hoping to talk with your son briefly. He's not in any trouble. But we do think that he may have information that would help us know whether or not someone else may have committed a crime."

"You're not talking with Leaf without him having a lawyer present!"

"Mr. Donegan, I'm sure I don't have to tell you that your son doesn't actually have a constitutional right to counsel unless he's being taken into custody. Smart lawyer like yourself – you remember that from law school like it was just yesterday, don't you? Now, we're not here to take him into custody. And as I said, we don't actually think he's done anything wrong. So again, I'm hoping we can simply have a conversation with him – with you and your wife present of course."

"What's this all about?" Mrs. Donegan asked from behind her husband at the door.

"Willow, let me handle it," Dave snapped back.

"It's about a video that Leaf posted online – we'd like to know where it was filmed and whether the footage was altered in any way."

"A video? I'm afraid you must be mistaken, Officer. Leaf wouldn't post anything online – let alone a video – his father

230

and I don't allow it. Too much negative energy online – especially with all the people posting comments."

"Mrs. Donegan – Willow – may I call you Willow? – I'm a mother as well. And I'm afraid that there are times that my son does things that I don't know about, especially when they're things that he knows I wouldn't like. Now, I hate to be the one to tell you this, but your son does post things online. In fact, he's quite good at it and has a few thousand followers for his video channel. Now, again, we're not saying there's anything wrong with that. There's nothing illegal about it. It's not a police matter, exactly."

"Then why are you here?" Mr. Donegan interjected.

"Well, again, Mr. Donegan," replied John, "our concern isn't that Leaf posted a video. Our concern is over what appears to be seen in the video that he posted. I'd be happy to show it to you, if that would be helpful. But we do need to ask Leaf a few questions about it. And I'm afraid that if we can't ask those questions here at your home – with you and your wife present, of course – then we'll need to go back to our Chief and get additional instructions from her, likely with input from the county Prosecuting Attorney."

"The prosecutor?" Mrs. Donegan exclaimed. "Dave, this isn't the time to play at something you don't do every day. Look, if I'm at my clinic and someone comes in with a gunshot wound the first thing I'm going to do is call an ambulance, not try to rearrange their aura and hope it stops the bleeding, ok? This is the same thing. You work with patents, not police. We should call a lawyer."

231

"I am a lawyer, Willow."

"I mean a *real* lawyer. One who knows what the hell he's doing when it comes to criminal matters."

Dave Donegan's face turned crimson, to the point where John was reasonably certain that if they weren't already at the Donegan household they likely would have needed to make a call there that evening for a domestic disturbance. But John knew Dave's type. And he knew that no matter what happened now, no matter how bad things might get for him or his wife or his son, there was no way that Donegan was going to call a "real" lawyer – not after the way his wife had neutered him in front of his son and two complete strangers.

Donegan turned his head toward the inside of the house and called out, "Leaf!"

"Yeah, Dad?" The boy was close at hand.

"You do anything especially stupid recently? Hurt anybody, steal anything, something like that? Just nod or shake your head – don't say anything out loud – the officers can't see you but they can hear you." There was a pause and then Dave spoke again. "You're sure?"

"Yeah. I'm sure."

"Ok. Well then let's all have a friendly chat with these two nice officers. Come on out here."

Dave Donegan opened the door fully. Willow stood looking at her husband with a mixture of disgust and anger. Leaf looked frightened, but also just possibly a bit proud. He'd been wanting to get attention for his videos. This wasn't exactly the kind he'd hoped for, but it was a start. Leaf walked out the door and onto the front steps of the house, followed by his parents.

The porch was crowded now – with all five of them standing together in a circle in the coolness of the early evening. Above them, in the waning light among the cedars and firs, bats darted frenetically in chase of their prey. Down the street, Agnes was barking.

"Leaf," John said, "I do apologize for interrupting you and your family on this lovely evening. But, as I think my partner Officer Strickland mentioned, we need to talk with you about a video you posted. I think you posted it yesterday and I bet you know which one we're talking about."

"Yeah."

"So, I'm guessing you haven't shared the footage with your parents?"

"No," Leaf said quietly – almost so quietly that he couldn't be heard.

"Ok. So, we can share it with them now – or you can share it with them after we leave – but my guess is that you and your folks are probably heading toward a pretty lengthy family discussion. Sorry to bring that on you, buddy. I remember dreading those when I was a kid about your age. Anyway, it's your call. Want to share the video here and now, or just have us ask you questions about it and your folks wonder what we're talking about?"

Leaf looked from his mother to his father, and then back again. Both officers, though they didn't share it at the time, thought the kid looked terrified. After a moment, Leaf spoke again "Can't we just talk about it?"

"Well, I don't have any real problem with that. But if I were your mom or dad, I'd probably want to know what all this was about. So I'd probably like it if everything were out in the open."

"Yeah."

John Wilkerson pulled his phone from his pocket. "Should I pull it up?"

Leaf looked dubiously at Wilkerson's aging phone. John was not an early adopter of new technology by nature. Even if he had been, however, his salary at the Bainbridge Island Police Department would not have brought the latest and greatest in cellular technology within reach.

"Does that thing even get video?"

Wilkerson chuckled. "Well, yes it does. At least assuming I can get a good signal down here. Looks like two bars. May take a few minutes to load."

Leaf weighed the relative discomfort of taking initiative against the discomfort of continuing to stand on his porch between his parents and two members of law enforcement. "I'll be right back," he said as he darted back inside the house. The four adults stood in awkward silence.

"Really nice out this evening," Wilkerson said. No one took the conversational bait and his words were left hanging. "Yep. Just about perfect weather. Hope it lasts for the weekend. You got plans this weekend, Sarah?"

234

Before Sarah could reply, Leaf reappeared with a tablet computer in his hand. "Ok – this should work better. I'm on wifi." With a few keystrokes he navigated to his video channel, selected a video, pressed play and held the tablet so that the adults on the porch could see. "I didn't think we were doing anything wrong. I mean it's kind of stupid – I know – but everybody at school does it."

On screen, Leaf and a couple of his friends, including Sarah's son, David, were shown spray painting the walls of the abandoned cannery on the south end of the Island. Leaf's work, an enormous penis and testicles, showed particular artistic promise.

The adults watched the short video to its conclusion. Willow's eyebrow twitched every time she heard Leaf swear; he had quite the vocabulary. Standing next to her, Sarah watched with horror as she saw David taking part in the mischief.

As the video concluded, Leaf looked up at his parents. "I'm sorry. I didn't think we were doing anything wrong."

Wilkerson chuckled.

"Well, Officer," Dave Donegan said. "We've all seen the video. Seems like a harmless prank to me. What questions do you have for my son? Honestly, man, stop laughing and be professional for a moment. You interrupted our evening and now you don't have the decency to be serious for a moment?"

Regaining his composure, Wilkerson ignored Mr. Donegan and turned his attention to the boy. "Leaf, I believe you may have a future as a filmmaker. The camera angles – the way you captured the moment – really made me feel like I was there. Of course, I was there – not this time – but years ago. I used to spray paint those same walls when I was about your age. Now, I wouldn't be treating you right if I didn't let you know that I got picked up by the police for doing that one evening with some friends. Criminal mischief, they said it was. I didn't think it was worth making a big deal over – after all the place had been abandoned for decades and my fellow students had been painting that place for years. Just like you are now. But anyway, it is apparently one of those things that the kids do – like painting the names of graduating seniors in the roadway near their houses – that isn't technically legal. So, I wouldn't go about filming it or letting people know you're doing it – or you might get caught. Understand?"

Leaf nodded at him.

"But here's the thing, Leaf. As funny as that video was – and like I said it really took me back to when I was a kid and painting those same walls – as great as it was, it isn't the video we're here to talk about."

"It's not?"

"Nope. We want to talk to you about the one with the crabs."

"Really? I'm not even in that one."

"I know. Remember, I said I didn't think the video showed you doing anything wrong. But you've got to admit, the footage you posted is a bit unusual."

"It's awesome, right? I mean, kind of gross – but really cool."

"Not sure I'd call it cool, exactly. But it did get our attention. Leaf I need to ask you – and I need you to tell me the truth – did you edit that footage? Add anything in, maybe - something that wasn't there originally?"

"I edited it down – shortened it a bit. I mean the crabs aren't exactly tearing up the screen for the majority of the footage. But that's it. Didn't add anything at all."

"I see. Well, now that's a problem isn't it. If you didn't add anything, then we need to figure out if what you filmed was real – 'cause if it is then somebody's missing a head."

"I'm sorry," interjected Mr. Donegan. "What is this about? What is the other video you're describing?"

"You want to show him?" asked Wilkerson.

"You remember the camera you got me? I dropped it into a crab pot - recorded some awesome Dungeness."

"I see. And what's this about a head?"

"Well, I dropped it late Sunday and it recorded overnight and into Monday morning, right? Anyway the footage is pretty boring Sunday and then it goes black when it gets dark. But in the morning when the sun comes up, there's another pot nearby the pot with my camera – and it totally looks like it has some dude's head in it. Probably not real – but I didn't fake the footage or anything. Guess somebody's just got a weird sense of humor."

"And you posted this online?" asked Mrs. Donegan.

"Yeah. I mean, it's pretty gross looking and the footage isn't as clear as I'd like. But it's the kind of thing that's likely to go viral and get like a hundred million page views. Hasn't happened yet – but it could."

"Let us see the video, Leaf," said Mr. Donegan.

Leaf pulled the video up on the tablet and pressed play. His parents stood, transfixed at the footage while the two officers watched their reactions, and those of Leaf, to the scene playing out on the screen.

"When did you film this, Leaf?" asked his father.

"I pulled the pot and the camera out of the water yesterday."

"So what we're seeing was filmed yesterday morning?"

"Yes."

"Oh, Jesus," exclaimed Mrs. Donegan. "We had crab last night. Leaf, we had the crabs that you caught that day. Remember? You brought them home and we had them for dinner."

"Yeah?"

"You fed us crab that had been feeding on a human being. Don't you get it? Your crab – our dinner – that head…" Mrs. Donegan didn't manage to finish her sentence before the revulsion of the thought took over. Wheeling around, she grasped the railing of the porch and emptied the contents of her stomach onto a well-manicured azalea.

"I'm sorry about that," said Wilkerson. "We didn't realize Leaf had brought home any of his catch. But I think you can understand why we needed to ask him about the footage. Now Leaf, I'm going to ask you this one more time because I need to be completely clear. Did you edit that footage to make it look like there was a head in the pot?"

"No."

"And do you know anything about how that other pot got there, or how the head got into the pot?"

"No. It just showed up."

"Ok. Thank you, Leaf. Now there's just one last thing I need to understand – one last thing that I'm hoping you can help me with. I need to know where you placed your camera. I mean exactly where. Can you help with that?"

"Oh that's easy," said Leaf. "The camera's got GPS built right in. I can pull the coordinates from the footage."

"That would be really helpful, Leaf. Thank you. Can you do that now?"

"Wait, Leaf," interjected Mr. Donegan. "Don't do that yet. Officer, I may not be a criminal lawyer – as my wife so kindly pointed out earlier – but I did at least go to law school. I don't think you want Leaf to pull the GPS coordinates from the footage. In fact, I don't think you want him to alter the metadata on the recording in any way. If what we're seeing on that video is real, then Leaf shouldn't be tampering with it. Rather than have him try to dig the GPS data off of the recording, I'd recommend you just take the recording. Put it into evidence and let someone in the department do the work of getting the data. That way if that thing is real, and you manage to figure out who did it, there will be less of a question about the authenticity of the video."

"Thank you, Mr. Donegan," said Wilkerson. "That is excellent advice. I really appreciate it. Leaf, can you get us the camera or the memory card or whatever has the footage on it? You'll get it back, I promise – but it may be a little while before you do."

Leaf reentered the house to go retrieve the camera and flash drive.

"I'm awfully sorry that we had to bring this up," said Strickland. "But we really do appreciate your help."

Leaf returned with the camera in its case and handed it to Wilkerson. "I put the flash drive back in the camera. It's all there."

"Thank you, Leaf," said Wilkerson. "Thank you all. We'll try not to disturb you again, but may have additional questions. If we do, what would be the best way to contact you?"

"Please call me any time," said Mr. Donegan – handing Wilkerson a business card from his wallet. "We'll do everything we can to help put this to rest."

Chapter 19

Earl ordered another beer for himself and one for the leggy blonde sitting to his left. His bladder was about to burst, but he didn't dare go to the john for fear that when he returned she'd be gone. This was the first time in a long while that he'd managed to catch the eye of an attractive young woman – at least one who wasn't selling him overpriced coffee – and he was determined to play out the hand. She'd been talking with him for over an hour now. Flirting with him. Touching his shoulder and his knee. "Not too bad," he thought to himself. "Still able to turn heads after all these years."

He hadn't seen her around before. At least he didn't think he had and he was pretty sure he would have remembered. Thought she might be a Navy wife. They must get awful lonely while their husbands are off on that submarine for months at a time. And she looked to be the right age – mid- twenties or so – maybe with a little kid at home and out looking for a night on the town and a bit of fun to make her feel sexy. He could help her with that – he was sure of it.

"What would you think about getting out of here?" Jasmine asked him. Her voice was low and sultry, with a lilt that reminded him of honeysuckle and sweet tea.

They hadn't finished their last drink, and he hadn't figured out a way to surreptitiously take the little blue pill he had wrapped in tissue in his pocket – he kept it with him just in case the opportunity arose. But she was asking and he wasn't about to say no.

"Sounds great. Where would you like to go?"

"Let's start with your car. You've got a car outside, don't you?"

"An old pickup."

"Oooh, even better," she purred. "Bet it's got a nice big bench seat in the front, doesn't it? Might be a good place to get more comfortable."

Earl slapped a couple of twenties on the bar. He didn't know what the tab was so far – substantially less than forty dollars – but he didn't care. Something that hadn't happened in years was happening. He'd never felt more alive.

Jasmine took Earl's hand and pulled him from his barstool toward the door of the bar. Moments after they left, a large fellow with a beard and wearing a leather vest stepped away from a booth in the back and also headed toward the exit.

"Know any place quiet around here, Earl?" Jasmine let her fingertips trace lightly across Earl's chest. "Any place where a lady could... enjoy herself... without being disturbed?"

"I do indeed."

Earl led Jasmine to his pickup. Fancying himself a gentlemen, he opened the door for her. A couple of empty paper cups cascaded out of the truck and onto the pavement. For a moment, he feared she would see the amount of trash in the floorboard of the truck and lose interest. But to his surprise and delight she climbed right in – sitting sideways on the bench seat to avoid putting her feet and bright red spike heels into the pile of trash on the floor. He shut the door behind her and climbed into the driver's side.

The truck sputtered to life and Earl drove west while Jasmine gently stroked his thigh. "Might not need that pill after all," Earl thought to himself.

Five minutes of ecstasy, anticipation and desperately needing to relieve himself later, Earl turned off the highway onto a quiet logging road. As he focused on Jasmine's fingers and the ever-present danger of premature ejaculation he failed to notice the motorcycle that trailed behind. It too turned off onto the logging road and – cutting its lights – followed the pickup.

Earl slowed the truck to a stop, cut the engine and turned off the lights – leaving the radio playing in the background. Jasmine turned it up. Said it was her favorite song. Said it made her want to dance. She rolled down her window. Leaning across Earl's lap – her breasts brushing his thighs – she rolled down his window as well. Earl felt a tightening in his otherwise flabby pelvis. Opening her door, she exited the truck and walked in front of it – one foot crossing over the other like she was on a catwalk, swaying her hips and tossing her curly blond hair. She was dancing now: writhing her hips to the tune. Earl turned up the volume.

"She's quite the dancer," Earl thought to himself as Jasmine moved in the moonlight in front of the truck. As he watched, his cock twitching in his jeans, she began tugging at her blouse – unbuttoning the top few buttons. A hint of lace peeked out from between her breasts. He couldn't make out the color so he turned on the truck's parking lights. That was better. He could see everything more clearly now: beautiful lace – black or maybe dark blue. She turned around. Facing away from him and

243

bending slightly at the waist, she let her hands ride up her thighs, pulling up the hem of her short skirt and exposing sinuous curves and more dark lace.

He was fully aroused now – breathing heavily – lost in lust. So focused was Earl on the scene before him that he never noticed the scene behind: the motorcycle that parked a short distance behind; the man who dismounted and walked to the passenger's side of the pickup with a gun in his hand; the extension of the man's arm to just inside the window of the pickup or the flash of the muzzle. One shot.

Earl's body slumped forward over the steering wheel. Jasmine stopped dancing and buttoned her blouse. Opening the passenger door, the man reached in and placed the gun on the seat next to Earl. He moved Earl's arm nearer to the gun – taking Earl's hand and forcing it to hold the weapon – pressing Earl's fingers to the warm metal – and closed the door.

Jasmine walked toward the truck, passed it, and waited at the motorcycle.

"Nice moves," the man chuckled.

"Thanks. Was running out of song, though. You sure took your time."

"I was enjoying the show." The man mounted the machine and Jasmine climbed on behind him.

Her knees gripping his waist, the two rode away back toward town.

When the logging crew arrived early the next morning, the only thing deader than the battery in Earl's truck was Earl himself. The cops were called and by 10:00 a.m. the once-peaceful logging road was now a swarm of activity, with members of the Kitsap County Sheriff's office and a representative of the county coroner combing through the pickup.

"Suicide," said the coroner – noting the gunshot wound to Earl's temple and the gun lying close to hand.

"Don't think so," said the Deputy Sheriff as he walked around the vehicle. Stooping to the ground on the passenger side of the truck, he carefully picked up a coffee cup from just underneath the door. *Exxxpresso Coffee* was emblazoned on the side – matching a handful of similar cups in the floorboard of the truck as well as the bed. "If he offs himself while he's just sitting in the truck, how does this cup fall out of the other side? Think he opened the passenger door for some reason and then got back behind the wheel before pulling the trigger? Doesn't make much sense to me." He thumbed through the dead man's wallet – retrieved from his pocket – pulling his driver's license and noting several thousand dollars in cash in the billfold. "No. I think maybe someone else was here with Mr. Earl Beauregard McAllister last night. Maybe someone he brought with him. And I believe I'd like a word with her."

"Her?"

"Just a guess. Seems to me maybe the most likely reason McAllister here comes out into the woods at night with a full moon is he's feeling a bit amorous. Finds himself a lady friend – maybe one of our working girls, from the look of him I'm guessing he doesn't have too many people asking him for dates – and makes his way out here."

"A reasonable inference."

"An educated guess – well-educated. I used to bring young ladies out here in my own pickup back when I was in high school. 'Course I don't think any of them were wearing spike heels. My dates weren't quite that sophisticated, I'm afraid. And they weren't on the clock. But we did have our share of fun."

The coroner raised an eyebrow.

"I'm not pulling your leg – about my dates or your dead friend's companion. Come take a look." Deputy Sheriff Carlton Williams beckoned the young coroner over and pointed at the ground. "Look on the ground – right outside the door of the truck – what do you see?" Without waiting for a response, Williams continued, "small spike marks in the ground. Looks almost like when you aerate your lawn, right? Those are high heels. Not just any heels, though. Those are professionals. The kind of heels a lady might wear when she's wanting to get a man's attention. And McAllister here, I'm guessing she got his attention good. The heel marks go all the way in front of the truck. It looks like she spent some time up there. The ground's all torn up from them. Maybe she's fighting with him. Maybe they're struggling. Maybe something else – hard to say. But she spent a while up there in front of the truck. Looks like maybe she walked back down the road a ways too – but then they stop. Maybe she took off the heels? Maybe someone picked her up – can't tell."

"Wow. Ok. I don't see any other prints, though. If they're struggling in front of the truck, doesn't he leave prints too?"

"Maybe. Maybe not. He's a big guy – but all his weight is

spread out over the whole of his feet. Her weight is heavy on those sexy little points. He could walk around here all day and maybe not leave a print – you're not leaving any. But her prints are going to get noticed. I'm guessing she wanted attention when she put those heels on, but they may end up giving her more attention than she'd bargained for."

"Yeah. Well. How about this. I'll have my guys take possession of McAllister here. We'll do the workup – cause of death and all that. Spoiler alert – likely to be close-range gunshot wound to the temple. I'll leave the stiletto-wearing phantom to you. Deal?"

"I wouldn't have it any other way."

With some help from Williams, the coroner loaded Earl's body into the back of his van and set off down the bumpy road back toward the highway. Now free of the coroner's questioning eye, Williams walked back and forth along the road behind the pickup, stooping here and there to examine something in the roadway, and then walked back toward the cab of the truck. "What were you doing, Earl? Hoping to get laid? Sure. But specifically, what were you doing?" He pulled his patrol car alongside the pickup, opened the hoods of the two vehicles and got jumper cables from his trunk.

Connecting the battery terminals of the two vehicles, he let his patrol car run just long enough to bring life to the truck's battery and started its engine. It's parking lights came on and the radio burst loudly into life – classic rock.

"She's dancing," Williams mused. "You're in the truck and she's dancing for you. So she's either drunk or she's a pro –

you're not good looking enough to get a sober amateur to dance in front of your fat ass. Now if she's dancing then you're sure as hell not pulling the trigger.. And if she's dancing she's not shooting. No hole in the windshield. Shot came from the side…. So, what? She gets back into the car and then pops you? No chance. Entrance wound square in the temple, exit wound on other side – no damage to inside the cab; you're looking straight ahead and watching the girl. Bullet is out in that field over there somewhere… Shell casing in floorboard. No obvious signs of struggle in the vehicle – just a shitload of trash. So the shot is fired from inside the cab. But she's not the shooter. Neither is he. Someone else. Boyfriend? Not if she's a pro. But if she's a pro why was his wallet fat with cash? She's going to take that. No – something else going on….. A hit? Could be. Who would want our boy dead?"

Williams pondered these and additional questions while sifting through the trash in the truck. A collection of coffee cups. Most were marked with the logo of either *Exxxpresso Coffee* or *The Coffee Grind*. Stuck under the seat, barely visible under the litter, was a manila envelope. The envelope was empty, but when Williams opened it his nostrils awakened to the all too familiar smell of cannabis. "Interesting," he said to himself. "Earl, you don't really fit the description of a dealer. But here you are dead in the middle of nowhere with a few thousand bucks in your wallet and an envelope that smells like weed. So what's your story?"

He waited for the wrecker from the impound lot to finally arrive on the scene – a frustrating interval since one of the deputies could have simply driven the truck back to the lot but departmental procedures didn't allow it – and then headed back

248

out toward the Sheriff's office. Driving along the highway, however, he saw the familiar sign for *Exxxpresso Coffee* and decided it might be worthwhile to pull in for a quick chat.

The line at the kiosk was long – at least ten cars deep – but Williams didn't plan to wait in it. He pulled around the corner of the building – past the privacy fence that kept passing motorists from seeing exactly what was taking place at the window – parked his patrol car and walked up to the door. The sight of his uniformed figure approaching the business seemed to make the drivers of three vehicles lose their taste for coffee and return to the highway before they'd reached the window. Williams chuckled and knocked on the door.

The curtain covering the window on the door slid back and Cindy's face appeared. Customers continued to leave the line – cockroaches scurrying away when the lights are switched on. Cindy opened the door.

"Carlton Williams, you get your ass in here before you put me out of business!"

"Cindy – always a pleasure to see you." Williams did his best to focus on Cindy's eyes and face, trying to remain professional despite her being dressed in some sort of patent leather bondage harness matched to a set of sensible clogs. "How long has it been?" He stepped inside the kiosk and she shut the door behind him. Inside, Cindy and her daughter Melinda had been taking turns at the window. The air was hot and damp. As Cindy started to converse with Williams, Melinda took over the window for the remaining customers.

"A few years. Five, maybe ten? You remember my

daughter, Melinda?"

Williams nodded. "Nice to see you again, Melinda. All grown up, I see." Williams winced as the words came out of his mouth. Melinda was indeed considerably more mature than when he'd last seen her as an adolescent with her mom at the grocery store. Melinda stood in front of him dressed as a schoolgirl with pigtails, knee-socks, a bustier and a strip of fabric that was clearly intended to convey the impression of a skirt despite the fact that it didn't extend much past her vulva, exposing ruffled shocking pink panties underneath. The dissonance between his memory of Melinda the actual schoolgirl and the current reality of schoolgirl-as-fantasy Melinda was discomforting at best.

"To what do I owe the pleasure of your visit, Officer Williams?" asked Cindy. "Can I get you some coffee?"

"Well, I'd like to say this is a social call, but I'm afraid I'm here on official business. And no coffee for me, thank you."

"Uh oh. One of my girls do something wrong?"

"Almost certainly, but nothing I'm aware of. More interested in one of your customers. You know a guy named Earl McAllister? Big guy – drives an old pickup."

"I do indeed. He's a regular."

"I thought he might be. What can you tell me about him?"

"Comes in just about every morning like clockwork. Don't think I've seen him yet this morning – he must be running late. Not a choirboy, I mean none of the fellas that come in here are – but he's not one of the ones that tries to get grabby. He likes to look. Good tipper. He's offered to tip extra a time or two if one of the girls would give him an extra show. 'Course the girls all know that's not the way we do business around here. Isn't that right, Mel?"

Melinda looked over at her mother and nodded, knowing full well that Cindy's statement wasn't entirely accurate. The girls did know that Cindy didn't approve of that sort of thing. But the girls also knew that when Cindy wasn't around they could make a bit of extra cash by exposing what little skin wasn't already exposed when a customer asked. And Melinda knew from firsthand experience that a barista could make serious money by letting a customer do more than simply observe. But what she knew and what she told her mother were very different things.

"I'm not here to make things difficult for you or your girls, Cindy. You know what happens when things get out of hand – you've seen that over at *The Coffee Grind* and I trust you'll keep things under control even if they aren't always exactly within the letter of the law. But this Earl fellow, I need to know if there's anything else about him you've seen that's unusual. Anything different from the other customers."

Mel spoke up. "Mom, isn't he the guy who picks up the envelopes?"

"He is indeed. So that's something different about Earl than the others, Carlton. A few of our customers – not regulars exactly like Earl but still folks that come in maybe weekly or so – they'll sometimes drop off envelopes with us. We hold 'em and then Earl will usually pick them up within a few days. He's always real thankful. Says we're helping him out. I figure it's the least we can do for him – he's probably our single best

251

customer. And you know this entire business is about customer service."

"That's what I'm afraid of," Williams replied, trying to avoid allowing his gaze to linger on Melinda's nearly bare backside as she bent over in front of him to retrieve a gallon of milk from a small refrigerator beneath the counter. "Why's he getting his mail here?"

"No idea," Cindy replied.

"Feels weird to me, Mom," replied Melinda. "I told you I thought it was weird. Guy's a creep to begin with – something's not right."

"You worry too much, Mel. Honestly, Carlton, ever since she enrolled at the community college – she's majoring in criminal studies…"

"Criminal justice, Mom," Melinda interrupted."

"Whatever. Ever since she started with those courses she's been finding criminals around every corner in the county."

"Sounds like she's got good instincts. Maybe we'll see you in the department in a few years, Melinda."

"Don't encourage her, Carlton, honestly."

Williams laughed. "Any idea what is in the envelopes?"

"Of course not! I don't go around sticking my nose into other people's business, and I'm sure as hell not going to open someone else's mail. Wouldn't feel right."

Melinda looked from Williams to her mother and back again. Williams, sensing that she knew something her mother did not, directed the conversation back toward her. "How about you, Melinda? Any idea what might be in the envelopes?"

"Well…"

"Melinda, you didn't! Honestly, didn't I raise you better than that?"

"Better than what, exactly? We're running a peep show disguised as a coffee shop. Seriously, I wouldn't get too self-righteous, Mom. Yes, Officer, I do happen to know what is in the envelopes – at least what was in one of them. A fellow came by a few weeks ago and dropped one off. I was here, hanging out with Lucy. Anyway, the guy comes through and drops off the envelope and Lucy knows the guy…"

"Sorry," interrupted Williams, "who is Lucy?"

"She's my cousin – goes to Bainbridge High. Anyway, Lucy was here and she said she knew the guy. He said he was a lawyer or something – and she said he wasn't a lawyer, was connected with *Herbvana* – you know the weed shop up in Poulsbo? Anyway he drops off the envelope and we're both wondering what the whole thing is about. So… well so we opened it. But we made sure to seal it back up again."

Cindy looked at her daughter with exasperation.

"Well, the good thing is that this not being an actual postal facility, this doesn't feel to me like you two were tampering with the mail – I seem to recall that's a crime, although maybe you haven't gotten to that part of your studies yet. So, Detective Melinda, when you opened the envelope, what did you find inside?"

253

"Cash."

"Really. Any idea how much?"

"Well, yeah. I mean we counted it. Twenty thousand dollars."

"Jesus!" exclaimed Cindy. "Melinda every last bill better have made it back into that envelope. You start stealing from our customers you might as well be stealing from me. I won't stand for it."

"We put it all back, Mom. But I told you this was weird! I mean, I didn't tell you we'd opened it because I knew you'd be mad. But I'm serious. People don't just leave each other fat stacks of cash at a coffee shop – tits or no – something's wrong here."

"See what I mean, Carlton. She's just plain suspicious."

"No, Cindy. She's not just suspicious. She's right. People – normal folk at least who aren't trying to hide something – don't do things like this. So let me make sure I get the story straight, Melinda, a guy came through who was connected to *Herbvana* and he dropped off an envelope with twenty thousand in cash for Earl to pick up. Do I have that right?"

"Yeah."

"Well that makes things a bit more interesting."

"What is this all about, Carlton?" asked Cindy.

"It's about your buddy Earl. The guy you say was your best customer."

"He's likely to be here any minute. Why don't you just wait

a while and ask him what it's all about. He's a nice enough guy, I bet he'd be happy to explain."

"I'm afraid he's not going to be your best customer anymore."

"Did he get himself locked up? I hope he's not in some kind of trouble. I really did think he was harmless and nice enough, even if some of the girls did think he was creepy."

Williams looked at Cindy. After all the years he'd known her and everything that she'd gone through in her life up to this point she'd managed to retain her innocence and trusting nature. He admired that, even if he didn't fully understand it.

"Cindy, do you remember when we used to go parking?"

Melinda raised an eyebrow but kept her mouth shut.

Cindy blushed. "Why yes, Officer Williams, I certainly do. That was quite a while ago."

"And do you remember where we used to go?"

"Oh, a bunch of places. There was the old quarry. And the campsite over near Seabeck. That was a nice spot."

"Those were nice. My favorite was the old logging road out toward Belfair. I remember this one night when you… well anyway, I remember this one especially enjoyable night up on that road."

Melinda's mouth was agape now. Her mother had never mentioned dating anyone before she married her father, and as Williams mentioned their earlier exploits Cindy had begun blushing and giggling like a schoolgirl.

"I remember that night, Carlton. It's a wonder we didn't get caught."

"One of my fondest memories of high school. Couple of crazy kids, weren't we? Those were good times."

"Um," said Melinda, "first of all, I'm right here so before you two start a reenactment, maybe take it somewhere else? And second, what does this have to do with Earl and envelopes of cash?"

Williams' face turned from wistful to grave. "An excellent question. Well, it so happens I was back out on that very road this morning. Earl McAllister was there too. And in his truck I found a lot of *Exxxpreso Coffee* cups – he was indeed a very good customer – along with an empty manila envelope."

"So, what's the big deal? What's going on, Carlton?"

"He's dead Cindy. They found his body this morning – slumped over the steering wheel in his pickup."

"Holy shit!" interjected Melinda.

Cindy gasped. "You know, he didn't look healthy. Was it his heart?"

"Coroner's looking at him now so I can't say anything official. But no, I can tell you I'm pretty certain it wasn't a heart attack. It was a bullet. My question is, did he fire it or did someone else? And if it was someone else, who and why?"

Chapter 20

Wilkerson drummed his fingers on his desk, betraying his lack of trust in his colleagues. The Bainbridge Island Police Department didn't have the most sophisticated IT or forensics personnel. But when he'd dropped Leaf's camera off with them earlier that day – with supreme confidence that he could have extracted the GPS data from the file with the benefit of about ten minutes and a quick web search – he still hadn't expected them to take the better part of the morning to get him the results of their work.

Sarah walked up, handing him a cup of coffee. Taking a sip of her own, she grimaced. "I'm getting too used to professional grade coffee. This stuff we make here in the station tastes like death."

"It's pretty bad. But then again it's free."

"True enough. Any word from forensics?"

"Not yet. And I've got the boat and the diver on standby. He's getting anxious. Me too. Don't want to try to do this at night – we need to get started."

"Good thing it's summer. A few months from now it will be dark by four in the afternoon. At least this time of year we've got a good window of daylight. Plus, it isn't raining. You've got to learn to look on the bright side of things, John."

"Right. I guess the bright side is that we'll have good weather when we go out and look for a severed head?"

"Something like that," Sarah laughed.

John's desk phone rang and he snatched up the receiver. "Wilkerson. Yeah. Perfect. That would be great. Thanks." He hung up the phone and looked at Sarah. "We're in business. They were able to grab the GPS coordinates from the camera – shooting them over to me now in an email."

"Great. I'll go tell Sandra. You about ready to head out?"

"Have been all morning. Want to get this over with."

"Me too. Be right back."

Sarah walked down the hall to Sandra's office and disappeared around the corner. Wilkerson, receiving the promised email from the forensics team, printed it off and shoved it into his pocket. He returned from the printer just as Sarah returned to the desk. She'd thrown on a light jacket on over her uniform.

"Sandra says she hopes we come up empty handed."

"I do too. Pretty warm out there. I'm not sure you'll need the jacket."

"It's warm out there now. But I'm not sure how long it will take to find what we're after. As soon as the sun starts to go down it's going to get windy. I just want to be ready."

The two officers left the station and drove down to Eagle Harbor and the boat launch used by the police department. A police skiff, the pride of the department, sat tied up at the dock, with a pickup truck and an empty boat trailer sitting in the boat ramp. As they parked their squad car, a stocky man wearing a dive suit hopped off the tailgate of the truck and waddled toward them, looking for all the world like a neoprene duck with a beer gut.

"Max!" called out Wilkerson. "How've you been?"

"Never better, Johnny boy. Yourself?"

"Oh, you know. Living the dream. Like today, for example. Looking forward to a nice relaxing day on the water."

"Right. That's why you call out a frog – for relaxation."

"Point taken," said Wilkerson. "Max, I want you to meet my partner, Sarah Strickland. Sarah, this is Max Gruberman. Know each other since what, Max, third grade?"

"Sounds about right. Johnny here was the class clown. Used to crack us all up by making fart noises with his hand in the back of his knee. That never stopped being funny."

"Yeah, well I seem to recall Mrs. Windthorpe didn't feel that way. She'd send me to the principal and then my folks would get involved and then – well let's just say it didn't usually end well." Wilkerson laughed a boyish laugh which Sarah found charming.

"It's nice to meet you, Max," said Sarah. "I appreciate you helping us out today."

"No problem. So what are we doing exactly? I know I'm diving but that's about it."

"We're looking for a crab pot," said John. "A very special one."

"No kidding? What's so special about it?"

"A couple of things. First, it isn't set up to actually catch

259

crabs. Second, it may or may not be using appropriate bait."

Max gave him a quizzical look – trying to decide whether John was pulling a prank. He didn't think his old friend would drag him out onto the water – bringing his partner along no less – on a lark. But the whole thing didn't make a lot of sense. In any event, the Police Department was paying him to do the thing he loved doing more than anything else – diving in the Puget Sound – so he decided not to argue and to just go with the flow.

Together, they climbed aboard the boat and pushed off from the dock. The water was choppy – the wind that Sarah expected had started earlier than usual – causing the small craft to bounce in the waves. Max and John continued chatting while Sarah looked out over the water – watching the parade of beautiful homes on the shore and the scattering of sailboats darting back and forth on the breeze – the beauty of the trip almost making her forget its ghoulish purpose.

After exiting the harbor, John turned the bow of the boat to starboard, directing it south along the shore of the Island and toward the scattered buoys bobbing on the surface. He picked his way through them carefully, doing his best not to run over any of the lines connecting the floats with the crab pots below, all the while carefully studying the depth finder and GPS device mounted to the pilot station. Finally, he slowed the vessel to a halt and threw a Danforth anchor over the side.

"Well, this is the spot," John said.

Max looked around. There were a handful of buoys within a twenty-meter radius of the boat. "You weren't kidding? We're really going after a crab pot?"

"I wasn't kidding. But we're not looking for any of these," he said – gesturing at the buoys. "Here's the deal. There's a kid that lives on that beach up there who dropped a pot out here a few days back. He put a camera in it and the camera picked up another pot in the background – not the kid's pot – that had what looked like a human head in it."

"You're joking."

"No, I'm not. And the kid claims he didn't doctor the footage. We pulled the GPS information off his camera. The pot was in this very spot, give or take about three or four meters – our IT guys say the data is about that precise. So if the footage is accurate, and if the kid wasn't lying, and if the pot hasn't washed away with the tide or been snagged by a boat or who knows what else, then somewhere below us you should find a very unusual crab pot."

"That's a lot of 'ifs'."

"I know. But we've got to check it out. Oh, a couple other things. First, the pot on the video – the one we're looking for – it had the doors to the pot held open. Looked like maybe zip ties but hard to tell. So you might look for that. Second, the video showed a pretty nasty crab eating the head. Try not to have anything snack on you while you're down there."

"I'll do my best." Max finished collecting his gear, putting his dive tank on his back and put on his mask. Sitting on the edge of the boat, he let himself fall backwards into the water, collected his bearings, and then began to dive downward, following the anchor rode down toward the bottom, using the line attached to the anchor to bring him back to the GPS coordinates where John had stopped the boat before allowing it to drift in the tide.

The water was surprisingly clear despite the amount of chop. But after the descending through the first ten feet he entered a plankton bloom – the tiny organisms swirling in the wake made by his passing. The plankton made it almost impossible to see, but as he descended down another ten feet or so they quickly disappeared and the water became quite clear but also very dark – the sun unable to penetrate the living cloud. He switched on his dive light. "Hard to believe a camera would pick anything up down here," he thought to himself, "must have been at a really low tide, otherwise all you'd film is dark."

Max continued downward, feeling the pressure and cold of the water mount from outside his dry suit with each additional foot in depth. Just over fifty feet down, he reached the anchor. Keeping his fins from hitting the muddy bottom, he rotated his body in the water to once again be right-side up and began to cast his light around him. A sea of derelict fishing gear and assorted trash lay on every side. Here and there, schools of baitfish darted to avoid predators. A half-dozen crab pots were visible – cages looming in the distance giving the impression of a cluster of prison cells in dense fog. Some thirty feet away, a large cylindrical object lay on its side in the mud, wedged between two rocky outcroppings.

He moved slowly along the bottom, trying to search as methodically as possible and – although it was difficult to estimate distances in the dark – to always stay within fifteen to twenty feet of the anchor. To aid in the search – and also the cleanup, Max was passionate about leaving a dive area better than he found it – as he came across each abandoned crab pot in the search radius he gently loosened it from the mud other debris and piled it near the anchor for collection at the end of the dive. After thirty minutes of this combined search and clean-up operation, he found he'd exhausted the area around the anchor. There was no head to be found.

Max, pleased with his collection of trash from the Sound – and also relieved that he hadn't come across a severed head – swept his dive light one last time over the eerie landscape of the sea floor. Once again, the light caught the shape of the large cylinder. "What is that?" thought Max. Leaving his pile of abandoned crab traps he swam over toward the object, trying to decide whether it was a pipe or an abandoned water heater, and in either case whether he could or should try to retrieve it along with the derelict gear. As he approached, however, he caught sight of one additional crab trap – just past the cylinder and on its left-hand side. Max pointed his light directly at the trap. Several large Dungeness shells lay strewn in the mud between the trap and what was now clearly a pipe of some sort. And then he saw it.

He approached the trap. Marshall's head lolled slowly in the current. The head was now largely picked clean of meat; the jaw was missing. Patches of hair remained attached to the scalp, which was now peeling from the skull – a combover of flesh. Empty eye sockets stared at Max from the gloom.

Max tried to remain calm and collected, reminding himself that he'd assisted in the recovery of bodies before. "This isn't any different" he told himself. But it was different. Never before had he been sent to recover only part of a body. Never before had he seen a severed head. And although he didn't yet know it, never before had he been prey during the recovery process.

He approached the trap, maneuvering his body between it and the pipe and bringing his feet down on the muddy bottom so that he might take hold of it and bring it back to the anchor. But as he reached out to grasp the sides of the trap, he felt a quick tug on his left ankle and he lost his balance. His feet flailing, Max was dragged backwards by a powerful force. Long tentacles crept over every inch of his body, curiously touching and tasting him throughout. One grasped at his regulator – ripping it and its vital supply of oxygen from his mouth. As Max struggled against the creature, he realized he was being dragged backwards into the pipe – the Giant Pacific octopus' lair. A sharp pain tore into his left calf as the octopus' beak pierced his skin through his dry suit and injected its venom. Unsheathing his dive knife with his right hand, he began slashing wildly – blindly – at the arms of the creature. Time and time again Max found his target, the tentacles recoiling as the knife sliced deep. And suddenly he was free. Max kicked as hard as he could out of the pipe and toward the surface. Dropping the knife he reached down and grabbed his backup regulator, thrust it in his mouth, cleared it of water and breathed deeply. Though Max would in later years claim that he'd fought the animal for a half hour, the whole affair had taken only seconds.

Kicking wildly with his right leg, Max breached the surface like a pot-bellied dolphin. John and Sarah, startled at his sudden appearance and thinking he was putting on a show, chuckled and applauded. But their mirth was short lived as he ripped the mask from his face and screamed for help. He had surfaced approximately forty feet from the boat. "Too far," John said to himself and quickly started the engine. Putting the engine in drive he turned it to face toward Max and gunned the motor – a short burst – before throwing it back into idle. The boat lurched forward toward Max. Sarah grabbed a life ring from the boat threw it to Max in the water. As soon as Max looped an arm around the ring, John and Sarah together pulled on the rope attached to the ring, dragging him to and then into the boat.

Max lay on the bottom of the boat. Blood-tinged seawater poured from the torn dry suit. Seeing this, Sarah pulled back the neoprene and revealed the wound – a clean triangular cut. A wedge of flesh had been removed – extracted with surgical precision – from Max's calf: through the skin and deep into the muscle. He was bleeding profusely. Sarah ripped off her jacket, rolled the sleeve tightly, packed the rolled fabric into the wound and applied pressure. "He's losing a lot of blood. Get us back to the dock now and call the ambulance to meet us there! He'll be in shock soon. Go!"

John switched on the boat's police lights and siren, threw the engine into drive and pushed the throttle to fully open. Pulling hard on the wheel he turned the boat back toward the entrance to Eagle Harbor.

Just north of the entrance to the Harbor, aboard *The MaryJane*, Lilith was bent over in the cockpit of the boat forcing the last few bits of Marshall's body into his last crab pot. Delighted to be finished disposing of his body, she was congratulating herself on a job well done when she first heard the police siren. At first, she dismissed it – assuming it was coming from onshore in the neighborhood on the bluffs above

265

and to the west of the boat. As the siren got progressively louder and higher in pitch, however, she realized it was coming her direction. Standing up, she looked for the source of the sound, only to pick out the police lights of the oncoming boat, still south of the entrance to Eagle Harbor but appearing to head directly for her.

"Fuck!" Lilith said under her breath. Hastily, she threw the last crab pot over the side and ran up to the flybridge to start the engines and head away from the oncoming police boat at a deliberate – but hopefully not obviously hasty – speed. As she climbed the ladder, that last pot sank to the bottom of the Puget Sound, pulling with it the neatly coiled line on the deck, and the attached buoy, all of which quietly slid over the side of *The MaryJane.*

Chapter 21

When Max woke, the first thing he noticed was the smell. Primarily antiseptic, but with notes of fecal coliforms and death – like the world's worst whiskey. The second thing he noticed was that his entire body ached in the way it had after each wrestling meet during his high school years. And the third thing he noticed, as he shifted his weight to roll onto his side, was that he'd been catheterized. He didn't know what day it was, but it was turning out to be unusual.

John Wilkerson noticed Max' stirring and pressed the call button for the nurse. A buzzer sounded and a voice – only slightly less nasal than the buzzer itself – replied "Yes, what do you need?"

"I think he's beginning to wake," replied Wilkerson.

"Ok. I'll let the doctor know."

Max opened his eyes and looked around the dimly lit room. He was flat on his back in a hospital bed. An intravenous bag hung from a stand near his head, its tentacle-like tubing trailing down and into his arm via a needle. Electrical leads ran from a machine on his left to his chest where they were affixed with adhesive pads. Pain, hot and biting, seemed to start in his left calf and radiate upward into his thigh. And in the center of his field of vision, John Wilkerson's face floated directly above him.

"You're leaning in awfully close, Johnny boy – you going to kiss me or just stare?"

"Jesus, it's good to see you awake, man. How are you

feeling?"

"I've felt better. You look like shit. Where am I?"

"Bayview."

Max took in this new piece of information. Bayview Medical Center was the area's best-known trauma center – over in Seattle – the place where you ended up if you'd been shot. Had he been shot? He didn't remember being shot, but then again he didn't remember much at the moment.

"You should have seen it," John continued. "They airlifted your ass in the helicopter. You got to ride in style. I had to take the ferry over – you beat me by at least an hour."

"I always did want to ride in one of those things. Did I enjoy it?"

"You tell me. Do you remember any of it?"

Max slowly blinked his eyes and weakly shook his head. "I don't. Why am I here? Did one of your idiot colleagues pop me by mistake?"

As Max spoke, the room began to swirl around him – a surrealist painting of a hospital room – and he slipped back out of consciousness just as a doctor who didn't yet appear old enough to shave stepped into the room.

"He was up and talking for just a few moments," Wilkerson said.

"He's probably going to be in and out for a bit," said the doctor. "But his vital signs are stable. It would be great if we knew exactly what happened to him, but apart from the hole in his leg we're not seeing any obvious signs of trauma and my suspicion is that he'll be around soon enough. In the meantime, let's let him sleep."

Wilkerson eyed the doctor with suspicion. Did the adolescent physician really think that he was going to shake his friend awake? Did people actually do that? He decided against arguing with the guy and sank back into his chair. It had been almost thirty-six hours since he and Sarah had dragged Max into the boat – and apart from the time apart while he was *en route* to the hospital and a few trips to the toilet, he hadn't left Max's side since. What had happened under the water? What had he seen? His obsession with the question was only exceeded by worry for his friend.

Wilkerson sat, wondering about the nature of Max's injuries – and also whether it was safe to go and grab a bite to eat before Max next gained consciousness – when his phone rang. It was Sarah. After staying with John and Max in the hospital late into the night, she'd returned home to play the role of mom; the life of a working mother required such concessions.

"Hey, Sarah."

"Good morning. How's the patient?"

"He's come to a couple of times, only once long enough to have any kind of a conversation, but still unresponsive at the moment. He's been pretty incoherent so far. I haven't been able to get anything out of him, but then again I haven't pressed him."

"I wouldn't force it. We'll figure it out eventually. In the meantime, we may have already gotten what we needed."

"How's that?"

"Station took a call this morning from one of our local game wardens, goes by the name of Bridgewater. Anyway, he's patrolling early this morning out in his boat and comes across a crab buoy."

"Yeah, so? There's a ton of them out there."

"Ah, but not this morning. Remember the regs, officer. Crabbing's only allowed from sunup on Thursdays to sunset on Mondays. Today's Wednesday, so when Bridgewater saw a buoy that was still in the water he naturally had some questions about why it was still out there."

"Got it. So what's the deal with the buoy?"

"When our boy pulls it up? Let's just say he's a bit surprised by what he finds inside."

"Let me guess, it wasn't a chicken carcass?"

"Not unless the chicken had especially big ribs and a hairy back. Anyway, Bridgewater? Guy's a piece of work. Says there's nothing in his rules about using, let's just say, unusual, bait – except maybe you can't use game animals themselves as bait – but nothing in the regs about body parts. So he's bent out of shape about the fact that the pot's in the water on a Wednesday and doesn't even think for a second about the fact that it's got a section of some poor guy's midsection in it. Apparently, they're only hiring pedantic psychopaths over at fish and game. He evidently only called the station because when he mentioned it to his chief the guy had some common sense and explained to Bridgewater that he was probably looking at evidence of a crime outside his authority – something a bit higher up the food chain in terms of criminal culpability."

"Wow. So what do we do from here?"

"Well that's the interesting thing. He found the buoy, right? Well, it's got a guy's name and contact information on it."

Wilkerson let out a quiet whistle. "You don't suppose that whoever killed our victim was dumb enough to leave that kind of a calling card, do you?"

"Doesn't seem like that was the intent – especially since the pot on the video didn't have a rope attached. But one way or another, Bridgewater found a buoy with contact info tied to a pot with a ribcage in it along with a bunch of happy crabs. Maybe the killer just got sloppy."

"Maybe, but I doubt the name on the buoy matches the killer. There's sloppy and then there's just plain stupid."

"There's no rule that says to be a criminal you have to be smart, John. Anyway, I'm going to go out and meet Bridgewater and take possession of the buoy and the pot. It took quite a bit of convincing to get him to agree to give them to us; he kept saying they were evidence of poaching. I'm grabbing them before he changes his mind."

"Good call. In the meantime, I'll stay here with Max. Hopefully he'll wake soon and be coherent enough to tell me what happened on the dive. Talk soon."

Wilkerson hung up the phone and chuckled to himself. He didn't envy Bridgewater his upcoming encounter with Sarah; if Bridgewater balked at giving her the crab pot and buoy he feared that there might be yet another body that needed disposing.

Some two hours and three trips by Wilkerson down the hall to the vending machine later, Max finally awoke and remained coherent. "It was pretty awesome, honestly," he told Wilkerson. "I mean, really a once in a lifetime kind of thing. I've seen octopus before that were pretty big, maybe seven or eight feet across. But this girl was much bigger. Figure she got her beak into my calf and at the same time had a tentacle wrapped completely around me and ripped my regulator out of my mouth. Hard to say, exactly, but that's probably six or seven feet from beak to the tip of the arm? So maybe twelve or fourteen feet across? Incredible. Just wish I'd gotten a good look at her. And I really hope I didn't hurt her with the knife. Just trying to get away, you know? Didn't really want to hurt her – certainly didn't want to do any lasting damage."

"You know you're crazy, right?"

Max laughed. "I'm not crazy. Look, she did what she was supposed to do. I came into her territory. I put myself right in front of her lair – that pipe or whatever it was. I was fair game. Totally my fault for putting her in that position. I'm guessing she'd been sitting in there just picking off crabs as they approached the pot – there were a ton of shells down there. Anyway, I'm just lucky I could get away."

"Yeah. Lucky. So, anyway. You say you saw the pot and it looked like it had a head in it?"

"No. I didn't say it looked like it had a head in it. I said it did have a head in it. No question. I couldn't tell you how long it's been down there. But there's a skull and a small amount of flesh left on it. Pretty gruesome thing to look at."

"You think it's real?"

"Far as I can tell. Looked real enough. To be sure, we'd need to be able to get it to the surface, right?"

"Yeah. But you're not going anywhere near the water any time soon. Not on my watch, at any rate. Plus, Sarah called a while back – while you were getting your beauty rest – she said we've got another pot, already retrieved, that has a ribcage in it. So unless we've got two bodies to deal with..."

"You've still got to pull it, John. Get somebody else if you're not going to let me back down there. But you've got to pull it. Can't take the chance that you've got two dead guys and don't know it."

"I'm going to let my Chief make that call. I'm not going to go risking somebody else to fight the Kraken without her approving it."

"The Kraken was mythical. The hole in my leg pretty much rules out myth. That, Johnny boy, was a Giant Pacific Octopus. Really wish I'd gotten a better look at her."

"You're an idiot."

"Yeah, but you love me. I saw the way you were fussing over me – like a mother hen."

"Fuck off, Max."

"Buy me dinner first."

"Ok. You're obviously well enough for me to leave. So I'm out. Enjoy your stay at Bayrview. Try not to get plague while you're here. I understand it's going around."

Wilkerson exited Max' room just as headed for the door just as a nurse was arriving to check Max's vital signs. "Your patient's complaining of a sharp pain in his rectum – thinks maybe the octopus got a tentacle up there – thought you should probably know."

"Oh dear, said the nurse. I'll tell the doctor. He may want to do an exam."

"Probably a good idea," said Wilkerson.

The thought of Max trying to talk his way out of a rectal exam put a bounce in Wilkerson's step for the duration of his transit back to Bainbridge. When he finally arrived back on the Island it was early evening, well past the time he should have clocked out from work. But Sarah's car was still in the Police Department's parking lot and so he pulled in as well. He found her sitting at her desk. Sandra Glickman sat across from her looking thoughtful.

"Oh, good, John – you're here," said Sandra. "We were just talking through a few things. If you've got a minute, we could use your perspective as well."

Wilkerson pulled a chair around from a nearby desk. "Ok. But anything except crab pots and octopi – I've had enough for a day."

"Octopuses," corrected Sarah.

"Whatever," said Wilkerson.

"Let's not get bogged down in grammar," interjected Sandra. "Here's the situation, John. We've got another body. Well, *we* don't. But there's another one. Maybe connected to the first one, maybe not. But it would make two dead bodies found in the county in a matter of days. So, they're connected in time for sure."

"What do we know about the second one?" asked John.

"I was just explaining some of this to Sarah. Let me back up and fill you in. Think you know there's regular communication between the police departments in the county and the sheriff's office – just part of normal policing, really. If there's a crime spree in Poulsbo it probably isn't going to stay there, you know? It's going to come across the bridge to Bainbridge, or maybe head south to Silverdale – maybe spread to Port Orchard – who knows. But the point is that we all try to keep each other in the loop on stuff that happens in the county generally so that we can all be ready. So this morning we got word that the Sheriff's office had come across a body. Guy was shot in the cab of his pickup truck between Gorst and Belfair. Sheriff thinks it may have been a hit."

"Seriously?"

"Yeah. Single shot to the head at close range with no sign of struggle. Made to look like it might have been a suicide, but they've got some evidence to suggest otherwise. So they're looking into it. Anyway, and here's the weird bit, the guy they found and the name on the buoy that our friends at fish and game found? The two guys almost certainly knew each other. The guy on the buoy is one of the owners of *Herbvana* – the weed shop over outside of Poulsbo. The dead guy was the LCB officer assigned to the area: the guy whose job it was to make sure that *Herbvana* operated within the law."

"That's too close to just be coincidence," said Strickland.

"Feels that way," said Wilkerson. "Sheriff have any idea who did the job?"

"They've got some partial prints," Glickman replied. "They're running them now – expect to know something within a day or two. In the meantime, I want you guys to find the guy who owns Sarah's buoy – Marshall Owens. Don't talk to him just yet. But find him. And find out everything you can about him. I want to know where he lives, who is friends are, how he spends his evenings. Everything. If this guy so much as sings in the shower I want to know the tune. Understood?"

The officers nodded in assent, and Glickman walked back to her office.

"What do we know so far?" asked Wilkerson.

"Not much, I'm afraid. When Sandra spoke with the Sheriff he mentioned the LCB stiff, we'd just run an initial name search on Owens – that's how we figured out he was connected to *Herbvana*. He shows up on the LCB database. We put two and two together and made the connection. Not sure if Sandra told the Sheriff about it, so we may have a day or two before they figure it out. Looks like Owens lives here on Bainbridge – a place up on the north end of the Island tucked back in the woods. We can get someone to watch the house. But we're going to need to work with the Sheriff in terms of watching *Herbvana* as its not in our turf."

"I know a guy who works out there – fellow by the name of Carlton Williams – good guy. I'll give him a call and see if we can't work together on it. If they're connected, this is going to get big fast. Will have guys swarming in from Olympia if we're not careful. Maybe if I can get to Carlton soon enough we can coordinate efforts and keep control so things don't get out of hand."

"Sounds good," said Sarah. "You work on that and I'll see what else we can learn about our crabber. Maybe he's got a neighbor that doesn't like him. That always helps. Also, we know he's crabbing so I'm guessing he's got a boat. I'll run his name through the Department of Licensing database and see if we can't find a registration. If it isn't in his driveway on a trailer, it's got to be moored around here somewhere and there aren't that many options. We find the boat, maybe we find out a bit more about him and the victim."

"Ok. We've got a plan. Let's see if we can't get something definitive on Owens before some idiot from Olympia tries to take over the case."

"Sounds good." Sarah switched off the light on her desk and prepared to leave for the evening. As she walked toward the exit she turned. "Hey, John?"

"Yeah?"

"Take care of yourself, ok? I mean, I know you always do. But seeing Max go down like that? That was hard – and I don't even know the guy. I don't want to see you bleeding out any time soon."

"Why Officer Strickland, I believe that's the nicest thing anyone's said to me in a long time."

"I'm serious, John."

Wilkerson walked over to her and took her hand in his. The two of them stood alone among the scattered desks. Reaching up to brush her strawberry blonde hair from her face, he tenderly caressed her cheek. "I'm not going to let anything happen to me. But more importantly, Sarah, I'm not going to let anything happen to you either. You're not just my partner. You know that." Leaning forward he kissed her forehead. "But we've got to be careful. Sandra finds out about us and we'll both be in a lot of trouble – or one of us will need to go looking for work elsewhere."

"I know. I'm just tired of pretending."

"Me too. I love you. I even like that goofy kid of yours."

Sarah laughed. "And he's pretty smitten with you. Could use a father figure around, you know?"

"Tell you what, let's get through this mess and then maybe we approach Sandra together? Make a full confession. What's the worst she can do, fire me? She's not going to fire you; you're her favorite. Even if she fires me, I can probably get on with the Poulsbo PD or do some private security or maybe even go over and join the Seattle force. We can make it work."

"I'd like that."

"Then it's settled. All the more reason to figure out what's going on with Owens. Soon as we're done with this mess I can get down to the important work of making an honest woman out of you – maybe spray painting your name on an overpass or water tower or something."

Sarah laughed. "Not an overpass. We don't have one on

the island. I'd never see it. Make it a water tower."

"It's a deal."

Chapter 22

Ed Jorgenson stared out the window of his office lost in thought. He was tall – well over six feet in height – with broad shoulders and a shock of blond hair that seemed always to be slightly too long even immediately after it had been cut. He liked to think it made him appear youthful. Many of his constituents thought he simply looked poorly groomed.

He'd been the Kitsap County Prosecuting Attorney now for the better part of a decade and, although he enjoyed the view of Sinclair Inlet from his office window, he was restless. Crime was relatively low in the county, the homelessness that plagued Seattle and the cities on the eastern side of Puget Sound hadn't yet fully made its way across the water and there hadn't been any real civic embarrassment since the incident at *The Coffee Grind* involving the whipped cream, the barista and the Silverdale City Councilman. All in all, things were good and his constituents would likely keep electing him to his current post in perpetuity. But comfort begets complacency and Jorgenson was anything but complacent. Ambitious by nature and the oldest of six children whose father passed away just before the youngest was born, Jorgenson graduated early from college and law school – joining a prestigious Washington, D.C. firm at the tender age of twenty-two. After honing his skills as a litigator he was voted into the partnership of the firm just shy of the age of thirty and then practiced for half a dozen more before everything fell apart.

His mother was dying – ovarian cancer had spread throughout her body quickly and without mercy. And so

Jorgenson chucked his east coast practice and moved back home. Back to help her in her last days, to help her die, and to be nearer to his much younger siblings, a couple of whom were still in school at the time of their mother's passing. After settling her affairs, he waived in to the Washington State Bar and got a gig at a mid-sized firm in downtown Seattle. They were pleased to get someone with DC experience and he was grateful for the job. Within a year of his arrival, the partner who had hired him got herself elected as Governor and he began to lead the firm's litigation practice. And that was when he figured out that the life of an elected official looked pretty good compared to the life of a practicing lawyer. One election cycle later he found himself the duly elected Prosecuting Attorney for Kitsap County and planning his next leap.

But as it turned out, his next leap wouldn't come as easy as the previous ones. The problem wasn't that he was unqualified – it was that the position was already occupied by a woefully unqualified but extraordinarily popular incumbent. So he abandoned the idea of running for Congress and set his sights on the Governor's mansion. Now, several years later, his former colleague was preparing to retire and he was thinking about taking her place. All he needed was some big win – something that would propel him forward and make his name known throughout the state as a viable candidate – and he was confident he could do the rest.

"So let me make sure I've got this straight in my head. You pulled Maldonado's prints off McAllister's truck and you've got a witness that puts him in the bar at the same time as McAllister?"

Williams nodded. "The print isn't one hundred percent – it's a partial. But it's still a really solid match."

"And we know that Maldonado's a Hornet?"

"No question. He wears the colors and we've got surveillance of him at the cleaners."

"You don't think he's the kind of fellow that just likes a nicely pressed shirt?"

Williams laughed. "No. That's not his style."

"Pity. Might be a change for the good. Tell me about the witness – the one that puts Maldonado at *The Hideaway* with McAllister."

"That's where it gets tricky. It was a tip on the crimespotters hotline. Came in the day after the paper broke the news of McAllister's death. Anonymous. We've got it recorded but there's not much there. The caller is a woman – sounds reasonably young but with a lowish voice and a southern accent. Says she was in *The Hideaway* and saw McAllister leave with a red-headed woman and Maldonado close behind. Says she's sure it was McAllister from the picture in the paper."

"How did she recognize Maldonado."

"No idea. She doesn't say."

"And she didn't give her name?"

"Nope. Says on the tape she's afraid to give her name. She's afraid of Maldonado."

"She should be. He's a thug." Jorgenson tapped his pen on his desk and focused his eyes on something off in the distance.

"If the Hornets are going to start knocking off LCB agents, that's kind of a big deal. Bigger than just any one dead fat guy in the woods. But if we could crack it – bring Maldonado in, say, and squeeze him, make him talk… Well that might be kind of a big deal too."

"There's one more thing."

"What's that?"

"I know a guy over in the force on Bainbridge."

"You have my deepest sympathies."

"Nah – it's all good. He's a good guy even if his beat's a bit challenging. Anyway, I don't know if this is related or not, but they've got kind of a weird situation over there. Found a body - pieces of it anyway – put in crab pots and dropped off the eastern side of the Island. They're reasonably sure it is a man. And one of the pots had a buoy attached with a name and contact information – Marshall Owens. They don't know much they do know is that he's part owner of *Herbvana* – the pot shop just outside of Poulsbo. That's McAllister's turf – he would have been the LCB agent supervising the shop."

"How stoned would you need to be to leave your name attached to a body?"

"Good question. They're operating on the assumption that Owens is connected to the body somehow but not necessarily that he's the killer. Anyway, they asked us to watch *Herbvana* for any unusual activity since it's in our turf. We're on it – guys are actually fighting over the gig since there's pretty good ice cream across the street. But we haven't seen anything weird yet.

Actually haven't seen Owens at all since we started watching the place. His car's there but he's nowhere to be seen."

"You go over to *The Hideaway*?"

"We did. I went over there myself."

"You ask if anyone there saw Owens the night McAllister was there?"

"Nope. Did not. Hadn't heard the guy's name until after we found McAllister's body. You think Owens had to do with McAllister getting shot? We don't have any record of him being a Hornet."

"Not necessarily, just checking things of in my mind. So what's your next move?"

"We're going to pick up Maldonado. You want to play?"

"Not just yet. I'll let you start. But I would like to be there and hear what he has to say."

"Sounds good. Will ring you when we've got him in cuffs."

Williams started to drive back to the office, only to find that half his work had been done for him already. Maldonado, by way of his quick temper and slow wit, had managed to get into a scuffle with a parking enforcement officer on Bainbridge. He'd stopped in for a cinnamon roll at a local shop and, not finding anywhere to park legally, left his motorcycle parked sideways in a spot reserved exclusively for electric vehicles. The good and self-righteous people of the town, unimpressed by any of his multiple obvious scars, his leather vest with the Hornets logo or the sheer size of the man, were nevertheless affronted that something so crude as a shovelhead v-twin would be parked in the holiest of holy parking spaces. Three separate well-meaning citizens called the cops and Sandra Glickman felt obliged to send someone out to keep the peace.

But the peace hadn't been kept. When Maldonado walked back to his bike, sticky bun in hand, he took issue with the officer who was writing the ticket. Words were exchanged and in a matter of seconds – before the incredulous eyes of diners sitting in the window of a nearby café, Maldonado's pastry and the parking officer hit the ground in quick succession. This posed a conundrum for the observing witnesses, many of whom had more affection for baked goods than the city's parking enforcement officials, but nevertheless more calls to the police – and the 911 dispatch – were made and soon the area around Maldonado's bike was cordoned off with every on-duty member of the Bainbridge Island Police Department. But Maldonado wasn't there. Depressed by the loss of his snack – which had ejected itself from the napkin in his left hand when he struck the officer with his right – he'd wandered back to the bakery to satisfy his craving. Moments later his reverie was interrupted when six officers, guns drawn, approached him mid-bite and he was taken into custody for battery on an officer. Williams heard all this, and more, on the departmental radio in his car and quickly turned around to head to Bainbridge. He called Wilkerson to let him know he was coming.

As Williams drove to Bainbridge, Ed Jorgenson sat staring out the window of his office. Taking his phone from his pocket he scrolled through his contacts, selected one and clicked the link for the personal number, ignoring the office line.

"This is Elizabeth."

"Liz, it's Ed."

"Hi, Ed. What's going on back in Port Orchard?"

"A beautiful day here in the county seat. Can't wait to get out of here. Hey, I know you're busy running the state and everything, but I'm hoping I might ask a quick favor."

"As long as it isn't something that will put me in the papers. I've been taking a beating since the last legislative session." This was true. Governor Elizabeth Ramsey had signed a patently unconstitutional ban on apple imports from California in an effort to placate angry farmers in Wenatchee. Her own internal memoranda - many of which had been leaked to the media – showed that she knew the law was illegal and should be struck down but she went ahead and signed it just to shut up "those apple maggots in the central part of the state." The Seattle papers had run a series of investigative articles in the ensuing weeks, each painting a progressively worse picture of Ramsey. To top it off, they seemed to be purposefully using photos that were taken of her while either her mouth was open or her eyes were closed. She wasn't sure which she disliked more, the written criticism or the unfairly realistic photojournalism.

"I've seen that. You'd think they'd cut you some slack. It's not like you're running again – what's the point in it, really?"

"The point is that they're assholes, Ed. The whole bunch of 'em. Never met a reporter that I didn't think would have his personality improved by asphyxiation. Anyway, I've got a meeting in a couple of minutes so not a lot of time. What's the favor?"

"You don't know it yet, but you've got another problem in

the LCB. You had one, anyway – guy named McAllister. He's dead – we found the body a few days ago. There's at least one other body that appeared this week that's somehow connected to one of the shops McAllister was overseeing. We've got reason to believe that a local gang is involved in some way, but we're not yet sure how it all ties together."

"Kitsap's more exciting than I thought."

"Not really. This is anomalous."

"So where do I fit in?"

"With the LCB overlay, your AG's going to want to take this over. I'd like you to make sure that doesn't happen so that I can run with the case."

"You looking for the publicity?"

"Absolutely. I have it on good authority that the Governor of the great state of Washington isn't running for reelection next fall. Could be a great opportunity for someone who'd maybe recently busted up some sort of crime ring involving a rogue weed cop and a biker gang."

"You don't want this job, Ed."

"I might, Liz. I'm dying over here."

"Ok. But don't say I didn't warn you. I'll talk to the AG and hold him off."

"There's one more thing."

"Yeah?"

"It would be really helpful if you could call the LCB director and get the agency to work with us. Partner with us to handle the case? They're going to have info that we're going to need to break this open."

"Not a problem. He owes me a favor."

"You're the best, Liz. Now I owe you a favor."

"Oh, Ed. You owe me so many more than one. I just hope you're in position to deliver on them when I need them. I'll talk to the AG and LCB – will make the calls by the end of the day. Good luck."

Jorgenson hung up the phone, put his feet up on his desk, and smiled.

* * * * *

Wilkerson and Williams sat in stunned silence at Wilkerson's desk. Maldonado, arrested barely four hours ago for battery on a police officer, was walking out the door of the police station accompanied by his lawyer – a greasy fellow with a lazy eye who'd arrived less than an hour after Maldonado making a single phone call.

"Could you get counsel lined up that fast if it was your ass in jail?" asked Wilkerson.

"I don't think so. And did you see how the guy introduced himself to Maldonado when he came in? They hadn't met before."

"Maybe Brandeis works for the Hornets?"

"Could be. Even criminals need lawyers."

"Especially criminals."

"I've been working with Jorgenson – filling him in on the McAllister matter and your situation with Owens. Was hoping that Maldonado might be the link – that we could get something out of him."

"Not today, apparently."

Sarah Strickland walked past and pulled up a chair. "Weird day, huh?"

"Very," said Wilkerson. "Sarah, Carlton, let me introduce you two. Sarah, this is my friend Carlton Williams – he's with the Sheriff's office. Carlton, this is my partner Sarah Strickland. We've been working together on the Owens matter. In fact, her son David is the guy who brought it to our attention."

"Nice to meet you," said Williams. "Seems to me that the bit with Maldonado and McAllister is pretty straightforward. One guy killed the other. Not sure about the 'why' just yet, but no real mystery as to the 'what' or the 'how.' But I'm struggling with how your guy Owens is connected. What's your theory?"

"It's changing by the minute," replied Strickland. "Actually haven't even had the chance to brief John on this. But here's what we've got as of today. We've had Owens' place watched for several days now, as well as *Herbvana*. He's a complete no-show. We've talked with his neighbors – discreetly. They haven't seen him either but they don't seem too upset about it. Seems he wasn't especially beloved. Only real development is down on the water. Running the DOL search showed that he's a boater and when we did a bit of poking around we found his boat – *The MaryJane* – moored down at Winslow Marina."

"Guy's running a weed shop and his boat is named *MaryJane*?" asked Williams.

"Guess he thinks that's clever," replied Strickland.

"Well, I'm guessing weed paid for the boat," said Wilkerson.

"Right," continued Strickland. "Anyway, we found the boat and did some talking with a few of the barnacles at the marina. One of them – older lady named Beatrice – seems like she keeps a pretty watchful eye. Knows everything about everybody at the place. She said she hadn't seen Owens around but that there's a young woman who has been using his boat. Goes by the name of Lilith. Anyway she gave us a full description of the woman and it's a dead match for one of the employees at *Herbvana*."

"Now that's interesting," said Williams. As he spoke, his phone rang from inside his pocket. Pulling it out to shut it off, he noticed the number and decided instead to answer. "This is John. Oh, hello. Yeah, nice to meet you too. I am. Yes. Really? That would be great. Tomorrow is fine. Sure. Ok. See you then." Williams hung up the phone and looked over at the other two officers, who eyed him expectantly. "That was someone named Eleanor Fritzell. She's with internal affairs at the LCB. Says she wants to talk with me about McAllister. And apparently she wants to talk with me soon – sounded like someone lit a fire under her ass."

As he spoke, Sandra Glickman came around the corner. "Wilkerson, Strickland, I don't know what you've managed to stumble into but it's got some people very excited. I just picked up a call from the Governor's office. We've been officially asked – by which I understood instructed – to work closely with Jorgenson and the LCB on the Owens case. Apparently there's going to be a meeting sometime soon between those two and they want BIPD working the matter to be there as well." Rounding the desk, she realized that Williams, whose back had been to her as she approached, was not one of her officers. "Oh. I'm sorry, I didn't mean to interrupt. I'm Police Chief Sandra Glickman."

Williams stood and shook her hand. "Carlton Williams - Kitsap County Sheriff's office. Was just meeting with Jorgenson earlier today to talk about Maldonado – we've got his prints at the scene of a recent shooting of an LCB officer. That call you just got? You're not alone. Moments ago I got a call from LCB telling me that I'm supposed to work with them on this same case. The meeting is tomorrow morning at Jorgenson's office."

The next morning, after Sarah hugged David twice before leaving for the office, she picked up John at the police station and the two of them drove the thirty miles to Port Orchard. Passing by *Exxxpreso Coffee*, John jokingly asked Sarah if she'd like to stop for a cup, or at least drop him off so that he could get an Americano.

"You make an honest woman out of me and I'll give you all the half-naked coffee you can handle."

"Officer Strickland!" he said in mock surprise.

They pulled into the parking lot, made their way through the metal detectors at the courthouse and up to Jorgenson's office where they were shown into a conference room. One by one,

Carlton Williams, Eleanor Fritzell, Steve Fujimoto and Ed Jorgenson joined them in the room. The exchange of pleasantries and introductions was brief.

"Thanks for coming," said Jorgenson. "Here's the situation. McAllister was dirty. Eleanor here had been investigating him for a while – recruited Steve to be her eyes and ears. The whole inquiry started with an anonymous tip that he was taking cash from *Herbvana*. She's done the legwork and can confirm he seemed to be spending a lot more money than you'd expect for a mid-level guy at LCB. He wasn't the best paid guy but was quite the big spender. So they put *Herbvana* under surveillance – and McAllister – to see what they could find. And they found quite a bit. Eleanor, want to walk us through it?"

Fritzell shifted slightly in her seat and swallowed hard. "Sure. There are three things that are important here – important for you to understand. First, in order to be a licensed cannabis dealer you've got to have a certain minimum level of security. The agency won't issue a license without a detailed security plan. And that security includes cameras. If you go into a shop, production facility, grow operation, whatever, that's licensed by the State, you're likely on camera the whole time you're on premises. *Herbvana* was no different. Second thing you need to know is that every cannabis licensee is tied into the LCB's online inventory tracking and tax system. We've got a seed-to-sale system that they're required to use. That means that our computers are connected to theirs. We can see into their computer system any time they're online. Got it?"

"Now the third thing is kind of big. This is something most of the licensees themselves don't really understand – we like it that way – but if their security cameras are connected to their computers – and they almost always are – then we can watch them through their own cameras from down in Olympia. Most of our own agents don't even know this. Again, we keep it quiet. But it can be really helpful when you've got a problem. Unless the licensee physically yanks the power from the cameras, or takes the computer offline, we can see everything. Doesn't even matter if they disable the camera from their computer – it's hard wired into the system. They must actually unplug them or shut off the power to cut the feed. This last bit is important because, at *Herbvana*, they've tried to shut down those cameras on a few occasions."

"After the initial whistleblower call came in, we flipped the switch down in Olympia to start recording everything that came into view of *Herbvana*'s cameras. If there was cash going to McAllister, we wanted to catch it. All that make sense?"

"So, basically, you've been recording everything that's happened at *Herbvana* for a few weeks now?" asked Williams.

"Yes," replied Fritzell.

"And you don't need a warrant or something?" asked Wilkerson.

"Our agency takes the position that if you're on LCB-licensed premises we have the right to see everything."

"Isn't there a Fourth Amendment problem with that?" continued Wilkerson. "Without a warrant that feels problematic."

"As a prosecuting attorney, it warms my heart to hear you

ask the question," said Jorgenson. "The fact is, it does feel like it might be a problem. But until someone challenges it, that's a problem I'm not going to worry about. At the moment, I'm more interested in what the cameras caught – what the LCB recorded. Eleanor, please continue."

"This is where I get out of my depth, honestly. It's hard for me..."

"Fair enough," replied Jorgenson. "What the cameras caught is the untimely death of Mr. Marshall Owens."

"The crabber!" gasped Strickland.

"More like the crabbee," replied Jorgenson.

"I'm sorry?" said Fritzell.

"A crabber is someone who goes after crabs," said Jorgenson. "Therefore, linguistically speaking, seems like a crabbee would be someone who is himself gone after by crabs. But this, I'm afraid, is where Eleanor's part of the story ends and where the BIPD must pick up the story. I understand you've recently found some of Mr. Owens' fishing equipment?"

"The guy was put in his own pots..." said Strickland.

"Wow," said Wilkerson. "So, yeah. Well, it's like this. We've had three reports of human bones showing up off the eastern side of the Island. One was a femur that just washed ashore. The second was a kid who dropped a camera into his crab pot and ended up filming another pot that had what looked like a human head in it. We sent a diver down – he couldn't retrieve the pot but confirmed that it's down there. The third is one we actually have in our possession. It had part of a ribcage in it.

Unlike the second pot there was a buoy attached to this one – the buoy had Owens' name on it. We didn't have a position on whether he was or wasn't the killer. Seemed stupid that a murderer would leave his name attached to part of the body of the victim, but then again some criminals are stupid. Never occurred to me that the name on the pot might be the name of the victim. Guess we were the ones who were stupid."

"Not stupid," said Jorgenson. "The whole thing is just odd and unexpected."

"So who killed Owens? You said you've got it on tape."

"I don't think I'm qualified to answer that," Fritzell replied.

"I'm confused," said Strickland.

"The video shows a struggle," replied Jorgenson. "Owens threatens a guy named Bartholomew Jones, the other owner of *Herbvana* with a pistol. Jones grabs Owens by the throat. In the midst of all of it, a woman, we think she's an *Herbvana* employee but don't have her name yet, she kicks Owens and he falls. The fall kills him."

"Lilith," said Strickland.

"Who?" asked Jorgenson.

"We did some work canvassing the marina – figured since we were dealing with a crabber the person had to have a boat. Owens had a boat but no one on the marina had seen him use it for weeks. But one of the people we interviewed said a young woman who calls herself Lilith had used it recently. Her description of Lilith matches the description of a woman we've seen working at *Herbvana*."

"Well, Lilith is pretty skilled with a knife," said Jorgenson. "The cameras didn't just catch Owens' death. They also caught his dismemberment. This woman – Lilith – butchered Owens on the floor of the storeroom. She kept the body in some sort of storage container in the back of the shop. A couple times she takes pieces out of the container and puts them in a cooler, which she then drags out of the shop and puts in her car."

"She's going crabbing," said Wilkerson.

"It appears that way," said Jorgenson.

"Wow," said Strickland. "So how does McAllister figure into any of this?"

"Although we weren't ever able to see any cash changing hands," replied Fritzell, "we do have video of McAllister in *Herbvana* a few days after Owens' death. He's angry. We don't have audio on the recordings so we're not quite sure why he's there or what gets said. But he gets into an argument with Jones. At one point – now it's kind of hard to tell based on the camera angle – but at one point we're pretty sure he finds Owens' body. He doesn't respond well – there's vomit involved. But by the end of the interaction this Lilith person seems like she's taken control. She's whispering in his ear and has her hand on his crotch. McAllister's way out of his league here. We don't know what she says to him. But we know he goes away smiling. That interaction is the last time we see him on the *Herbvana* security footage. And it's just a few days before we learned he'd been killed."

"I've seen the video," said Jorgenson. "And I've read the report that Williams' here prepared when he found McAllister's body. Unless I'm mistaken, he thought there was a woman with McAllister the night he was killed."

"That's right," said Williams. "We found high heel marks in the soft ground outside his pickup."

"I'm guessing that woman was Lilith," said Jorgenson.

"Only one way to find out," said Wilkerson. "Let's pick her up and bring her in for questioning."

"Not yet," said Jorgenson. "Here's the thing. We can't forget that Maldonado was involved. He's part of the Hornets and they had a lawyer spring him from your custody faster than I think I could get out of jail – and I've got the Governor on speed dial. If Lilith was there when McAllister was killed then she's part of the Hornets too. Picking her up won't help – their lawyer will just spring her before we make any headway. We need more info. Need to build the case before we make the move."

"So what's the play?" asked Williams.

"We pick up Jones," Jorgenson replied.

"The other owner? If Lilith's a Hornet what makes you think he's not connected?" asked Strickland.

"He could be. But after watching the video, I don't think he is. He's rocking back and forth with his head in his hands after Owens hits the floor. She's the one that dismembers the body – he's not there. And she's the one that flips McAllister. Either Jones is one hell of an actor or he's soft. Real soft. Lilith is anything but. If one of them's a Hornet or connected somehow, it's her."

"So why pick him up?" asked Williams.

"Just watching on video, the guy reminds me of my baby brother. Sure as a kid he got into trouble occasionally – hanging out with the wrong crowd – but he was basically good. My bet is that if we can get to him, talk with him, get him to understand the situation he's in and how he can get himself out of it? I think we can get him to tell us what he knows – maybe even work with us to get Lilith on the record that she helped kill McAllister."

"And if your bet is wrong?" asked Wilkerson.

"Then we're no worse off than if we'd just picked up Lilith."

"Well," said Williams, "you're the quarterback here. We'll pick him up."

Chapter 23

"I'm going to be straight with you, Barry. The way I see it, you've got a choice. You can help us out or not. Now I can't make you any promises. I can't tell you that if you play nice with me then you have won't have any trouble. All I can tell you is that if you do help me, I will do my best to help you." Jorgenson took off his glasses and put them on the table between himself and Barry.

"I want my lawyer."

"I'm sure you do. And you've got a right to counsel, Barry. I'm going to respect that right. But before we get you on the phone to a lawyer, I'd like to have you just listen to me for a minute. Just listen. Don't say anything. Don't answer any questions. Ok? 'Cause here's the thing, Barry. I think you've been taken. I think you've been set up. And I don't have any interest in putting the wrong guy behind bars. Not my style. Got too many of the wrong people behind bars already. Seriously. You're selling weed legally out of your shop and we've got thousands of people in jail for possession. Makes no sense. I don't want to spend any more time putting the wrong people in jail. What I want to do is just paint for you a story, Barry. Tell you what I know for sure and what I think I know. And at the end of that you're going to get a lawyer. The only question's going to be who you choose for that very important role. Ok?"

Barry looked straight ahead. "I'm not telling you anything until I've got my lawyer."

"I'm counting on it. Got some folks here I want you to hear from." Jorgenson rapped his knuckles on the table. Three sharp knocks. The door at the back of the room opened and Steve Fujimoto and Eleanor Fritzell stepped in. "Please, come in – take a seat. Barry, you remember Steve, don't you? From the LCB?"

Barry nodded in recognition of Steve, who smiled at him. He placed his briefcase on the table and took a seat to Barry's left. Eleanor remained standing.

"Barry," said Jorgenson gesturing to Fritzell, "this is Eleanor Fritzell. She's with the LCB as well. Steve, why don't you share with Barry some of the finer aspects of the LCB's security camera protocols."

"Happy to. Barry, I know that you're aware of the security cameras that you've got over at *Herbvana*. Believe you've got three – on the outside of the building, one in the sales floor and one in the storeroom. Right? And they're connected to the shop's computer. Right? So far, I'm guessing this isn't much of a surprise. But there is something that you might find surprising. See, the shop's computer – like similar systems at all our licensees – it's connected to the Internet. And part of being a licensee in our cannabis system means that people in our agency can access it. We've got the right to look at the shop's records at any time."

"Now, Barry," said Jorgenson, "Steve here doesn't just mean the shop's sales records. Nope. He means all the records. Including what's going on in the shop – what might get recorded by the cameras."

"That's not cool, man. You can't just go around spying on people like that!"

"Oh, but we can, Barry. Or, rather, Steve and Eleanor here can. It's part of their job and part of what you agreed to when you applied to open *Herbvana*. But here's the thing, you promised you wouldn't tell us anything – you'd let us talk to you without answering back – and I'm going to hold you to that promise. I'm going to insist that you don't say anything to us until we've finished explaining what we need to explain – laying it all out for you. This last bit is important. So, please, do us all a favor and keep quiet for a bit. I promise we'll go as fast as we can. Steve – can we show him?"

"Absolutely." Fujimoto reached into his bag, pulled out a thick folder, and placed it on the table – relocating the bag to his feet.

"Barry," said Eleanor, "the funny thing about those cameras is that they can't ever really be turned off unless they're unplugged or the power goes out. And if someone tries to turn them off, well, a little alarm goes off over at LCB that lets us know. Now in some cases we don't really care. But in some cases we do. And a few weeks back, that little alarm went off because someone tried to shut off the cameras at *Herbvana*. Now it didn't work – shutting the cameras off, I mean – but it did stop the cameras from recording onto the *Herbvana* computer. Understand? The cameras are still rolling but nothing's getting saved on the home system. But – and here's where things may get interesting for you, Barry – we had already switched on our own recording system back at LCB headquarters. So even though things weren't getting saved at *Herbvana* they were getting saved down in Olympia."

Barry's eyes widened. A look of severe discomfort spread across his face.

"Now, I know what you may be thinking, Barry," said Eleanor. "You may be thinking 'what did they see?' or 'what did I do?' or something like that. Or you may be thinking 'why would they start watching?' Let me answer that third one first. We'd actually been watching for a few months. We started watching because we were suspicious. In fact, we are suspicious by nature. That's our job. But we weren't actually suspicious of you or anyone at *Herbvana*. No. I hate to say it, but we were worried about one of our own. One of our own officers, that is – Steve's former partner, Earl. In fact, we assigned Steve to Earl because we had some concerns. We were worried, Barry. Worried about whether Earl was trustworthy. We'd gotten some information – whistleblower calls – from people who said he was dirty. They said he was taking cash from some of the shops – basically extorting money from them. We had to find out what was going on. And so we started to watch him. Started to dig into things a bit. That's when we started getting really worried. He had a lot of cash. Cash we couldn't quite explain based on everything we knew about him. Cash that just didn't make any sense."

"Now, when we started to watch him, that meant that we started to watch really closely the shops that Earl was overseeing – the licensees in his territory. And after Steve had been assigned to partner with Earl for a few weeks, we asked him to keep a close eye out for anything that seemed out of the ordinary. Steve was very helpful – he kept track of a lot of things that didn't make a lot of sense for us, things that it seemed like Earl was letting slide with some of the licensees – but he didn't catch Earl doing anything really strange. We were kind of hoping that Steve might see Earl taking cash from one of the shops, you know? I mean we didn't want him to be doing that – but if he was doing it we wanted to know about it. Anyway, we never did. And things just didn't really add up."

"But again, there was that odd thing about the cameras. When we put two and two together and realized that someone had tried to shut off the *Herbvana* camera system – and *Herbvana* was in Earl's territory? Well we thought that was pretty interesting – especially since Earl didn't mention anything about it in any of his reports. So we went back and started looking at the *Herbvana* recordings. That was… enlightening."

"I'd like to show you a bit of what we've seen, Barry – if you don't mind," said Jorgenson. "I think it may help you understand where I'm coming from on this. Steve, why don't you show him the first one."

Fujimoto opened the folder, taking care to keep the contents shielded from Barry's view, and pulled out a single piece of paper. On it was printed a screen shot of the *Herbvana* storeroom – obviously a picture taken from the perspective of the security camera. In the frame, Barry could see himself, Lilith and Marshall standing near the desk. Marshall looked angry.

"Recognize this night, Barry?" asked Jorgenson. "This is the last night anyone saw your partner, Marshall, alive – the night he died. Now here's the thing. Normally how this would go down is that you would tell me you didn't kill the guy and I'd tell you I think you did and we'd go round and round and you'd get your lawyer and then we'd have to prove our case, and all that. Right? You've probably seen it all on television or in the movies hundreds of times. Standard playbook – straight over tackle murder case. But this is a bit different, isn't it? This time we've got a neutral spectator in the room."

"Lilith…" whispered Barry.

"Not even close," said Jorgenson. "I'm talking about the camera itself. It's not picking a side. Not deciding who we should believe or discredit. I doubt Lilith would be so objective. But we're not done yet, Barry, so please don't say anything – wouldn't want you to say something you might regret later."

"Anyway, like I was saying, this time is different because of the camera. Steve, can you pull the next photo?"

Fujimoto took the next picture from the stack in the folder and put it on the table.

"Now in this one," continued Jorgenson, "we see something a bit different. Your boy Marshall's got himself a new toy, doesn't he. Can't tell exactly the caliber from the photo – but that's a revolver. And, unless I'm mistaken Barry, he's pointing it right at you. Right at your chest. See? He's got this look in his eye – doesn't look friendly does it? And you're looking surprised – maybe a little bit frightened, but who wouldn't be with a gun pointed at you. I've had that happen a time or two to me while I've been in this job – not a good feeling. Not good by a long shot. So, yeah – you're frightened and Marshall's angry and he's pointing a gun at you. Lilith? She's hiding back there in the corner of the room. Not being much help. Not yet at any rate. So now my playbook – the one where I just say 'Barry's a murderer' – that's getting more complicated. Steve, show him the next snapshot, would you?" Steve complied and slid the next photo over.

"Now what do we see in this one that's different than the last? Well, for starters you've got our boy Marshall by the throat. Damned impressive, if you ask me. Guy had a gun pointed right at you and you made a move for his throat. I've seen the video – really wish we could play the whole thing for you but it just isn't possible here at the station – anyway you're quick. Lots quicker than I would have guessed – and obviously much quicker than Marshall expected. You got him good. But here's the thing – the way I see it? The way it comes out on the screen? You're defending yourself. Guy's got a gun pointed right at you – you've got a right to defend yourself. The law doesn't expect you to just stand there and get shot. Law lets you try to defend yourself and it looks to me like that's exactly what you're doing. And apparently you're doing it well 'cause you haven't been shot, right? Next pic, Steve. Yeah. This one. Honestly, Barry this one gives me the willies. You know what I mean? That creepy feeling on your arms? Anyway this one does that to me – even more than some that come later that made Ms. Fritzell here lose her lunch – it's this one that gets to me. What do you see? Don't answer that. I'll tell you what I see. I see you and Marshall locked in. He's got a gun on you. You've got him by the throat. You're bigger than he is but he's holding his own pretty well. At least he was. 'Cause in this one your friend Lilith has made her move. See where she is there? It's kind of hard to tell with the shelving partly in the way. But if you look carefully you can see part of her face. And you can see a whole lot of her leg. She's giving him quite a kick, isn't she. Here, let's show you

305

the very next pic – about a half second later on the camera feed – thanks Steve – here it is. You look at these in quick progression and you can get a sense of just what's going on. I'm guessing she damn near castrated him with that kick. I mean she finished the job later – we'll get to that in a bit – but with that kick she turned the tide of the fight, didn't she? She kicks him so hard he loses his balance and a split second later – let's see the next picture, Steve – yeah, here it is – a split second later he's toppling backward with you on top of him. Whacks his head pretty good on the way down, doesn't he? I'm guessing that's what actually killed him – a good blow to the back of the head will do it. And you might have managed to do it without Lilith's foot. But then again if it weren't for Lilith's foot the two of you might still be locking horns in the storeroom. Marshall might still be alive. So when I look at these I think to myself: shit – hard to charge Barry with murder when he's defending himself. Might actually be better to charge Lilith with something since she deals the blow that sets Marshall's death in motion. Maybe charge her with manslaughter. Yeah – probably makes sense. We charge her with manslaughter and be done with it."

"Want anything to drink, Barry?" asked Fritzell. "I could use a coffee." Barry shook his head – declining the coffee. "Ok. Just let me know if you change your mind. Ed, where do I go to get coffee around here?"

"Down the hall – second door on the left."

"Thanks," said Fritzell. She stood up and left the room.

"Poor thing," said Jorgenson. "She's sitting at a desk all day down in Olympia and doesn't really deal with this sort of thing. Turns her stomach. I get that. So she's going to go get coffee

306

right when we start talking about the weird stuff. Now, Barry, I've walked you through most of that night with Marshall. And I'm not going to show you any more from that night – but I'll just tell you that I know – I saw on camera – you argue with Lilith a bit and then it looks like you help her drag Marshall's body toward the back of the shop and hide him somehow. Can't see exactly how he's hidden – the camera angle doesn't pick up the back wall. But, yeah. I know that you helped move the body and then you left and she spent some time cleaning things up around the place. I mean I'd have loved it if you called the cops and reported that the guy was dead – but I'm not sure I can blame you for not doing it. But that's when the footage starts to get weird, Barry. Really weird. Steve, can I have the next one in the stack?"

Fujimoto reached back into the folder and pulled out a picture – handing it to Jorgenson.

"Yeah. This one." Jorgenson slid it across the table to Barry. "You're not in this one. In fact, you're only in one or two more of our collection. Between you and me and Steve here, that's a good thing. We wouldn't be having this conversation if you were. I wouldn't be wasting my time. Take a look at it. Hard to make out exactly what's going on there, isn't it? I mean without context. That's the way it is with bodies sometimes. When you just see parts by themselves they don't always look human. But that? That's all too human, Barry. That's your buddy Marshall on the floor – what's left of him anyway. And that's your girl, Lilith, with him. Can you see what she's doing? She's been working away on him for a while with that knife of hers – the one in her hand – and now she's... well let's just say that's maybe the unkindest cut of all – what she's about to do."

Barry looked at the photo – Lilith's hands frozen in time. One tugging the shaft of Marshall's penis. The other closing in with the knife. Taking it all in, Barry slowly began to conclude that it was just possible his romance with Lilith wasn't going to work out – possibly she wasn't the girl for him after all.

"Here's the thing, Barry. What she's doing right there – cutting him up into pieces? I mean you could almost forgive her for her role in killing him. Maybe she didn't mean to – you know? But whatever excuse you – or a jury – might make for her with the kick flew out the window when started carving him up. From a technical, legal standpoint – her doing this is what we refer to as fucked up shit. Makes me sick to see it. Made Fritzell sick too. Only real question is whether a judge would even let a jury see it – might be too much for them too."

"So where do we stand? We've got a dead guy whose been cut up into tiny little pieces. Pretty bad, right? It gets worse. Steve, how about the last few pictures as a group? Now you're probably wondering why Steve and Fritzell are here, right? Well, here's why. This little vignette."

"These were snapped just a few days after Lilith did her work with the knife. You're in this one, along with Lilith. But Earl's joined the party. And boy does he look pissed. The guy was a blowhard. Wasn't he? A real piece of work. Anyway we've got a few good shots. Here's one where it looks like he's putting his finger into your chest. Not very nice. Not super professional. Here are a few where it looks like he's doing some sort of quick inspection of the place. In this one he's real close to the camera – along the back wall – maybe he's found something you're not supposed to have? Can't tell for sure. But this next one? Bingo! That's one hell of an expression on his face – nice and up close for the camera. You can't really see what he's doing. But you know what? I think I know what he's doing. I think he found Marshall. Or at least part of him. Know why I think that? This next picture. Yep – here it is. Remember I said that the sight of Lilith carving up Marshall made Fritzell vomit? Well, I'm thinking our boy Earl had the same kind of reaction. Here's the action shot – Earl emptying his stomach in the direction of that back wall at your shop. Can't be too many things that would make him puke like that. How's that for a guess? Don't answer – not just yet – but I bet I'm close."

"Now of course that wasn't the end of Earl's visit to *Herbvana* that day. Nope. He stuck around for a few more minutes. But just like in the fight with Marshall – and just like dealing with Marshall's body – Lilith took over, didn't she? Here she is talking with Earl. You're out of frame here. But there she is up close and personal with Earl. In fact – now I could be mistaken – but I'm pretty sure in this frame she's got her hand in Earl's most sensitive area. Right in the man zone, so to speak. Geez, I don't think I'd want her hand anywhere near there if it were me – but then I've seen that other picture – you know, the one where she's lopping off Marshall's cock? Now in these last few pictures we see Earl leaving the shop and going outside – jumping into his car. There's Steve in that last frame – sitting right in the passenger seat. Funny thing about this series, Steve was outside the whole time but Earl had asked him not to come in. Now why would that be, I wonder."

"Tell you what I think – I think he didn't want Steve going in because he didn't want him to know what was going on inside. Didn't want him to see something and report it back to Eleanor;

that's basically her role – trying to keep the agency's officers honest. But Earl wasn't honest, was he? I'm guessing you knew that after whatever conversation took place in those last photos. But did you know he was on the take before that? Did you know Marshall had been paying him off? We don't know how much he paid – how much in total, anyway. But we know he paid him twenty thousand in cash on at least one occasion. And we know he made multiple payments. From the look on your face, I'm guessing you didn't know any of this. And that's good for you, Barry. That's very good."

Jorgenson paused and studied Barry's expression, a mixture of fear and surprise, while trying to decide how much more to tell him. He wanted Barry's cooperation but despite his best hunch he couldn't tell for certain whether he could be trusted.

Eleanor stepped back into the room. "Sorry I was gone so long," she lied, "it took me a bit longer than I expected to find the coffee. Where are we?"

"I was just explaining to Barry here that we know that Marshall had been paying off Officer McAllister. Was about to explain the most recent developments in the matter. Want to jump in here?"

"Sure. Barry, Ed here has probably explained it already – but I work with the LCB's internal affairs department. And honestly that's usually a pretty boring job. Most of our officers are squeaky clean. Which is good for me because it means I don't need to worry about them going off the rails. Now Earl McAllister? Major derailment there. And that would be bad enough. But you add to that the fact of your partner's death and it gets more complicated. Unfortunately it doesn't stop there."

Fritzell glanced over at Jorgenson. "Do we tell him?"

"I think we have to. You want to or should I?"

Fritzell squirmed. "I think I need to find the ladies' room." She stepped away from the table a second time and exited the room.

Jorgenson chuckled. "I shouldn't laugh. She really is just a bureaucrat – not a real cop. Wouldn't make it a day in actual law enforcement. Ok, Barry, here's the deal; McAllister's dead. We found him a few mornings ago slumped over the steering wheel of his truck. He'd been shot in the head. Whoever did it did their best to make it look like a suicide but it wasn't a suicide. It was a hit."

"Now, first of all I want to say that we don't think you did it. So don't spend a second thinking about that. Not a second. No – we think we know who did it. And we think we know who ordered it. See, here's the thing. Our team got some partial fingerprints from the outside door handle on Earl's truck. They're pretty decent matches for a fellow we know – a member of a local gang that's done a few other jobs in the area. Honestly, they're not the most sophisticated crew. This was probably some of their best work. But even when they're not as careful they've been a tough nut to crack. Very tough. They're very good at keeping secrets. And just when we get close they manage to weasel out with the help of piece of shit lawyer – maybe you've heard of him – Cal Brandeis."

The sound of Cal's name snapped Barry to complete attention. Biding his time throughout the prosecutor's exposition, he'd been waiting simply for it to end so that he could call Cal and enlist his help. But how did Cal factor into this? How was Cal connected to Earl? These and similar questions flooded his mind.

"Now this Cal fellow. He's an interesting link in this chain, isn't he? Funny thing about lawyers, they always leave a pretty good trail of where they've been – professionally I mean. Now in this case, that trail brings Cal and Marshall together. You knew that, right? When you started *Herbvana,* Marshall helped you fill out the paperwork – he was working for Cal at that time. Anyway, now here we are a few years later and Marshall's dead and the guy who Marshall was paying off is dead – I'm ninety percent sure killed by one of Cal's clients. Now this is a small world – but that's too close to just be a coincidence. So what I'm trying to figure out is – who is it that wanted Earl dead enough to have him killed? Sure, plenty of people probably hated the guy. Near as we can figure, he was extorting half a dozen weed shops – Steve's been really helpful in nailing that down – and he was making a killing doing it – if you'll pardon the expression. To be honest, at first I was pretty skeptical that any of his victims would have had anything to do with it. No – most people that are getting worked just keep on getting worked, you know? They don't lash out. They don't make waves. They just keep taking it. Seems like that was where Marshall was at. Paying all that money every week – just a cost of business, I guess."

"But Lilith… well maybe that's a different story. She's got no qualms slicing a man into bits. Got no problem using him as bait either. Did you know that? I mean, what she did with him? Sank his ass in crab pots and let the Dungeness do their work. Nasty little critters. Weird thing about it, though, she used zip ties to keep the doors to the crab pots open so none of them would get trapped. So there's that. She's got a heart of gold – when it comes to crabs."

"She's vegan," Barry said quietly.

"No kidding? Well, that explains the doors. Too funny, really – a vegan willing to have a guy killed. Never did trust vegans – starting to understand why."

"You think Lilith killed Earl?"

"Well, no. I think that Lilith had someone else kill him. Although the idea she might have killed him herself did cross my mind. You know that gun that Marshall pulled on you? The revolver? Lilith took it. We've got her on tape picking it up. What she did with it after that we're not quite sure – but she could have popped him – or she could have given the gun to whoever did. Looked like a small caliber piece on the video – might be a match for the hole in Earl's head, might not. Here's the thing, Barry – we've already talked with a fellow who we're pretty sure had his hands in this. Got his prints. And as soon as we picked him up and started talking to him, you got involved? None other than Cal Brandeis, Esq. And I can't help but think that it feels odd that within just a couple of weeks one of Cal's clients gets killed *and* a guy who was extorting that same client gets killed only to have Cal come down and defend the likely killer. And there are two links that I can see between these two events. You're one of them. Lilith is the other. But I don't see you on video trying to kill Marshall. And I don't see you on video slicing his cock up into slivers or pissing on his body. And I don't have anyone that can say they've seen you on Marshall's boat in those last few weeks, but I've got a very nice and extremely nosy old woman who swears that she saw a tattooed young lady take his boat out on a couple of occasions during that time – even talked with her once – and that she said she was going out crabbing but didn't ever seem to come in with any crab. So unless you're some kind of criminal mastermind, and I honestly just don't see that being true, then Lilith is the key."

"And that's really why we're here today. I'd like your help. And I know that if you help me then I will do my best to help you. But if you don't help me? Well, I've already got you on film struggling with the guy who ended up dead and fed to crabs all along Bainbridge Island, don't I? I mean that alone should be enough to put you away for a few years. Even with good old Cal defending you, if I decide to take you down, you're going down."

"But, like I said, if you help me then there's a chance – a real good chance, mind you – that you don't do any time. Don't even get charged with anything. And you can go along your way and run your shop and live your life."

Barry looked at Jorgenson and then back down at the table. He wanted nothing so much as to be able to do exactly what was being proposed – just go back to his shop and his weed and his routine. At the same time, however, something was stirring inside him. Feelings he'd only felt it once or twice before – most recently when Marshall had confronted him and demanded that he sell his stake in the shop. Anger. Rage that someone he'd trusted hadn't turned out to be the person he'd thought. Frustration that he'd been taken advantage of. And this time, unlike when Marshall turned on him, the feelings were compounded by a deep sense of loss that someone he loved not only did not have reciprocal affection but may have actually intended him harm.

"What do you need me to do?"

"First thing I want you to do, Barry? First thing I want you to do is to ask for a lawyer. But not Cal. No – I want you to ask for a public defender. They're overworked and occasionally ill prepared, but they're honest. And I don't think Cal is honest. I'm still not sure exactly how he fits into all this, but I'm sure he's a cheat. You ask for a lawyer and I'll get you the best public defender we can find. Maybe even a volunteer defense attorney from a big law firm over in Seattle. We'll get you damned good representation and make sure you're protected. You, Barry. Not Lilith, not Cal, not whoever did the hit on Earl – you."

"Why do you care who represents me – I mean other than Cal?"

"Because I don't want there to be any question that you were treated fairly. I don't want there to be any way for anyone to try to say that the help you might give me to put Lilith and whoever killed Earl behind bars was illegitimate or inappropriate and to have it thrown out as evidence. I want to be able to rely on it. And I know that starts with getting you a lawyer that you – and I – can trust."

"Ok," Barry said. He looked into Jorgenson's eyes. They were stern and focused but also reassuring, reminding him of the eyes of so many men he'd known growing up – father figures to him – men he'd always wanted to have respect him and to earn their trust.

"Ok. I'll do it. I want a lawyer. Please get me a lawyer."

"Thank you, Barry. I appreciate that. And I appreciate the trust you're putting in me right now. I won't do anything to betray that trust."

Chapter 24

Barry finished counting the cash from the day's sales – a large stack of twenty-dollar bills, a few fifties and some smaller denominations. Business had been good. Opening the safe, he stowed the cash inside, closed the door and spun the combination lock.

"Thanks for covering the shop this afternoon. It's hard to get away now that Marshall's not here. I really needed the break."

"Not a problem," said Lilith.

"I hope you don't mind," Barry continued, "but I asked Cal if he would pop in tonight after closing. He should be here any time now."

"Yeah? What for?"

"Earl. I mean, I want to talk to him about Earl. Figured you should probably be here too. We had our little run-in with him a few weeks back but we've hardly seen him since. Just want to talk through with Cal what our options are."

"We're not going to tell Cal about Earl."

"I think we should. He could help. Plus, he's *Herbvana's* lawyer, right? We can tell him anything and he's got to keep it a secret. He has to or he loses his license. It's like talking to a priest but without all the religion."

"I don't trust him."

"I don't blame you. He's a crook. But he's our crook. I

think as long as he's getting paid he'll do what we want. We've certainly paid him enough."

"Not sure you can ever pay him enough to trust him. I'm not comfortable with this – don't do it."

"I'm going to. We need the advice."

"Let's talk about this first."

"Nothing to talk about. We need to know how to deal with Earl."

"I'm serious, Barry."

"Me too. And it's my decision. Marshall and I were co-owners, remember? He's dead. That makes me the one in charge. I own the place. What's it to you?"

"I'm sorry, what did you say to me? You own the place? The fuck you do. I own over half of it. You signed the papers yourself."

"Yeah. About that. I've done some digging there – talked with Cal earlier. Seems I couldn't have actually given you any of it. Any transfer has to be approved by LCB. So those papers you had me sign are invalid. Good thing too, otherwise I'd feel like you'd cheated me."

Lilith stared at Barry in stunned silence. "You can't cut me out of this. I won't let you."

"I don't have to cut you out. You were never in. Just because you tried to take it from me and failed doesn't mean I've done anything to you. You did it to yourself. Just like you killed Marshall."

"I didn't kill him."

"Didn't you, though? You're the one that kicked him in the balls. He and I might still be fighting over the store if you hadn't. And you're the one who cut him up into pieces and got rid of the body. I sure as hell didn't have anything to do with that. What did you do with the pieces, anyway?"

As Barry finished speaking, the lights from Cal's car flashed across front window of the store.

Barry, opening the door to let him in, glanced over Cal's shoulder and across the street to the Poulsbo Creamery. A sheriff's department car sat in the parking lot. "Come in, Cal. Thanks for making it out here so late. I really appreciate it."

"No problem," said Cal. "Anything to help a client. What's up?"

"Lilith and I were just chatting. Feel like we could use some advice."

Cal looked over at Lilith, who was standing in the doorway between the sales floor and the storeroom and glaring at Barry with a level of vitriol typically reserved for ex-spouses or members of Congress. He'd obviously walked into the middle of an argument and wasn't yet sure if he was there to solve it or, preferably, profit from it. "Uh. Sure. How can I help?"

"Let's go back into the storeroom where we've got a bit more space and someplace to sit. You go on back. I'll lock up so we're not disturbed."

Cal walked uneasily toward Lilith in the doorway, who sighed heavily and retreated back into the storeroom. Barry made pretense of locking the outside door and then joined them.

"So Cal," started Barry, "hypothetically speaking, if two people are fighting – like physically fighting – and not getting anywhere, but somebody else comes along and strikes a blow that causes one of the two people to fall down and get killed, who's responsible for that?"

"Hypothetically speaking?" asked Cal.

"Jesus, Barry," said Lilith.

"Yeah. I mean, the dead guy wouldn't be dead except for the action of the third person, right?"

"Well, I mean, possibly. There's this idea called 'proximate cause' in the law – different states think about the concept differently – but you could make an argument that in the case you've described the person who changes the outcome of the fight – the third guy – is the one who caused the death. In some states you might charge the first guy. In others you might go after both of them."

"Hear that, Lilith? I was wrong. We might both be in the soup."

"Shut up, Barry," said Lilith.

"What's this about?" asked Cal.

"Marshall," replied Barry.

"What about him?"

"Barry, I swear to God if you don't shut up..."

"Calm down, Lilith. Cal here is on our side. Here's the truth,

Cal. Marshall's dead. He's been dead for a few weeks now. I was just telling Lilith – right before you arrived – that I thought she killed him. But – according to what you were just saying – maybe Lilith and I both killed him. Kind of weird, isn't it? To have one dead guy but maybe two people who killed him? Never really thought two different people could kill the same person – guess the law's more complicated than I thought."

"Oh, the law's pretty complicated..." Cal's voice trailed off. The evening wasn't at all turning out the way he'd expected.

"I didn't kill him, Barry," said Lilith. "I didn't kill Marshall; you did."

"We may have to agree to disagree on that, you know? I mean, I had him by the throat – that's true. But he was holding a gun on me. That feels like self-defense. He hadn't done anything to you – but there you were kicking the shit out of him. Right in the balls, wasn't it? One hell of a kick, as I remember. Did you play soccer in high school? I bet you played goalie."

"You're not funny, Barry. You think you're being funny but you're not. You're just being a prick."

"See how she talks to me, Cal? You'd think we were married. Anyway, that's not why I asked you to come over tonight. What I actually want to talk to you about is Earl."

"Earl?"

"Yeah. Earl McAllister. He's the LCB Agent that's been assigned to us since *Herbvana* opened. He's been a huge pain in the ass since day one. Anyway, Marshall always dealt with him before he, well, you know – went away. But he came in a few

321

weeks back and… well there's no good way to say it…. He found the body. Marshall's body. We had it here in the storeroom for a bit while Lilith was getting rid of it."

"Jesus, Barry. Shut the fuck up."

"I'm telling you, Lilith, it's ok. We can say anything we want to Cal. He's our lawyer. He can't share it with anybody. Isn't that right, Cal?"

"It is indeed."

"Right. So anyway, Earl came in here and found the body and freaked out. I mean you would, right? It isn't every day that you see a body cut into a bunch of pieces. Oh, I hadn't mentioned that, had I? After Marshall was dead – I still think Lilith killed him – she cut him into a bunch of pieces so she could get rid of his body. Anyway, Earl freaked out. Lilith talked him off the ledge. Even convinced him to help us get the owners of the shop changed over – out of Marshall's and my name. Remember you said we'd need to find a way to do that? Anyway, she convinced Earl to help us – promised him a slice of the business – and then he went away. And that's kind of the problem."

"The problem?"

"Maybe problem's the wrong word. I mean, I don't exactly miss the guy. But I'm worried. I saw in the paper that they found his body – he'd been shot. What does that mean for *Herbvana*? Also, are we really on the hook for sharing the profits with him if he's dead? I mean I guess we would be on the hook if he were alive and splitting the profits was all that kept him from telling people that Lilith killed Marshall. Probably money well

spent – at least for her anyway, maybe for me too if I'm a…
what did you say?… 'proximate cause' of Marshall ending up
dead."

"You talk too fucking much, Barry," seethed Lilith.

"Tell you what, Cal, I'm starting to think that she doesn't like
me. Which is a shame since I've always liked her. Especially
liked her figure – always wanted to see it up close, if you know
what I mean, but she's never given me the chance. Anyway, any
idea about the whole Earl situation – who might have killed him
and why?"

"Did he have any enemies?"

"I'm guessing he only had enemies. Like I said before, the
guy was an ass. He even put the moves on Lilith about three
minutes after seeing Marshall's body. Was pretty rude about it
too, wasn't he Lilith? Didn't he suggest you should…"

"Yes," interjected Lilith. "He was rude and foul and filthy
and probably deserved to die."

"Whoa. Struck a nerve there, I guess. Did he offend you
that much? I mean you turned the tables on him – had him
eating out of the palm of your hand by the end of that
conversation. Did he really make you that angry? Wait, wait a
minute. Did you kill him?"

"What? No I didn't kill him. Why would I kill him? You're
talking out of your ass."

"That would be a talent. Seriously, though, I mean you were
mad enough to kill him, I bet. After he told you what he wanted
you to do with your mouth? You were livid. I remember the

323

look in your eye. Plus, you promised him you'd be partners with him here at *Herbvana* and then you tried to take my share of the business. If you'd managed to take my share and then didn't have to share with Earl, you'd have owned the whole thing, right? So you had a few pretty good reasons to kill him. Are you sure you didn't."

"Barry, I swear to God I didn't kill Earl but if you keep saying I did I'll kill you instead."

Cal chuckled. "I think I may be able to shed some light on Earl's death, or at least take suspicion off of Lilith here."

"Yeah?" asked Barry.

"I can say with certainty that Lilith didn't kill Earl."

"How do you know she didn't?"

"Well, because I know who did. Not exactly, mind you, but I have a pretty good idea who did. And I have a very good idea of who wanted him dead."

Both Lilith and Barry looked expectantly at Cal. Lilith raised an eyebrow, waiting for him to continue speaking.

"Marshall wanted him dead."

"Seriously?" asked Barry.

"Very much so."

"How do you know that" asked Lilith.

"Well, since this is an attorney/client privileged conversation, I can tell you. Marshall came to me a couple of weeks before the two of you did. He said he had a problem with Earl. Said he'd been paying him off for years and was getting tired of it – wanted to get out from under it. He asked for suggestions on how to do that. I mentioned that I have another client who does occasionally assist in helping to solve these types of problems. He paid a fee and gave me a name, which I passed along to my client. And just like that, the situation with Earl was solved."

"Amazing," said Barry. "How much did he pay? I mean, how much does a thing like that cost?"

"Depends on the job, generally. In this case? One hundred fifty grand all in. If I remember correctly, Marshall said he was paying twenty a week to Earl. All in all, quite economical, really. For two months' worth of payments to Earl he was rid of the problem."

"Jesus," said Lilith.

"No, Miss. Not Jesus. But close. She goes by the name of Angel."

"Wow," said Barry. "So, with Earl out of the way, I assume we don't actually have to pay him or his family anything, right?"

"It seems to me you didn't have any kind of enforceable agreement with him in the first place. I mean it would have been illegal for you to make the payments in the first instance. So, you're off the hook."

"That's fantastic. Really good news. Thank you. That just leaves me with a couple of things to resolve, really."

"What's that?"

"Well, first, what to do about you? I mean I've been looking over the books and it looks to me like you've been stealing from

Herbvana at every turn. That may have been ok with Marshall – probably was since you guys had a long history together – but it really doesn't work for me. The way I see it, you owe *Herbvana* at least a couple million dollars. Now, I could go to the state bar and complain about it – you'd probably lose your license – or I could go to the cops. Maybe I should go to both? And second, what to do about Lilith here. I mean, she had me sign some papers that she put in front of me that made it look like I was selling her part of *Herbvana*. But she can't really own part of it without the LCB approving it, and she never paid me anything for it, and as far as I can tell she was just trying to steal it out from under me. I've got to say that really hurt. I cared for her, you know? Stood up for her when Marshall wanted to fire her – gave her a job when she needed it – even shared my stash with her back before I got clean. And she knew how much *Herbvana* means to me; it was my dream to open this shop back before the plant was even legal to grow. The sad thing is I might not even have been all that upset if she'd ever shown me the least little bit of interest, you know? Maybe let me kiss her or something? I mean I still wouldn't have let her steal my shop from me, but I wouldn't necessarily be angry. But she never did. So what do I do about her?"

Lilith listened as Barry spoke; fury filling within her. After all the years she'd spent working alongside Barry and Marshall – all the indignities she'd endured - all the times she'd held her tongue as she'd felt the eyes of the two men leering at her, it had come to this. She was to be cast aside. She turned her back on the two men and walked to the shelving unit opposite them. Reaching into her satchel she withdrew Marshall's gun and turned to face them.

Her hands shaking with rage, Lilith clenched her jaw and squeezed the trigger. The sound of the shot, sharp and staccato, echoed off the stark walls of the storeroom. She fired a second time and the computer monitor behind Barry exploded – a shower of sparks and electrical smoke. She fired a third time; Barry slumped to the ground, hand clutching at his shoulder.

Cal froze momentarily, shocked by the sound of the first shot, and then reached inside his blazer. Retrieving a pistol of his own, he fired one shot. Lilith fell backwards, her body collapsing inward – a puppet whose strings have been suddenly cut. Cal turned to look at Barry, glassy-eyed and breathing hard, blood flowing from between his fingers as they pressed on his shoulder and upper chest. He leveled the pistol at Barry, taking aim at his forehead.

"Drop the gun. Drop it or I shoot." Carlton Williams' voice was almost supernaturally calm as he stepped from the showroom into view. "You hear me? Drop the gun or I'll blow your head off. You understand me, Cal? Drop it now."

Cal released his hold on the pistol and it fell clattering to the floor. Moving closer, Williams kept his service weapon leveled at Cal as he squatted down and took possession of Cal's gun, then stepped forward, cuffed his hands behind him and patted him down. Outside, sirens screamed toward *Herbvana*. Williams looked over at Barry, now beginning to lose consciousness. "Situation cleared," Williams said into his radio microphone. "Shots fired. Two down. Need EMT assistance now."

Williams grabbed Cal and shoved him roughly to the floor, the suddenness of the descent causing what little hair he had on the top of his head to come unstuck from the opposite side – his

327

comb-over now standing proud like a feather in a cap. "You sit there until I tell you to move. So much as twitch and you'll be bleeding out on the floor. Understand?" He moved toward Barry. "You hang in there, buddy. Help's almost here." Barry didn't respond.

In a moment, the room was abuzz with EMT personnel. "This guy first," said Williams as he pointed at Barry. Barry's chest was stripped bare. A small entrance wound just below his right clavicle trickled blood and led to a larger, ragged-edged exit wound just between his shoulder blade and his spine in the back. On top of it all, front and center for Cal to see, was the microphone that had been taped to Barry's chest.

"Son of a bitch," said Cal.

"Counselor," said Williams, "I believe you know you have the right to remain silent. If I were you, I'd probably do just that."

As Barry was carted out on a gurney to a waiting ambulance, the EMTs turned their attention to the Lilith's lifeless body, lying in a heap. It was intact, save for a gaping hole in her head where Cal's bullet had found its mark. Williams thought her frame bore a striking similarity to what he'd seen of Marshall's body after Lilith had finished her work with the fileting knife: disjointed-appearing arms and legs stuck out of the Lilith pile at odd angles. On her back, visible above the waistband of her jeans, disappearing under her blouse and then reappearing on her bare shoulders, Williams discerned the gnarled branches of a giant tree tattooed on her back. "Beautiful work, really.," Williams thought to himself. "Shame it had to go to waste."

Epilogue

Barry switched off the neon HERBVANA sign in the window and prepared to close up shop. Nine months had passed – nine months of painful rehabilitation and even more painful reflection.

As soon as Cal had found himself staring at the inside of a jail cell he'd begun to talk. It seemed that his bar credential wasn't nearly as important to him as his freedom. His assets seized and his licensure stripped, he happily cooperated with Jorgenson – testifying against Angel, the Hornets and half a dozen other clients who'd enlisted his services as part of their criminal activities.

Jorgenson, meanwhile, was doing his best to make a name for himself with the prosecutions – all with an eye toward future elected office. But it wasn't going well and he was lagging in the polls. It seemed that Washington state voters ultimately didn't care all that much about what happened on the west side of Puget Sound. He couldn't get much name recognition in Seattle – a critical area to win any statewide office. The Seattle mayor was making tremendous strides in getting the busses to run on time and the average number of homeless individuals per city block seemed to be decreasing – two factors which, although excellent for the populace, were problematic for Jorgenson's political aspirations.

The more he'd thought about it, the more Barry realized that everyone had an agenda – everyone he knew had goals and aspirations. Some were good. Most were not. Even the most

329

outwardly altruistic wished to reap the reward of their actions. It was disillusioning. But, he told himself, maybe this was all a part of just growing up – of taking charge of one's life – being able to recognize when someone's working toward an aim.

As Barry closed out the till and shut off the lights to the storeroom, the outside door opened. "I'm sorry, we're closing up," said Barry.

"It's just me, babe." Jasmine's voice, soft and sultry, made the hair on the back of his neck stand up and his stomach tighten.

"Hi. How was your day?"

"No complaints," she replied. "I missed you." She kissed his cheek.

"I missed you too."

Printed in the USA
CPSIA information can be obtained
at www.ICGtesting.com
JSHW03225325 1023
50815JS00007B/21